ONE ROAD IN

HANNAH R PALMER

First edition September 2021

Cover Art & Design by Apartment 9 Media

Edited by Karl Palmer

www.hannahrpalmerauthor.com

Holidays always seemed to have the same impact on Mandy. She'd build them up, hundreds of blocks of excitement placed on top of one another until they'd inevitably fall down. Holidays were almost always better in her head than in real life. The way they turned out never lived up to the expectation she developed of them.

'Come on grouch, put the book down.' She raised her eyes over the top of the paperback to make eye contact with her dad. His face glowed a warm tinge of orange through her wide lens sunglasses. It wasn't that she didn't enjoy holidays at all, that wasn't the case. Mandy might have been fifteen but she wasn't entirely neurotic. She enjoyed the time spent with her family away from the greyness of the city, away from the constant chatter about work and money and mundane things like petrol and grass clippings. But at the end of the day, she knew these breaks were mere blips in her everyday life. They could be happy and joyous and blissfully ignorant of the real world and its problems for a week or two, but at the end of the holiday they'd return to their home with its endless flood of bills and chores. The reality of everything had that knack of breaking into the happiness of holidays and days out. And once it was in, no matter how hard Mandy tried, she was completely incapable of shoving it back out. God, maybe she was a bit neurotic.

'Earth to Mandy, anyone home?' A hand waved across her face, fingers fluttering in front of her eyes.

'Sorry, what?' she said, drawing her head up from the pages of her book.

'Ice cream - yay or nay, Mands?'

'It's Mandy. And yay, of course,' she replied with a grin.

'You'll always be Mands to me,' her dad said, turning his attention to Mandy's younger sister, Christine.

'Right you, shoes on,' he said to the younger girl.

'I don't see why I need shoes on to eat ice cream.'

Mandy snorted. Her sister was four years her junior, but was far more of a teenager than she had ever been. If she was this sassy at eleven, God help her family when she reached sixteen.

'Oh no, I'm afraid I'm unable to pay for your ice cream in sarcasm. You're going to have to come with me.'

It was the third time this had played out so far in the four days that the family had been at Rose Bay. It went like this: 1. Mandy's sister refused to do as she was told, accompanied by a witty remark; 2. Mandy's dad retaliated with added sarcasm, grabbing the youngest daughter around the waist and 3. The whole event ended with Mandy's dad flinging Christine over his shoulder and sprinting towards the sea whilst she cried out, claiming to be sorry between hysterical bouts of laughter. They were currently on stage 2. Mandy slipped her head-phones back over her plaited hair and jabbed her finger into the chunky play button. Synthetic sounds brimmed from the foamy ear pieces, spilling into her ears. She watched over the top of her book, smirking and enjoying the scenes in front of her. Somehow, it had yet to get old.

Her dad held her younger sister over his shoulder, her body flopping about and giggling as he sprinted down towards the water. Perhaps this was what happiness felt like. Perhaps she had already found it in moments like these but she was unwilling to allow herself to enjoy them, to live and relish them in the moment.

'Ooh, Mum,' she said, tugging the headset down to rest around her neck. 'Do we have any pictures left?'

'Yes I think so, check the beach bag,' her mum replied, her own face buried into her favourite Jackie Collins novel, the corners of which were peeling and splitting with age. Mandy shoved her hand deep into the straw bag and rummaged around for the familiar cardboard feel of the disposable camera. Her dad had a fancy Olympus but refused point blank to take it anywhere near the beach. *If so much as a single grain of sand makes its way into the complicated mechanics of this thing, I'll blow a gasket,* she imagined him saying. The camera emerged, a smudge of yellowing sun cream smeared on its front.

'Ah great, three left. Smile.' Mandy held up the camera and waited for her mum to tip her large sun hat back to reveal her tanned, freckled face. The camera clunked and creaked as Mandy slid her thumbnail into the grooves of the plastic wheel, churning the film onto the next available image. 'Be right back,' she said with a grin, running down to the water to find her dad dangling her younger sister into the salty waves. She clicked the camera, capturing Christine's wide toothy grin. She wondered why she wasn't able to hold onto her happiness like this camera held onto wonderful holiday images.

'Just one picture left,' she said to herself as she walked back up to her mum, her voice more sombre than anticipated.

'We'll save it, have a family snap when your dad stops torturing Christine,' her mum replied. 'Help me roll these mats up. We're going to hire some of those ridiculous swan shaped pedalos after ice cream.'

Mandy began clearing things from the grainy sand, slotting them into the oversized beach bag. She wound the cable from her headphones tight around her yellow Walkman and placed it on top of her book. She quite liked the idea of a pedalo, the bizarre prospect of cycling across the top of the water and directing your swan to a far off land to explore. Even if they did look utterly ridiculous.

'I want my own one, can I go in my own one? Dad? Can I?' Christine whined between mouthfuls of silky white ice cream, remnants of the sugary substance clinging to the corners of her pink lips.

'Well I don't know, there are four of us so I was quite hoping we'd all go in one, to be honest, Christine.'

'Oh come on, I'm 11 and you lot are embarrassing. I'm too old to come with you!' Christine planted her hands on her hips, practicing her teenage attitude far before the beginning of her teenage years.

'Your older sister is coming with us.'

'Hey, don't bring me into this,' Mandy said, nudging her headphones away from her ears to hear her bickering family that bit clearer. 'Besides, I don't know if you've noticed but there are spaces for four people - I don't even know if these things will work with just one person in them.'

'Yeah, you'll end up going around in circles, Chrissy,' her dad said, jabbing his finger into her side and sending her into fits of hysterics again.

'We agreed - no more tickling! Please, no more!' she screeched, swatting her dad's hands away.

'Well that settles it, we're all together,' Lorraine concluded, nodding towards a sunny yellow and white pedalo drifting in the water and spinning in slow, pronounced circles. Its lone pilot frantically pushed his feet into the pedals, making his already embarrassing situation worse and drawing a wave of laughter from those queuing for their own plastic vessel.

'Fine,' Christine groaned, clambering into the boat and jiggling up and down with excitement. Mandy sat to her right and glanced at her parents who were awkwardly sliding into the two back seats.

'Right, let's go,' Christine yelled, barely waiting for her family to sit down before driving her legs against the pedals. 'This is your captain speaking,' she mocked, bellowing into cupped hands and lifting her head high above her family. 'Please make sure you keep your arms and legs inside of the boat at all times, or else the crocodiles will chomp them off.'

'Who decided you should be the captain, huh?'

'I'll take no rude comments from the passengers, unless they fancy jumping overboard,' Christine retorted, dodging the droplets that flew from her dad's hands as he ran his fingertips across the top of the cool water. 'Oi,' '— she said, scooping up her own handful of murky British water '— 'behave!'

The water was still, bar the splashes and droplets that flew through the air between Christine and her dad. Mandy and her mum continued to pedal despite their ribs hurting from laughing at the other half of their boat, and soon enough they were bearing up to the side of the luscious green island that was situated in the middle of the channel of water.

'So what is this island, exactly?' Mandy asked.

'Not entirely sure. There was a sign at the top of the beach that said it was uninhabited by people but it's full of birds and plants. That's it essentially.'

'Who knew there were so many beautiful shades of green? Look how wonderfully healthy all of the plants look.' Lorraine gawked at the fauna from the side of the pedalo. 'It is very small though. Doesn't surprise me that no one would live on it,' she said, leaning back into her seat and basking in the late afternoon sunshine. 'The mainland is so close. Not much point living out here.'

'Can we get off and take a look?' Christine tilted her head, adopting her classic puppy-dog eyes that would be sure to work their magic on her parents.

'Oh no, I'm not sure that's the best idea,' her mum replied. 'It doesn't look like we're supposed to.'

'Dad?' Christine asked again. Her eyes widened in the way she was sure would twist her dad's arm, but he didn't budge. She puffed out her bottom lip and lifted her eyebrows.

The hardness in her dad's face melted away. 'I don't think it would hurt, would it? Just a quick look?'

Mandy and Lorraine glared at him, unimpressed by his overruling. 'Oh come on,' he said, resting a hand on his wife's knee. 'Live a little. Besides, there are no signs telling us we *can't* go on there.'

Mandy glanced at her mum's more stern face and shrugged in agreement. 'We can hop on, spot a bird or two, and hop back off again. No one would ever know.' Her dad grinned at her, the playful nature of his personality twinging at the corners of his eyes.

'Fine, whatever,' Lorraine sighed. 'But if we're caught you're dealing with it, Gavin.'

The girl's dad saluted, pulling his back ramrod straight and planting a mock-serious expression on his face. 'Right-o, pull over when you're ready Captain Christine. Prepare for landing.'

The pedalo veered to the right and curled round the back of the island, away from the potentially suspicious eyes of those manning the rentals on the mainland. The side of the plastic boat scraped along the edge of the island, smearing wet sand and mud up the smooth outer layer.

'Whoah,' Gavin jested. 'Carefully does it. Is the pilot drunk?'

Christine chuckled, pushing Mandy out of her side of the boat and onto the green, overgrown island. She clambered over the centre console, landing on the island next to her sister. 'Right, where shall we explore first?'

'We'll be on here for five minutes, then back in the boat, you understand me?'

'Yes, Mum, or should I say, First Mate Buzzkill?' Christine giggled, taking off into the thick layer of trees.

'I'm going to wait here and make sure the boat doesn't float away. Please, five minutes Gavin,' Lorraine pleaded. 'I mean it,' she said, frowning through a grin that tugged at her lips and threatened to break her matronly facade.

'Ye ma'am, you got it.' Gavin leaned over and kissed his wife before darting off into the tree line behind his two daughters. 'We'll be back before you know it.'

Lorraine rummaged around in the beach bag for her book. How did her family fill this thing with so much stuff?

Where did it all hide, squashed in the corners of the multi-coloured straw like a sand covered Mary Poppins holdall? Her hand passed by multiple bottles of suncream of varying strengths, the flimsy disposable camera, half finished packets of crisps, an apple, too many books for one child to claim to be able to read in an afternoon, and God knows what else.

'Ah,' she breathed, lifting the battered paperback up to her face and flipping the pages to her place. *Why do you always read the same things?* That's what Gavin always asked. It wasn't true. She didn't read exactly the same thing all the time, but when they were on holiday she loved nothing more than to jump into her favourite novel. The words comforted her, their familiarity lulling her into relaxation. It might not have made sense to everyone, but she enjoyed it. And she was coming up to a good bit.

The pages swallowed her whole as they always did. It didn't matter that she could quote this particular chapter word for word. The suspense between the lines, between the words that didn't need to be written, those were what got her. The paragraphs drew her in, and soon she'd read close to thirty pages. Thirty pages at what, a minute or so a page? It took a second to dawn on her. She dug her hand frantically into her bag again in search of her old Casio watch.

'Oh shit, oh shit,' she mumbled, her mind immediately catastrophising the situation. 'What. Is. The. Time?' she uttered. 'Ah.'

The watch floated to the top of the bag, summoned by her hand, to reveal itself amongst the debris of family life at the beach. *16:54. 16:54.* What time did they get off the boat?

'Oh my goodness,' she uttered, the realisation dawning on her that she'd been waiting for her family for almost forty minutes. 'Gavin!' she yelled, holding onto the side of the pedalo in the thankfully calm water. No one answered. Lorraine strained her eyes into the thick blanket of trees and shrubs, desperately hoping to lock onto one of her family members. No one surfaced. She leant forward, away from the boat, eager to run off into the trees in search of her children but aware that the boat would likely drift away if she left its side. She couldn't see anywhere sensible to tie the boat, and in turn felt tethered to it herself.

'They're just in there, they've lost track of time, that's all,' she whispered. 'You've got to stop overreacting like this.' She swallowed, a deep breath of fresh air. 'They're just in there,' she repeated, a mantra meant to calm her down.

She squinted into the trees. The trunks and roots of the plants merged together, the varying shades of brown and green bleeding and morphing into one until she could hardly make out any space between them. Was that a light, or did she imagine it? She brought the watch up to her face again: *16:59. Oh God, those five minutes felt so much longer.* 'Gavin?' she yelled again, spotting a hand on a nearby tree. 'Gavin, is that you? Stop messing around, we need to get back.'

Mandy finally peered from around a tree and came running out to meet her mum.

'Oh thank God,' Lorraine exhaled, the words gushing from her mouth. 'Where's your dad? Where's Christine?'

Mandy stared at her mum, unsure how to respond.

'Mandy? Where are they?' she mouthed.

'I —.' Mandy looked frantically to either side of the small island. 'I don't know.'

'What do you mean you don't know?'

'As in, I'm assuming they're still in there, but I don't know exactly where.'

'I'm not joking, Mandy. Where are they?' Lorraine raised her voice, her face taking on the rosy tint of panic.

'Mum, I honestly don't know. I thought they'd be out here with you.'

'Mandy, thank God! Where did you go?' Gavin cried, bursting out from the line of trees and shrubs. 'It's so thick in there, you can hardly see your hand in front of your face. So much for seeing loads of birds. I saw sod all apart from a load of damp plants and bugs!'

'Gavin?' Lorraine interjected her husband's exasperated rambling. 'Where is Christine?' Her jaw clenched and she finally moved away from the pedalo, letting it drift into the water. Mandy rushed over and grabbed the side of it before it made a break for it.

'What?' Isn't she out here already?' Gavin said, his eyes automatically darting back to the edge of the forest. 'I left her with you.' He turned to Mandy.

'No, no you didn't, Dad. She was with you the entire time.'

None of them answered Mandy's statement. The three of them stood in their respective spots on the island, staring from the trees to the edge of the land until it dawned on them. Not one of them knew where Christine was. Christine, the eleven year old girl, was alone somewhere on the uninhabited island.

'This island isn't big,' Mandy said. 'She can't have gone far.'

'I'll head back into the forest,' Gavin replied, striding towards the tree line. 'You two stay here in case she comes back.' He moved swiftly into the trees, the darkening forest swallowing any trace of him.

'I'm going to walk around the perimeter, Mum - she might have come out of the forest on the wrong side.'

Lorraine tried to argue, tried to say that didn't want to risk another daughter getting lost, that Gavin had the situation under control, that everything would be perfectly okay. But something stopped her, something wedged her breath in her throat and forced her to remain silent. Despite the warm evening air, the hairs on Lorraine's arms prickled and rose up to stand on end. There was something else on this island.

'Mandy, no—', she said, only to realise that her eldest daughter had already taken it upon herself to go in search of her younger sister. Lorraine was, once again, left alone , standing next to the pedalo, her hand resting on the plastic hull. The book was still hanging in her other hand, a reminder that ten minutes ago, everything felt fine. And now it felt anything but. She flung the book onto the backseat of the boat, disgusted at how she'd let herself slip between the lines and lose track of time. She slipped the old watch onto her wrist and checked the time again. *17:12.* Mandy and Gavin had only been gone a few minutes but time was stretching out in front of her like a tape measure - preparing to snap back to reality any second as if nothing out of the ordinary had happened. Or so she hoped. Her breath quickened as she struggled to remain calm. *17:17.* Where did those five minutes go? How was everything moving so quickly?

17:22. 'Oh come on, where did everyone go? I can't just stand here and do nothing,' she whispered. She scanned the edge of the forest again in search of any member of her family, but her gaze was not met by an ally.

'What was that?' she gasped, embarrassed that she'd asked the question to the emptiness in front of her. An uneasiness rippled through her stomach, lapping at the back of her throat. She strained her eyes into the trees, desperately willing her vision to be stronger and see that bit further inside the forest. There was an orange glow, no, two orange glowing objects hovering above the floor at the centre of the trees. Two orbs of blazing amber light revolving in the shadows. Lorraine gripped the edge of the boat, her fingers ramming into the hard plastic. The orange spheres lifted a foot off the ground and lurched forward. Lorraine jumped back, shoving the pedalo behind her into the water.

'Shit!' she hissed, scrambling around to try to grab the edge of the boat. The force of her trip shunted the plastic swan out into the water, too far away for her to reach. She placed one foot in the water, hoping that it was shallower than it looked, and started to wade towards the boat when she heard the unmistakable hissing of an animal. Her body turned slowly, the muscles in her jaw clenching and unclenching, her whole body riddled with nerves.

She swallowed. The amber spheres had moved beyond the tree line, beyond the darkness. They pulsated like flames; the further they moved out of the shadows the more Lorraine could see that these orange spheres were attached to something the likes of which she had never seen before. They were set inside a large, matte black, writhing creature. The surface of the creature was deep and dark and absorbed all light that came near it. It cast everything into shadow. There were no limbs, exactly. Rather, the entire body was composed of tendrils and ropes and slithers of shadow that stretched out and touched the edges of the island.

The hissing dropped to a low, guttural groan, each globule of spittle and phlegm audible inside Lorraine's eardrums. She backed further off the island into the water, desperate for her family to burst from the trees and rush to her side, desperate to decide that the pedalos were a daft idea, desperate for this all to be a dream and for her to wake up outstretched on her towel, sand clinging to the underside of her bare feet. Everything had changed so suddenly.

'Mum!'

Lorraine's head shot up to the left of the island, her attention whipped away from the shadowy creature. 'What the—,' Mandy's shouts were cut off by her shock as she registered what her mum was staring at. Just as her words trailed off into the cooling evening air, Gavin burst from the other side of the forest, without Christine, and ran straight to Lorraine.

'Gavin, watch out!' Lorraine cried, throwing her hands in front of her, willing the creature to remain where it was. Gavin spun mid air to see the creature slither back into the tree line, swallowed once again by the shadows that appeared to be growing between the plants and branches. 'Where is she?' Lorraine sobbed, throwing her hand up to cover her mouth. Her husband swallowed, unable to answer. Mandy stood to the side of the pedalo, watching as her parents broke down in front of her.

THE HAIG FAMILY stood in the shallow water for what could have been minutes, hours, or even longer. Their bodies took on a hollow air, their chests wrenching with every laborious breath and their eyes widened beyond belief in search of Christine and the creature that writhed from the depths of the trees. The coastguard would soon make its way out to the island. They'd be alerted to the family's struggle by the pedalo floating back towards the mainland, a drifting time capsule of their happy holiday possessions. The coastguard would be followed by police and volunteers holding heavy-duty silver torches, yellow high-vis jackets draped over their shoulders. There were so many people on the tiny island that

Lorraine began to fear it would sink, taking them, and Christine, wherever she was, down with them. Surely this many people would find her youngest daughter? How could there possibly be so many of them and they not locate her? The family held onto that idea until they could no longer. They held onto the idea that the youngest member of their family would one day come home. But of course, she never did.

2

Summer 1995

Sadie jammed her index finger into the gap between her collarbones. *Still beating, still breathing,* she thought to herself. *You're okay.*

The anxiety had gotten worse. It no longer crouched in the corners of her everyday, threatening to grab onto her torso or slide heavily against her chest. Oh no, there was no threatening anymore; the anxiety was very much there. Its pincers perforated and gripped her heart and lungs, convincing her time and again that somehow, despite the fact that she was very much still standing upright and walking and talking, her heart had failed to remember to beat. She shoved her fingers harder against her skin, counting the beats under her breath. Her inhalations quietened, easing lower so she could hear her heartbeat loud and clear. She willed the thudding to drown out her footsteps as they pounded against the concrete, surrounded by hundreds of others. Her shoes hit the ground, vibrations rippling through her body as they made contact. *One day,* she thought, *one day, my body will crumple onto this ground and my heart will give up beating.* It was a fear that stalked her.

She lowered herself onto the narrow plastic bench, thrusting her trusty, beaten up paperback into her face. Throngs of people surrounded her, all behaving in much the same fashion. Heads down, hidden by newspapers, fidgeting in the heat, thumbing through pages of well-worn novels. The train carriage rocked back and forth. The heat intensified, condensation and moisture clinging to the window frames. A young man flicked the door vent open, desperate to entice some cooler air into the car. Sadie noticed his attempt, but knew it was futile; he'd flick it closed again soon enough. A puff of hot, dusty air billowed in, hitting the man in the side of the face and, sure enough, he thumbed the vent closed as quickly as he had opened it.

The train's wheels thrummed against the tracks. The space in the train carriage began to close in around Sadie and the other passengers. The temperature rose again, the air quality lessened, and the people got closer. Sadie looked down at her hands, at the beads of sweat forming between the creases in her palms. A swelling sensation crawled up her throat; an allergic reaction? Was it possible to be allergic to the London Tube? The tightness closed in around her neck, squeezing around her tonsils. Her hand flung up and grabbed the metal pole closest to her.

Concentrate on the coolness. Ground yourself, Sadie. She closed her eyes and allowed the rocking of the carriage to translate into her body, her torso swaying in time with the wheels against the tracks. The sway calmed her frantic heart.

She swallowed deeply, pushing the dust-laden air from her lungs.

A hand gripped her shoulder. Sadie's eyes flung open, wide and hyperaware.

'This your station, love?' The gentleman that had nudged her looked down, concerned eyes peering out of curly hair.

She recognised him. He rode this same journey every day, the same as she did. 'Yes,' she said, shaking her head and grabbing hold of her bag. 'Thank you,' she mumbled, flinging herself out of the train and onto the sooty platform.

The London Underground was the number one place that triggered Sadie's anxiety. The lack of air, the intimacy of every other sweating, heaving body, and the rush of traffic towards open tracks. It crossed her mind daily how fortunate she was not to have fallen on the tracks, not to have tripped and plummeted against the rusting metal. She read about someone not long ago, some that had been pushed onto the rails by a passerby. They died, of course. The train driver had no chance. They had no choice but to let tonnes of metal and machinery course over the fragile human body, pulling it limb from limb. They had no choice but to end a person's life.

You never know what people are thinking, underneath the normal facade of their work suit, behind the crumpled edges of the latest broadsheet newspaper. Who knows what these so-called normal people are capable of.

A shout broke out from the crowd in front of her. Sadie threw her hand down over her belongings instinctively. She drew the bag across her body, a shield against the pulsating flow of people. There was some more yelling, a brief tussle up ahead, and then it was over. She let out a breath, relaxing her grip on her bang and letting her arm swing to her side.

The escalator carried her to the upper level of the tube

station. A young man tussled amongst two police officers, his arms held behind him and his chest propelling forward as he struggled against their grip. He looked like a pretty normal guy, eighteen years old or so. He was slight in build, his stature shrinking beside the two towering men in uniform. There was nothing special about the young guy, nothing to indicate what he'd done or what had driven him to make such a bad decision. Perhaps he hadn't made a bad decision at all. You never do know.

Sadie slid her ticket into the barrier and walked into the gate as it flung open, allowing for her escape into the somewhat fresher air of central London. The station tipped her out onto the pavement amongst hundreds of other bodies. Her feet began to carry her home on auto-pilot. The journey was an easy one that she'd done almost every day for the past four years or so since leaving Rose Bay. One tube, one twenty-minute walk, and done. Simple and pain free, save for the stress brought on by the thousands of other people that felt the need to make the identical journey. Unless it was raining, of course. That was another story entirely. When Britain had rain, the whole city was engulfed in an angry shade of grey, raindrops and thunder and bitter cold water showering down and bouncing off the pavement. Luckily, today was bright and sunny.

She'd made silent acquaintances with a few others that travelled the same path as her. There was the gentleman with the obnoxiously loud headphones thrusting his music taste into the world and the mature woman whose power dressing commanded the attention of whatever space she was inhabiting. And there was the same ticket conductor with the same fluorescent orange vest and the same honest smile that had more of an impact on peoples' days than they probably realised. She'd often had imaginary conversations with them, or one sided ones out loud. Conversations where the recipients weren't sure if they should be answering, or if they should move away from the lady who was making small talk with her handbag.

'Oh no, thank *you,*' Sadie uttered under her breath, swerving out of the way of an important looking Londoner who walked directly into her, their eyes trained on something fascinating that resided behind her forehead. 'I don't mind moving at all, not a problem,' she grumbled, hugging her bag tight to her stomach. She squeezed her body closer against the throngs of people as they spewed from the belly of the tube station. 'You're welcome,' she said a little louder. An older lady turned around, her coiffed hair flopping over her glasses. 'Oh shit,' she mumbled, embarrassed that she'd been heard. The woman's eyes passed over her, her jaw firm, red lipstick bleeding into the feathered skin of her upper lip. A giggled escaped Sadie's lips as she slipped amongst a crowd of teenagers. *How mature,* she thought as she sped up along the pavement, bustling her way through the crowds of people until she found herself at her normal crossroads.

The crowds thinned, revealing the dirty grey pavement and, finally, some remnants of fresh air. Sadie dug her hand into her oversized bag and pulled out her yellow Walkman. The headphones were well-worn and the buttons had grown shiny with hours of use, but this was all part of the ritual to get her home. She slipped the headphones over her wavy brown hair, nestling the grey foam on top of her ears and pressed the 'play' button. The music picked up where it left off earlier that morning with a satisfying clunk. The electronic sounds filled the headphones and spilled into her ears. She never understood how there were people out there that claimed to dislike music. The creativity and passion of it all made Sadie's heart sing. She slowed her pace to enjoy the music as she began her walk home.

The energy of the city still overwhelmed her if she let it. The crowds, the creativity, the terrible air quality, the sprawling buildings like limbs reaching up to smog-filled skies. She couldn't put into words what made her come here and decide to stay, but it had a hold on her that she doubted would ever change. It was the kind of hold that, no matter how anxious the city made her, would refuse to let go.

The city spread out in front of her. People filled every inch of it, each one with their own story. Bjork sang her home, or wailed, as her mum would say. Her mum had never understood the appeal, but that made Sadie like her even more. Enjoying her music became a kind of exclusive club, something that not everyone understood. She turned right down a busy street and slipped down an alleyway, a well-known shortcut that trimmed her journey by a few minutes. The bricks changed colour here; they started the well-known washed out grey of Central London and, the further she moved down the alley, the darker they got.

Grey turned to red, stone to warm brick. The white, commanding balconies of Piccadilly and Waterloo slid away, replaced by dark black snaking staircases and fire escapes. The closer Sadie got to her home, the more the greyness of the city slid from under her feet, warming with the clay redbricks.

Her home was humble, as most homes had to be in the middle of the city for a young professional. She lived with a flatmate who had, more-or-less, been foisted upon her by the estate agent, but it was the only way she'd been able to afford rent, so she readily accepted. Luckily for the both of them, they got on like a house on fire. Her key slid into the lock of the main door and, leaning her body against the heavy wood, she heaved her way into the hallway. Her flat was the first behind the main door. It had felt like a great deal when she'd first accepted. There were no stairs to contend with, wide doorways for furniture, and well-lit rooms that faced out onto the street. Of course, the estate agency had handily failed to mention how noisy it was to live on the ground floor of a flat in London, but that was nothing that her headphones and some Pearl Jam couldn't resolve.

'Honey! I'm home!' she yelled, kicking her shoes off at the door and flinging them around the corner.

'Did you pick up some milk on your way home?' a warm voice came in reply. Tabitha stood in the kitchen fussing over something in a frying pan, her back turned to the door. She'd scraped her hair high up on her head, the dark curls clipped in place with what looked suspiciously like a bulldog clip. Sadie walked over to her, glancing at the comical placement of the item of stationery.

'I may have forgotten.' Sadie grimaced, leaning against the countertop to face her friend. 'Can it wait until tomorrow or do I need to go out again?'

'Depends,' Tabitha sighed, stirring the contents of the pan. 'Could always substitute the tea we would have had with the wine we do have?'

'Glad that settles that then.' Sadie grinned, pacing over to the fridge and sweeping two wine glasses from the cabinet. 'Good day?'

'Not so bad,' her friend said, shunting vegetables from one side of the pan to the other. 'We've got building work going on in the office so I'm forever welcoming a new cohort of unknowns through the foyer with a Barbie grin plastered across my face, but aside from that I can't complain.' Tabitha loved her job, she'd told Sadie multiple times. But she also liked the currency of having a little moan, as we all did. 'How was yours?' she asked, turning her head away from the stove.

'You know, it's not so bad. I think, if I keep slogging away, I'll get somewhere eventually, you know?' Sadie swilled the wine around the edges of the glass.

'Hmm. You think this is a ladder worth climbing? You've felt this way for some time, Sadie.'

'In all honesty?' Sadie lifted her gaze from the light golden contents of the glass. 'I'm not that sure. But it pays at the end of the day. I guess I need to work out my options.'

Sadie watched Tabitha's back as her head bobbed up and down in agreement. Tabitha didn't think much of Sadie's job, but then, neither did Sadie. She had searched for a job that held her passion many times, but there was nothing that grabbed hold of her and screamed *apply to me!* If she thought about it long and hard enough, she might find that it was something else that was keeping her from feeling fulfilled, from being truly happy. But she couldn't let those thoughts in and admit defeat, so she continued as she had done for the past four years since arriving in London.

Tabitha reached up above the oven-hood and fetched two bowls. She tipped the pan and let the contents slide out, nudging a bowl over the countertop in Sadie's direction. The two sat at the small kitchen table in comfortable silence.

'Father's Day this Sunday,' Tabitha mumbled between mouthfuls. 'I'm off out to meet Dad for lunch with my brothers.'

'Oh,' Sadie replied. 'That'll be nice.' She'd avoided any mention of Father's Day up until this point. She kept her head lowered to the table, focussed intently on her dinner.

'Are you doing anything with your family?'

Sadie had seen her family last Christmas. They'd come to visit London in the winter, to wander around Hamley's and drink hot chocolate in the cafes and nestle in pubs like families ought to, like they do in the films. All romantic and cosy but in the best possible way. Where the windows fog up with the warmth of nestled groups inside pubs, chattering excitedly about the festive season and their plans. Of course, it hadn't played out like that for Sadie.

Her mum and dad had come to visit. They'd stayed in a small, fusty B'n'B a few roads over from Sadie's home, dragging themselves away from the comfort of their seaside life and dropping themselves in the centre of one of the busiest cities in the world. The crowds terrified them and the fear of getting lost or mugged played on their minds the entire time. They hadn't spent a great deal of time talking to each other. Instead they wandered the roads of London in a tense quiet that made Sadie long for their departure minutes after they'd arrived. There were a few passive-aggressive comments made about old, stale arguments and hints at gaping wounds in their family, but everything bubbled beneath the surface. No one wanted to break face; no one wanted to discuss how they actually felt. These kinds of experiences made up the vast majority of Sadie's memories of her family.

'No, not this time,' Sadie smiled, the expression empty. 'They're visiting one of my uncles or something,' she lied. She hadn't mentioned Father's Day to her family. She'd sent a card home, but that was all. She was happy to let Hallmark do the legwork for her this time around.

'Oh, that's a shame. Have they come up to visit you so far this year? Feels like ages ago that they were up this way.'

Sadie shook her head. She had never divulged much to

Tabitha about her family, despite their close friendship. 'We had arguments a long time ago. It's made things...tricky,' she offered.

'I get you,' Tabitha nodded. 'Sometimes it's hard to move past things, sometimes those things need a little more time.'

Sadie smiled. One of those small smiles reassuring your friend that what they said was right, that what they were saying had meaning to you. But also one of those smiles that divulges that you may not have told the whole truth, and you were never likely to.

'Right —' Tabitha said, pushing away from the table and taking a few short steps over to the fridge. 'More wine, I think.'

Sadie swept up the empty bowls and placed them into the sink. 'I'll get to that later,' she said, taking the wine glass from Tabitha and swallowing a large gulp. 'Fancy a crappy film?'

'Always,' Tabitha replied as Sadie followed her through to their small living room area. Tabitha flopped onto the light cream sofa, flinging her feet onto the coffee table and nudging her slippers onto the floor. 'Your turn to choose.'

Sadie sat cross-legged on the floor, rummaging through their large collection of VHS tapes. 'Anything you fancy in particular?' she hummed. 'Do we fancy comedy, romance?' She whipped her head round to face her friend. 'Before you ask, no, I don't want to watch *The Little Mermaid* again. Please, anything but that.'

'Hey!' Tabitha shouted in mock offence. 'That's a classic and you know it.'

'How about something new?'

'New? No. How about something old?' Tabitha retorted, initiating their usual game. Selecting the film often took longer than watching it from start to finish. Sadie shot her friend a knowing glance; she knew where this was going.

'How about,' Sadie mumbled, thinking out loud. 'Ooh, I bought that new Arnie film the other day, where's that gone? I can't remember what it's called. Something about lies or truth or something equally unimaginative.'

'*True lies*?' Tabitha interjected. 'I hid that. I can't stand Arnie. You're not making me watch that thing.'

'Fine,' Sadie drawled, dragging the vowels out like a small child. '*West Side Story*?'

'Don't think I'm feeling a musical today.'

Sadie offered a few more options, unceremoniously dumping the video tapes behind her until she was surrounded by a plastic case fortress. 'Are you likely to say yes to any of these?'

'No...maybe not. Okay, how about...' Tabitha teased, nudging the growing tower of films with her toe.

Sadie turned, her head tilted and eyebrows raised. *Ghost*? Sadie grinned from ear to ear. The pair had seen *Ghost* countless times, maybe more than *The Little Mermaid*, but always ended up going back for more.

'Oh go no then, I thought you'd never ask.'

Sadie unclasped the chunky plastic box and slid the cassette into the player. The familiar scent of dust and film and plastic escaped the box. 'Would it kill you to rewind this thing every now and then?' Tabitha hid her face behind a cushion, an overdrawn innocent look on her face. The tape whirred and clunked, and finally reached the beginning of the movie.

Sadie thumped onto the sofa, careful to guard her wine from spilling over the edges of the glass and onto the floor. She leant her head on her friend's shoulder and they watched the familiar film play out before them on the small, square television set.

'You can talk to me if you need to, you know.' Tabitha said, around a third of the way through the film.

Sadie sat up, stretching her aching neck. 'I know.' And she did know. 'I'm not sure where to start with it all, to be honest.'

Tabitha tilted her head but didn't say anything in response.

'It's all a bit of a mess. Some things happened when I was younger, before I moved here. I came here to start again, so when my parents visit, it dredges things back up, you know?'

Tabitha nodded. 'I do know. Sometimes we need to dredge those things back up, to talk through them and say what needs to be said.' It was almost like Tabitha knew more than she did, but that wasn't possible. 'Sometimes these things are painful,' she continued. 'You need to move at your own pace, Sade, but family won't be here forever.'

Sadie felt the sting of tears and swallowed another gulp of wine, concentrating on the acidic tang as it sank down her throat. 'You're right, but I'm not ready to talk to them properly. Not yet.'

Tabitha placed her hand on Sadie's knee and turned her face back to the film. Sadie focussed her eyes on Tabitha's fingers, staring at the cuticles that had separated and drifted part way down her pink fingernails. She desperately tried to hold back the tears that threatened to break free down her cheeks. She wanted to confide in her friend. So why couldn't she? She closed her eyes and imagined the words drifting freely from her parted lips. She imagined the burden of the truth dividing into two and the weight lifting to be shared between her and Tabitha but still, something stopped her. She couldn't share this secret, not with anyone.

The film whirred by. Both women had seen it far too many times and knew exactly what was coming next, but the familiarity of it all lulled them. Sadie relaxed into the end scenes, Tabitha's sweet floral perfume lingering in the air, an invisible comfort blanket. As the movie drew to a close, the usual Friday evening noises pulsed into the flat from the street below. The cheering of groups of young people off to the pub, the yelling of those who had already had a few drinks too many. Sadie considered, again, how lucky she was to have Tabitha.

'You know,' Tabitha said, breaking the silence, 'I could always come with you to see your family. If you don't want to be alone.'

Sadie inhaled. 'No, that's fine, really.' She shook her head. 'I don't want to see them any time soon. Thank you, though.'

'I really think you ought to think about it a bit more.'

Sadie's jaw clenched. *Stop pushing it, please.*

'It's just, our parents aren't getting any younger. I can't imagine how horrible it would be to pass up the chance to fix things before, you know...'

'I know what you're saying, but the answer's still no,' Sadie snapped, pushing herself away from her friend's shoulder and shifting further along the sofa. 'I can't speak to them right now. I just... I need to focus on myself for a while. I want to get myself a better job, get myself sorted up here so when I see them, they know I'm doing okay. So they won't see me as a failure.'

Tabitha nodded and let her eyes drop to the floor. She folded her hands across her chest. 'I'll sort the kitchen tonight,' she announced, lifting herself off the sofa and escaping into the kitchen.

'Sure? I don't mind helping,' Sadie offered, her last ditch attempt obvious to both of them.

'Don't worry, I'll let you do it tomorrow,' she answered, turning and pulling a thin grin across her face. 'Maybe you should get some rest? We could both do with some R&R?'

THE WATER WAS ALWAYS a bit too hot for Sadie's likings. That was the problem with rented property - you always had to compromise on something. The water was either scorching hot or pretty much frozen; there was never any in between. Her legs tingled, the heat prickling and raising her hair follicles as she lowered herself into the tub. Bright pink, shimmering bubble bath swirled into the water, a sweet, saccharin scent of strawberry lifting into the warm air.

She couldn't shake her earlier conversation with Tabitha. The words clung to her skin as she scrubbed, desperate to shed the uneasiness of her friend prying. She knew Tabitha was right. She also knew that there was no quick fix to the situation with her parents. She plunged her head under the cooling water. Her hair pulled out in tendrils, water echoing in her ears like a conch shell. The sweet smell of strawberries and sugar swilled across her body.

'Sadie!'

She sat up, water sloshing over the sides of the bath and onto the floor in a wave. Tabitha was banging on the door. 'Sadie, phone!' she yelled again through the wooden door.

Phone? Sadie thought. *Someone calling for me?* Seemed unlikely. 'Who is it?' Sadie responded, heaving herself out of the tub and grabbing a towel from the radiator.

There was a pregnant pause. 'It's your mum, Sadie.'

Oh God, what's happened? 'Erm, did she say what she wanted?' Sadie wrapped another towel tight around her dripping hair, tucking the end underneath. Her mum didn't call for casual chats.

'No, she didn't say. Just that it's urgent and that she needed to talk to you right away.'

'Okay, thanks.' Sadie unlocked the door and walked out into the hallway. Tabitha pulled her lips into a thin, tense smile and ducked into her room.

The phone stood ominously on a small, spindly wooden table at the far end of the hall, nearest the kitchen. It cast a long, thin shadow out onto the floor. The receiver lay face up, cast aside from its cream, plastic body. The small lamp flickered and threw a synthetically warm light over the table, luring Sadie closer. She couldn't work out whether she ought to run towards the phone or take as long as possible to get there. Her family didn't call, not ever. She walked over, wet footsteps following her, seeping into the carpet, and lifted the receiver to her ear.

'Hello?'

3

Summer 1995

There was nothing. No noise came from the other end of the line, apart from the low hum of electricity buzzing through the receiver.

'Hello? Mum?' Are you there?' Something shuffled in the background, righting itself, the thud of fingers as they grasped at the receiver.

'Sadie? Is that you?' An exasperated voice broke over the line, out of breath and panting, as if its owner had been running. Or crying. Or both.

'Yes Mum, it's me.' Sadie couldn't bring herself to say anything further. She waited for her mum to tell her exactly why she'd called. It certainly wasn't for a chipper late evening chat or to catch up on the family gossip. *We are the family gossip.*

There was silence. Sadie listened as her mum inhaled and steadied herself.

'What's wrong?' Sadie said, her patience fraying at the edges. She couldn't wait around all night for her mum to relent and finally speak.

'It's your brother.'

Sadie's heart plunged. 'What about him?' Goosebumps raised all over her body, vibrating to the top layer of her skin.

'He's...', her mum choked, pulling the phone away from her mouth.

'Mum, what about him?' Sadie pushed. It was coming up to the five year anniversary of the event that blew her family unit apart. When it first happened, her mum would convince herself that he was still at home, that he was hiding in his room, waiting for something or other to pass. The rest of the family knew that was her coping mechanism. She held it out in front of her, a shield to the reality of being down a child and being left with another that refused to fuel her delusions. None of the family knew how to broach the subject, so they let her be. How do you tell a grieving woman that what has happened is final, that it has to be? For anyone to have a hope in hell's chance of moving on, or even carrying on, what happened needed to be accepted? Her mum had never really accepted it. She never would. 'Mum?' Sadie pressed.

A swallow. 'He's come home, Sadie.'

She'd done this before, back in the first months of the disappearance. She'd call Sadie, or wake up in the middle of the night when she lived at home to tell her that he'd returned, that he was waiting for his family on the front doorstep. Of course, he hadn't. Sadie's mum had been drinking wine and a desperate hope, a dream, forged its way into her fraudulent reality.

What was it that Sadie could hear in her mother's voice? Was it hope? She thought it was. Hope and innocence, happiness and...fear? Maybe her mum could hear the falsehood in her own words, after all these years.

'Mum, we've spoken about this. He's not come home. He can't come home.' Sadie closed her eyes and placed a weary hand over her forehead. She took a deep breath. 'He's dead, Mum,' she whispered.

'No, you're wrong, Sadie. It's real this time. He's come home, he's here with me now. He's in the kitchen. Aren't you dear?' Sadie pictured her mum leaning her head around to the other side of the kitchen, yelling into the empty space there.

There was no response. Of course there wasn't. Sadie pitied her mum, but they'd been through this so, so many times.

'Mum, is Dad there? Put Dad on the phone. Please?' Sadie begged, desperate for a voice of reason.

'I can't,' she spluttered. 'I mean, he can't come to the phone right now. He's with your brother.'

Sadie raked a hand over her tired eyes. 'Mum, this has to stop. It's been five years.'

'Don't you think I know that?' she shouted. A breath rattled between her lips and she coughed down the phone. Sadie remained silent.

'Okay,' she finally said. 'Put me on the phone to Ben.'

'Oh, I can't do that, Sadie! He's with your dad, I told you. They've got so much lost time to catch up on.'

Sadie slipped onto the floor, all energy and desire to understand her mum leaving her body in a rush. Her forehead rested on her bent knees, the receiver still pressed to her ear.

'He has come home, Sadie,' her mum whispered. 'I know you don't believe me, I can hear it in your voice. But he's here, I promise.'

'Okay,' Sadie relented. 'Tell me what happened, Mum.'

Tabitha peered into the hallway from the kitchen, tilting her head and motioning to Sadie. 'Everything okay?' she mouthed, her lips forming the exaggerated words. Sadie shook her head and shrugged - who knows? She watched as Tabitha slipped back into the kitchen. The hallway stood long and dark again, as if no one else had been there at all.

'Sadie, are you listening to me?'

'Yes, Mum,' she lied. 'Ben's home, he arrived early this morning when it was still pitch black outside and, conveniently, no one else has seen him.'

'Oh no,' her mum corrected. 'People *have* seen him. The police have been over, the newspapers are crawling up the street. People know he's here.'

Sadie lifted her head from her knees, suddenly aware of the dampness still permeating her towel. She shivered, her free hand automatically rising to make contact with her throat. *Still beating.* She took a deep breath in. This was just another bottle or two or rosé speaking. There was no way this could be true.

'Oh look, your dad's just come into the kitchen. Hang on, I'll put him on.'

The moisture drained from Sadie's mouth, leaving her tongue dry and swollen. *There's no way...* Her eyes widened in the darkness as she waited for her dad to speak.

'Sadie, it's your dad.' She'd not heard his voice in months. He sounded as strong as ever. She'd never known anything to knock his composure. 'What your mum said, it's true Sadie. He's come home.'

Sadie's head dropped, her chin resting on the tops of her knees that peeked through the bath towel. Her eyes locked onto the strands of the carpet, desperate for something to hold onto, something small and menial and not utterly impossible. A slow, deliberate breath through the nose, her other hand laying atop of the carpet, the prickle of each individual fibre electric on her palm. Her heart raced.

'Sadie?'

'Yes Dad, sorry, I... I don't know what to say.' Sadie scrunched her eyes tight.

'No, I can understand that,' he replied, pragmatic as ever.

Sadie heard a short scuffle on the other end of the phone. Her mum jostled the phone back from her dad and began talking again. 'How about saying "that's amazing?" Are you going to come home, Sadie? You need to come home. I want you to come home.'

Her mum's voice trailed off, bouncing around in the holes of the phone receiver's earpiece, interspersed by the odd hacking cough laced with tobacco.

'Erm,' Sadie faltered. 'I don't know.' Her body tensed.

'You don't know? Your brother has come home, Sadie? Did you hear that part?'

'Yes, I am Mum, I did. I — I've got a lot that I need to sort out here. I can't just up and leave.'

'Not for this, Sadie?' The anger in her mum's voice deflated, the frustration seeping from her tone. 'Not even to come home? Not even for me?' She was virtually whimpering. Sadie had heard the injured animal voice before, but this time it had real meaning; her brother had actually come home.

'I'll try, Mum.'

'Fine,' she snapped, the vexation flooding back. The

receiver snapped back into the cradle, leaving Sadie to stand and listen to the haunting sounds of the dial tone. Water had dripped down her legs and gathered on the floor. A cool draft lapped at her ankles and tugged at the corners that were wrapped around her body. Tabitha peered her head around from the kitchen.

'Are you okay?' she asked.

Sadie nodded, her lips pressed together in a thin, straight line.

'Do you want to talk about it?'

'I don't know,' Sadie said, her voice barely above a whisper. Her eyes had yet to leave the telephone.

'I'll put the kettle on.' Tabitha slipped back into the kitchen, leaving Sadie alone with her thoughts.

Sadie made her way back to her bedroom in a daze. Her feet dragged her forward, heaving her along the corridor. She pulled on her pyjamas with limbs that felt as though they belonged to someone else, with hands and fingers wrapped in thick cotton wool.

She drifted back to the kitchen, following the whistling sound of the kettle and Tabitha's low humming. She often hummed. The sound was warm and friendly and familial; a sound that Sadie equated to home. Tabitha handed Sadie a cup of tea and placed her hand on her friend's shoulder. She didn't say anything, but the expression on her face was deafeningly loud.

'I don't know where to start,' Sadie finally murmured.

'You don't need to start at all,' Tabitha reassured her friend. 'You don't need to tell me anything, but you can. If you want to.'

Sadie traced her finger around the top of her mug, wiping condensation off and watching it reform, carried by the clouds that lifted from the hot liquid. She took a breath in. If she couldn't open up to Tabitha, then who could she open up to?

'My brother went missing five years ago. He was twelve years old and he... disappeared. No one knows where he went. There was no trace of him. It was almost like he never existed, in a way.'

Tabitha's eyes narrowed. She moved her hand across the table and rested it on top of Sadie's, giving it a gentle squeeze of encouragement.

'I think I've gotten used to him not being here.'

'I'd understand that.' Tabitha nodded, her warm brown eyes trying their best to empathise with an impossible situation.

'But he's come home.'

Tabitha pulled her head back with a start. 'That's incredible, Sadie!' she gushed.

'Is it?' Sadie's eyebrows arched, deep thought settling across her face. 'I'm really not sure. Where has he been? Why would he stay away for so long?'

'But he's home now, surely that's what matters? You can go home, you can see him. Maybe this will help your family?'

Sadie remained silent, her eyes trained on the depleting tea in her mug. She clenched her jaw.

'Oh,' Tabitha said, putting two and two together. 'That's why you don't speak to your parents, right?'

Sadie nodded.

'When he disappeared, it was like he took our family with him. I know we're still here, physically, but Mum has never been the same. She crumbled without him. And Dad sort of, well... he got harder, I suppose. I guess he thought of it as protecting what was left of his family. It drove me away. I couldn't stay around it, I could hardly breathe for being reminded that Ben had gone.'

Tabitha watched Sadie as she spoke.

'So what now? Tabitha asked. 'What does it mean for you? For your family?'

'I don't know.'

'You can get upset, Sadie. If you need to. You don't have to worry about crying or screaming or being angry or whatever it is you need to be.'

Sadie's head bobbed in a tiny, almost imperceptible nod. Her hands clasped together in front of her chest and she continued to stare at the table. 'We don't know where he's been, how he got home. We have no idea,' she whispered, more to herself than to Tabitha.

'If there's anything you need me to do, anything at all I can do to help you, you let me know.' Tabitha reassured her friend, reaching her hand across the table.

Sadie glanced at it, at the outstretched, warm fingers, at the eclectic mix of bangles and rings, but didn't reach for it. She nodded again. 'I don't think I can go home, not yet.'

Tabitha nodded, her eyes wide with the desperation to empathise with her friend. 'You need time, that's understandable.'

'And I've got that charity thing for work tomorrow. I can't miss that,' Sadie added.

'I'm sure they'd understand if you didn't go, Sa—'

'—no' Sadie interrupted. 'I want to go. I said I'd help, I can't let them down.' Sadie held onto the prospect of the next day's charity event like a lifeline that anchored her to her London home. She wasn't ready to let go of that tether yet.

Tabitha sat up straight, consciously trying to stifle the

shock that she knew was permeating her expression. 'You don't need to do that, Sadie.'

'I want to.'

'But no one would expect you —'

'It's fine,' Sadie huffed, standing from the table. 'You're not going to understand.' She marched across to the sink, tipping the rest of the warm liquid down the plug hole. 'I'm going to bed. I need some time on my own.'

Tabitha remained at the table, her hands still wrapped around her mug. The chair where Sadie was sitting moments ago stood empty, the mug dumped unceremoniously in the sink.

SADIE LAY ON HER BED, her legs outstretched and arms straight down by her side. She focussed on what she could see of the ceiling in the darkness. The moon was a bright white outside her window. The cool light dripped between the curtains and spread itself across the textured plaster pattern that coated the ceiling and walls. Odd shapes danced across the peaks of plaster, catching her eye; she willingly lost herself in their movements. Ever since her mum called, she'd had a sensation of nausea blossoming in her stomach. It was still there now, sloshing around in the pit of her tummy, gurgling and threatening to lurch up her throat. *There's no way he could be home.*

She was there for her parents when Ben disappeared all those years ago, back when they were children. Ben was a child, Sadie edging into adulthood and inches away from flying the nest to study law. She remembered it like it was yesterday. She loved her brother, but boy did they argue.

They'd feud with a kind of ferociousness only siblings understood.

The press interviewed her when he first disappeared. It took place in their front garden, a space reserved for water fights and picnics and sunbathing, now tarnished by the intrusive hand of the newspapers desperate for their exclusive scoop.

'Act natural,' the man with a fluffy microphone dangling at the end of a rod said to her, shoving a script on a piece of scrap paper in her hands. 'Show us how much you care, okay darling?' he urged. Sadie nodded, her body cold and numb despite the summer heat.

'Can you tell us a bit about your brother?' the woman next to the cameraman asked.

'Yes,' Sadie answered, tucking a stray piece of chocolate brown hair behind her ear. 'He likes riding his bike in the woods. He likes climbing on things. He likes exploring.'

'Speak up, dear,' the woman interrupted, nudging the fishing pole-microphone contraption closer to her face. 'And don't forget those notes we gave you in case you don't know what to say or need some help, alright?'

Sadie nodded. She tilted her head down, the warm sun beating on the back of her neck as she squinted at the small piece of paper. 'My brother, Ben,' she read, 'went missing two days ago.' Her eyes didn't leave the paper. 'He is the best brother anyone could wish for. He's caring, kind, and loves our family very much.' Her voice exited her body, commanded by the tiny words scrawled on the lined piece of paper. It was robotic, cold. The script was making things worse.

'That's great, love, very good,' the man behind the microphone said. 'It'd be good if we could get some tears, though,' he grumbled. 'Viewers would lap that up.' The woman rammed an elbow into his side and scowled before turning her body back round to face Sadie. She knelt down on the ground, placing a well-manicured hand on Sadie's knee.

'Sadie, do you think you can act a bit more, erm—', she stammered, thinking of the right phrase. 'Do you think you can let your guard down a bit?'

Sadie frowned. 'I'm not sure I know what you mean.'

'As in can you cry please?' the cameraman blurted, taking a swig from a can of pop and thudding the tin on the makeshift table beside him.

Sadie's face flushed red. Her fingers gripped onto her tiny script for dear life, the sweat dampening the cheap paper.

'I,' she stammered, 'I don't think I can do that.' She swallowed.

The cameraman rolled his eyes, moving back behind his rig and jabbing his fingers into various buttons.

'Okay Sadie,' the woman soothed, 'we just need you to open up a bit more.'

Sadie stared, her lips clamped together.

'As in, you've just lost your brother and he might never come home. It'd look better, it'd be better for you if you let yourself be sad about that, do you understand?'

Sadie did not. 'Yes, I guess so,' she answered.

'Okay. How about you tell us about the night Ben went missing? Think you can walk us through what happened?'

A red-hot rash flushed over Sadie's chest, prickling its way onto her cheeks and neck. *What* did *happen? What am I supposed to say?* Her mind went back to the agreed words she'd discussed with her parents beforehand.

'Erm,' she swallowed. 'I was out with my friends. We were out along the beach by the rowing club. It was quite late.'

'Yes,' the woman nodded, overly encouraging. 'And then what?'

'Then I came home and Ben wasn't there. We waited a while in case he'd run out with his friends. He does that sometimes, he goes out with them later than Mum and Dad say he can. But he didn't come home.'

'Could your brother's disappearance have anything to do with your friends? What were their names? Vedat and...Callie?'

Sadie's head shot up from her lap.

'Do you think they could have taken him?'

'What?' she blurted, eyes wide and panicked. 'No. No, of course not.'

The reporter dropped the question, saddened by the lack of drama. She shuffled through a handful of notecards, turning her back on Sadie and talking to the cameraman.

Sadie turned away to see her mum and dad talking to another set of interviewers at the other end of the garden. Her mum brought her hand up to her face, dabbing her cheeks with a well-used handkerchief. Her dad had his hand on her mum's knee, staring straight down the lens of the camera as if it were the barrel of a gun. The reporter stood next to Sadie, brushing grass trimmings off the knees of her grey suit, making eyes at the cameraman that said *we've got the money shot*. Even at that age, Sadie understood that these people didn't care for her wellbeing at all. Only then, when she realised that this was about something entirely different for them, did she allow herself to cry.

Sadie blinked back tears and let the memory of five years ago drift from her mind. A dull ache had settled behind her eyes, hammering in time with her heartbeat. She rolled onto her side, sliding her hand underneath the pillow. She closed her eyes, willing sleep to grant her some respite from her racing mind. If she could switch off long enough to sleep, just for a few hours.

SUNLIGHT PIERCED through the cheap curtains, spreading across Sadie's legs. She came to, the reality of last night still a dull thud behind her eyes. She swung her legs off the bed, slipping on a pair of flip-flops that doubled as slippers, and made her way into the bathroom to shower. Her pyjamas crumpled into a heap on the floor as she stepped into the bathtub, her arms moving on autopilot and her mind focusing on little other than the scent of her shampoo. Wash hair, shave legs, scrub face, get out of the shower, get dressed, drag a brush through hair. Everything was happening in order, as it should be. She pulled on a pair of flared jeans and a blush pink spaghetti strap top, running her hands through her shoulder-length, choppy hair. Her eyes caught her reflection as she left the room; what a happy outfit to wear on such an odd feeling day.

Tabitha was in the kitchen, already making breakfast. The clank of plates echoed down the short hallway. The whistle of the kettle, the closing of the fridge door as Tabitha rummaged for her favourite pineapple juice. The rattle of the cutlery drawer as it closed, Tabitha grabbing hold of the handle and shaking it to loosen whatever mystery utensil had jammed itself at the back. Sadie stole a breath and entered the room to the warm scent of toast and jam.

Tabitha swung round and greeted Sadie as she walked in. 'How are you feeling today?' she asked, pouring the cloudy yellow liquid into a short glass and placing it down.

'I'm okay,' Sadie nodded, wrapping her fingers around the

glass. 'I just need to get through today, then I can work out what I need to do.'

'You do know you don't need to go in today, right? I'm sure they'd understand if you couldn't make it.'

'I know,' Sadie responded, massaging her temples. 'I honestly think it'll help me clear my head. I'll be home around lunchtime.'

'Okay.' Tabitha swilled the juice around her glass. 'I'll be here if you need to chat about anything.'

SADIE WAS grateful for the fresh air that flooded her lungs. She stepped out onto the pavement, sweeping her hand over her forehead and into her feathered hair. She willed the strange mood she was in to lift, at least for the next few hours. A tension headache had been settling behind her eyes all morning and was now shifting to the back of her head. Her mind felt groggy and tired, and an uncomfortable, clammy sweat clung to her top lip.

Sadie's shoes hit the pavement with what felt to be a loud thud. The streets held fewer people this morning; they were always quieter on a Saturday morning. Despite the fewer people, every noise seemed to increase and clang in Sadie's eardrums. The shuffling and clunking of someone opening up the coffee shop, the whistle of kettles and the ding of tills as people prepared for a busy day of trading. All these noises and all the humdrum bounced around in Sadie's tired mind. It all felt so loud. It all felt incredibly warm and claustrophobic.

It was only a short walk to the church hall where Sadie's work was taking part in a charity event. They did it a few times a year, supporting local orphanages and gathering

funds for local children. All those children that had no
family, or lost theirs to some sort of tragic accident. It was
Sadie's job to man the charity stall today, collecting money
from children who wanted to buy packets of sweets or place
their names on the sweepstake to guess the name of the giant
stuffed bear. She usually enjoyed it.

The church hall was tucked down a side road behind a
busy street. Its warm red brick facade and well-tended to pot
plants out the front did their best to entice passers-by in.
Today the chalkboard out the front of the hall had the charity
event scrawled on in white chalk pen. *Someone's probably quite
proud of that attempt at decent handwriting,* she thought to
herself, struggling to read the loopy cursive and smudged
white marks that slipped off the edge of the board and into
the pale grass. *Oh well, at least they tried I suppose.* She bent
down to pick up a squashed Sprite can that had been
discarded just inches from the bin by the door. She flung it
into a bin a metre or so away from the can, the simple movement sending her temperature rocketing. She tugged at the
edges of her cheap leather blazer, the shiny fabric clinging to
her damp skin.

Sadie had barely made it into the hall before her manager
began yelling at her from the far corner. 'Sadie, hi! Over
here!' he shouted, waving his hands frantically as if she were
quite literally miles, not merely a handful of steps, away. He
was the only one at the stall and stood behind the large
sandy-coloured stuffed bear, cradling a cup of coffee. The
light blue of his shirt betrayed how warm he was; large sweat
patches bloomed under his armpits.

Sadie stole a breath and plastered on her best smile.
'Morning,' she said, sliding behind the table beside him. 'All
set?'

'Oh yes,' Graham replied, rubbing a pink hand over his balding head. 'Should be seeing some footfall any second now. Davina sends her apologies, she's not feeling well apparently.'

'Oh, that's a shame,' Sadie replied, knowing full well that Davina had gone out last night with some of the finance girls. Davina wouldn't be nursing anything today besides a hangover and a large portion of regret.

'So I'm afraid you're stuck with little old me all morning,' he said, sloshing coffee onto his shirt. 'Oh bloody hell,' he said, grabbing a used tissue from his pocket and dragging the warm patch of liquid further across the thin blue fabric. 'What a nightmare.'

'Oh it's not that bad,' Sadie lied, shuffling some coins around in the change tin. 'I'll go grab some more tissues.'

The hall was filling with people, mostly others manning various charity stalls and setting up fête style games in the hopes of luring families off the streets. Sadie rummaged around in the kitchenette at the back of the hall in search of a cloth or some thicker tissues. She opened cupboards to find stacks of fizzy drinks, their bright, nuclear colours held captive in the thin plastic walls. There were hoards of plastic cups and plates, but no tissues.

The kitchenette backed onto a large window that looked out to the other side of the street and as Sadie stood, her attention was drawn outside. A family was making their way along the road. Mum heaving her body against a double pram, Dad holding onto a toddler's hands, and a teenager trailing at the back. The teenager, a boy, seemed familiar from the angle that she was standing. He was lithe and tall, all limbs and barely any torso. His sandy coloured hair was shaggy and long overdue a cut, the sides bushing out under a worn black cap and dangling in strands towards his collar. He wore headphones over the top of the hat and slowed to change the track he was listening to. The rest of his family pulled away, leaving him to ram the buttons on his CD player. He jabbed at the small buttons, placing the contraption back into his coat pocket with care so the track didn't jump or skip. His gait and attitude were familiar. Sadie wondered if her brother would be anything like this young man, if he had grown taller and now towered over her and had shaggy blonde hair. Her mind slipped away from the woefully understocked kitchen.

'Sadie,' Graham said from behind her, his eyebrows raised.

'Oh God,' she jumped, 'sorry I got a bit side-tracked there.' She brushed her hands down the front of her jeans, registering a thin layer of dampness that had gathered on her palms. She winced at Graham, dragging her lips into yet another forced grin.

'Not a problem,' he said, grabbing a soiled cloth from the kitchen sink and dabbing it over the browning coffee stain. 'I've got it under control. You head back and man the fort, Captain.' Graham gave Sadie a curt nod and continued to scrub at the brown splodge in vain.

Sadie stood behind the stall, both eager for some form of customer and equally desperate to be left alone. Her fingertips played idly with the bear's ear, the soft fur comforting but plasticky in her hands. She loved soft toys and plushies as a kid. Both her and Ben did, though Ben grew out of them far quicker than Sadie. A memory teased its way into the forefront of her mind. Just a small one, one that she had no doubt a huge number of children shared in some way. She recalled sitting cross-legged, toes tucked under her knees on her bedroom floor, organising her toys into some kind of line, a shift pattern of sorts. She had to make sure each toy had the same number of nights up on the bed as the one next to it.

After a few minutes of staring around the hall, a mother and daughter sauntered over and placed a bet on the bear's name. Sadie smiled, took the money, and dropped it into the metal tin. The girl took a lolly from the pot and just like that the mother and daughter duo had moved onto a rather sad looking home-assembled version of Whac-a-Mole. *What am I doing here?* Sadie thought to herself, allowing her hand to float back up to her temples and massage them in an attempt to alleviate some of the pain that still lingered from her earlier headache.

Sadie let out a loud sigh, her breath escaping her lungs like a burst pipe. As she continued to wonder whether attending the fête was a complete mistake, her eyes wandered over to Graham who was still faffing in the kitchen. He'd left one of the bottom cupboards open and let some paper plates and plastic cups topple onto the floor. The inside of the cupboard gripped her eyes; eerie darkness drew her closer. She'd looked inside that cupboard only moments ago and knew it was filled with cheap bottles of fizzy drinks and straws, so why was it calling to her now? A shadow grew from the inner corner of the cupboard and stretched out, curling around the bottles and cans. Sadie squinted and tried to get a closer look, squashing her eyes closed to clear them. The shadow, if that's what she was seeing, was moving. A smokey black substance was peeling away from the main shadow and dripping down onto the floor. Sadie frowned, trying to make sense of the black matter that was both dripping and oozing and drifting to the floor, spiralling, curling out of the corners of the cupboard and coating the cheap linoleum by Graham's feet. And there it was, right at the very back of the cupboard, further back than she could comfortably focus her eyes. Two rolling, roiling spheres of amber tumbling in on themselves. Flames grew inside the spheres, licking and lapping and seducing Sadie's attention. She knew what this was. She knew where this came from. But she didn't know why it was here. An icy chill welled in the pit of her stomach.

Graham continued to chatter and flirt with another woman from a neighbouring business. The black soot tendrils snaked further out of the back of the cupboard, inching closer to his ankles. He didn't flinch, didn't move a muscle, and still, it crept closer until it appeared to be touching his leg. The pointed end of the shadowy creature traced the fabric cuff of his trouser leg, teasing Sadie, preparing to strike.

Sadie opened her mouth to shout, but her voice refused to comply and her limbs refused to budge. The curling black substance slithered its way into Graham's trouser leg.

'Graham!' Sadie shouted, the volume of her voice a surprise even to her.

Graham's head flicked up away from the blonde woman in the tight white shirt. The shadowy creature flinched, its liquid-like body turning rigid as Graham shifted his feet on the sticky linoleum. Sadie could make out a sigh and could see his chest rising and falling in frustration. 'Erm, I need a hand, sorry.' He turned and made his way over to her, pumping his arms and marching, failing to hide his irritation.

'Sadie, really? Is now really the best time to call me over? Can't you see I'm having a wonderful chat with, erm --' he stumbled, glancing back at the platinum blonde lady hovering by the radiators.

'Cassandra?' Sadie offered.

'Yes, of course, Cassandra. I knew that. Well, is now the best time?'

Sadie fumbled, her mind racing to find a suitable lie to prevent him walking back over there to the group of women. 'I, er,' she stammered. 'I need the loo.' She blurted the lie before she was able to think of something a bit more subtle. 'You'll need to look after the stall,' she said, virtually running out of the hall and into the cold, stone-floored bathroom in the hallway. A quick glance to the kitchen on her way out revealed that the shadowy rope of a creature had slithered back to wherever it came from. There was no sign of it.

Sadie grabbed hold of the faucets, concentrating on the coolness as it permeated her skin. The sink was at an awkward height, built for a child. She hunched over, her face inches away from the mirror. She took the opportunity to wash her hands and calm her breathing. She'd hoped to never see that thing in the kitchenette ever again. The memories of its existence haunted her for months after her brother's disappearance. The past year or so she'd managed to move on to a stage where she was no longer taunted by it. Sadie washed her hands, rubbing the cheap, syrupy, pink soap between her palms and fingers. She only had around an hour left to endure Graham's company, and then she could make a break for it. But she'd have to work out what to do next.

The soap suds swilled and swirled down the drain, leaving a fake sugary scent behind them. Sadie moved her gaze up from the plughole, her neck shifting vertebrae by vertebrae until she was facing herself in the mirror. Her heart lurched and then paused in preparation for coming face to face with the creature, with its marble-like eyes and smokey exterior. But of course there was no one in her reflection besides herself; nothing out of the ordinary. Her chest rose. Her heart hammered in her ribcage as if she had seen something unusual in her reflection, but something told her she was truly alone. She placed her fingertips on the edge of her neck in search of her carotid artery and only allowed her breathing to slow once she confirmed the presence of her erratic pulse.

Sadie returned to the stall. The poor, nameless bear teetered on the table next to Cassandra who had draped herself not-so-subtly over Graham. Her long fingernails danced across the back of his hand as she tilted her head, letting her crisp, bleach-fried hair dangle over her shoulder like singed cotton.

'Ah Sadie, feeling a bit better now, are we?' Graham asked, pushing away and raising an eyebrow.

'Yes thanks,' she murmured, turning her nose up at her boss' attempt at expressing his authority over her. Good thing she was used to him.

'You can head off now, me and Cassandra are happy to finish up, aren't we Cass?' he asked, turning his face close to hers and brushing his nose up against her heavily powdered cheek. The cheap scent of lavender and talcum powder wafted above the canoodling pair.

'Great, okay,' Sadie mumbled, grabbing her bag and jacket and rubbing her nose to avoid sneezing. 'I'll be off then. See you Monday,' she waved, a pang of guilt pinching at her chest at the realisation that she'd not brought up her family situation. 'Actually, Graham,' she stammered, turning back to face her rosy-cheeked manager. 'I've got some family things I need to sort out. I've not taken any holiday and there's nothing big going on next week, is there? Am I alright to take a few days off?'

'Yes sure, that's fine,' Graham mumbled, far more interested in Cassandra than caring for his member of staff. 'Take as long as you need,' he uttered, batting Cassandra's hand away from the back of his neck playfully.

SADIE DROPPED ONTO HER BED, kicking her shoes off and letting them drop to the floor. She rolled onto her front, facing the long floor-length mirror that leant against the wall by her door.

'You should go home,' she said to herself. The muscles in her jaw tightened and her back teeth grated together. Home. What did home mean to her now? Home was here with Tabitha, and her home cooking and humming and her obsession with Patrick Swayze. Home wasn't with her parents anymore, it hadn't been for a long time. Her home hadn't been contained by the walls of the house she grew up in for years. Her eyes felt heavy, they felt full of... what exactly? They didn't feel full of tears; Sadie hadn't felt the need to cry. But they felt full, regardless.

Sadie closed her eyes. She could hear Tabitha moving around in her room, draws closing softly and her slippers shuffling against the fluffy rug that coated half her floor. She knew Tabitha was right, that she needed to go home. But not yet.

The phone rang in the hallway, the shrill tone bouncing off the wooden floors. Sadie lifted her head to hear if Tabitha was already on her way out to grab it, but there was no movement from the room next door. Sadie rolled over and climbed off the high divan bed. The trill called expectantly. She gripped the receiver and wrenched it up to her ear.

'Hello,' she answered, expecting a sales call or someone for Tabitha; Sadie didn't often get calls. She hoped that it wasn't her mum. A second or two of silence followed.

'Hi, Sadie.' A cool voice, a languid, calm tone. It was so familiar.

Sadie felt herself swallow, the action happening without her blessing. Moisture drained from her face and throat, leaving a sandpapery texture behind. She gripped the side of the telephone table, the wooden flooring swirling and swaying underneath her feet. The familiar nausea from the night before returned with a vengeance. Somehow she'd managed to convince herself, deep down, that both her parents were mistaken in her brother returning home. But now she was hearing his voice; there was no way she could deny that.

'Sadie, are you there?'

She took a deep breath in. 'Yes, yes I'm here. Sorry,' she croaked, shuffling and spreading her weight between both feet so she wouldn't collapse to the floor. 'How did you get this number?' The question was out before she could stop it. She squinted, scrunching her eyes closed. *What a stupid question,* she scolded herself. *Is that really what you'd ask your sibling who'd been missing for years?* Her jaw clenched again, the muscles spasming under the pressure.

'I got it from Mum.' His voice sounded so familiar, and yet not quite right. It was thin and wispy, as if the words were the correct ones to say but there was no conviction behind them. Like when you listen to someone play a new instrument; all the notes were in the right places, but there was no feeling behind them, no musicality tying them together. His voice was a cheap imitation. 'Sadie, are you coming home?'

'I, I don't know Ben.' His name got stuck in her throat, the jagged letters spiking her gullet so much she could almost taste the blood. She'd not said his name in such a long time, let alone to him.

'Please come home, Sadie.'

There was nothing but silence from the other end of the line. Sadie fought the urge to slam the phone back into its cradle, her knuckles white with tension. Her heart drummed, desperate for her to choose flight over fight.

The tone of his voice didn't sound any different from how he'd sounded on the day he disappeared. It didn't sound any deeper, any richer, any more mature. But, Sadie supposed, if he'd not had a chance to live a normal life for the past half a decade, perhaps that made sense. He sounded innocent and young, not like he'd had five years of his life snatched from him.

'Sadie, are you still there? You've gone again. Is this a bad line?'

More silence from her end of the phone. Her voice wedged in her throat. She could hear Ben breathing, hear his footsteps as he paced the hallway of their family home, hear him gently drumming his fingers on the worktop. She pictured him wrapping the coiled cord around his fingers, pulling it tight to feel the skin pushing against the plastic, and then releasing it to coil down by his legs. He waited for her to speak, but she didn't. 'Sadie,' he whispered, 'please come home.' He kept talking. Despite her silence. 'I'd really like to see you. I think I need to see you, after what you did.'

Sadie choked on the air in the hallway. After what you did?

'What do you mean?'

'Well, you left Mum and Dad I mean. You abandoned them to cope on their own.'

Relief slammed into her chest so forcefully she felt sick. An underlying sense of unease and fear bubbled amongst the acid in her stomach.

'How did you get home, Ben?'

Now it was her brother's turn to remain silent. She waited, running her fingers through the coiled telephone cord. 'I'm not sure,' he eventually responded. 'I think, I walked,' he said, as if he'd been lost for a few hours, wandering around in the cornfields that backed onto the village hall. As if he'd stayed out for a while too long with school friends, as if he'd gotten distracted walking back from the corner shop again and sat petting the shop owner's dog. That's what they thought had happened at first. Ben was such a sociable, friendly kid, the family and the police assumed that he'd got chatting to someone in tow, and lost track of time. Nothing sinister.

'Ben, what do you mean? Where have you been all this time?' Sadie pushed the panic down lower in her voice, forcing the cap down on a bottle that was close to bursting. It took all her strength to stop from dropping to the floor and bawling.

'I'm not so sure, if I'm honest. Where have you been, Sadie?'

'Ben, what does that even mean?' she screeched. 'Why are you being so cryptic? You've been gone so long.'

Sadie heard someone shout in the background of the call, someone asking if Ben was okay, if everything was alright. No, it's not bloody alright, she thought to herself.

'Sorry Sade, I need to go now. Mum's sorting lunch.' And with that, her brother hung up. Sadie hovered, alone in the hallway, hot tears finally breaking over the crest of her eyelids and streaming down her face. Guilt and stress and fear and confusion wrapped tightly around her chest. The grief that she'd fought so hard to keep contained over the last twenty-four hours erupted from her throat and she tumbled to the floor, her legs collapsing under her like an old floppy doll. The door to Tabitha's room opened and her friend ran over to her, squatting down onto the floor and wrapping her arms around her as she sobbed.

'You need to go home,' Tabitha whispered in her ear after she'd finally calmed down. The two of them were still sitting on the floor in the hallway, Sadie resting her head on Tabitha's shoulder. Her eyes ached from crying, the skin taut and strained and red and raw. She could barely bring herself to move. She knew Tabitha was right.

'I can't, not tonight,' she whispered, her throat dry and cracking from the tears.

Tabitha ran her hand through Sadie's long, chocolate hair, twisting the ends in her fingers. 'I can come with you, if that would help.'

The offer came by surprise and Sadie sat up to face her friend. 'Oh, you don't have to do that,' she said. 'I couldn't expect you to come with me. It's fine, honestly.'

'Fine,' Tabitha said, 'but you are actually going to go, right? You can't stay here and pretend nothing's going on.'

Sadie nodded, placing her head back down on Tabitha's shoulder and breathing in the warm cedar wood scent of her perfume. She couldn't have Tabitha come home with her. She couldn't bring something from her new life back to her old, it didn't work that way. She couldn't risk it.

4

Summer 1990

'They say it captures those who drift too close to the island,' the boy whispered, leaning forward and twisting his face into a twisted smile. 'It drags them in with some kind of supernatural force, takes control of their limbs, and walks them to their own death. Some say it can shape-shift and lure innocent passers-by to its cave. It imprisons them, tortures them, and abuses them. Gauges out their eyes with its claws. Sticks their dripping heads on stakes surrounding the perimeter of the island to serve as a warning to others. It's gruesome, and emotionless, and grotesque. Some say at night, you can see its glowing eyes of fire between the trees, watching. Waiting.' He leant back, proud of his rendition.

'Oh shut up Vedat. How old do you think we are?'

'Young enough to know the stories, old enough to think

they're lies, Callie Elisabeth Murray' he replied, over-enunci-
ating her full name, dragging out the vowels into a posh
English drawl. He sat up straight and crossed his arms over
his chest, almost knocking over the glass bottle of cider that
was part-buried in the sand by his feet.

She frowned at him and smirked. Vedat was always
telling these stupid stories of things living over on the island -
dark things, demonic things. Things that don't bear thinking
about. The idea had possessed him since the day they met.
He told the tales with rigour, like he believed every single
word he was saying. Maybe he did. He was like a religious
pastor, committed to every word that left his lips. His face was
animated with the excitement of passing on this ancient
knowledge, his hair frantic in the breeze. His eyes lit up at the
mention of the beast on the island. He believed every single
word. But he was convincing no one.

'You need some new material - it's getting old,' Callie
giggled, throwing a handful of sand towards his face.

A few grains drifted into the makeshift fire between them,
sending golden embers crackling and spitting towards the
sky. There were three of them gathered on the beach around
the fire pit. Three students studying hard in their last year of
school, three old friends who thrived in each other's
company. And there was, of course, Sadie's younger brother
Ben, who relished in the enjoyment of being invited to hang
out with people so much older than him. They had all been
born here, in Rose Bay, to parents who were from the town
back when it was still a village, and who had never thought to
leave - they probably never would. The group had an
unbreakable sense of community, a sense of being, and
purpose, and naivety. It had wrapped itself around their
youthful bodies and formed a bond that made them feel

utterly invincible. Like so many seventeen year olds, they had
the whole world in front of them, waiting for them to make
the most of it.

Rose Bay held an odd sense of heritage and pride that ran
along the low, red brick wall that traced the shape of the
town, incorruptible and unwavering. There was one road in,
and once you were in, there was a slim chance of you getting
out. Why would you? Everyone knew everyone and everyone
knew everything. The pride was like a fortress - a shield
against outsiders, and the three of them were some of the
only three to consider moving away. On the proviso that they
would come back, of course. This was the year that they were
to leave: Sadie to study law in London, Vedat to study art and
drama in Lincoln, and Callie to study something science-y in
Surrey. They were to go their separate ways, seeds drifting in
the wind.

'You've not actually seen it though, have you Vedat?' Sadie
asked from the other side of the campfire. She sat cross
legged, her red tartan jacket peeking underneath the dark,
ripped jeans stretching over her knees. She was picking at
her shoelaces, fraying the plastic between her fingernails and
flicking it into the fire. She watched Vedat as he considered
his answer, the flames licking the reflection in her irises.

'Well no, of course I haven't. It hides itself well, doesn't it?
It's a master of disguise and deception, you know that.'

She snorted. She was sceptical and disinterested and the
perfect age to carry the expression well. She continued to
twist the ends of her long dark hair between her fingertips,
oblivious to the reactions of the rest of the group.

The girl shifted her eyes back to Vedat and giggled under
her breath. The stories of the creature on the island had been
rife in the village for years. The myth was everywhere, if you

knew where to look. In local art, local books and folk, immortalised by gossip and whisperings around campfires just like this one. Stories of missing children, of dying crops, of the sea filling with congealing blood and the fish suffocating; floating to the top in hoards. The usual. They were all there and they were all easy to spot. And that was before you remembered the lady that lived at the bottom of the hill, right at the north edge of the town. The lady whose daughter went missing all those years ago and was never found. But of course, they were all lies.

'You're ridiculous, Vedat. It's so funny that you still believe all that stuff, after all this time.' Callie had raised one eyebrow in a high arch on her forehead as she turned her face to the other girl sitting around the fire. 'Surely you don't believe this crap, do you Sadie?'

'No, of course not,' Sadie shrugged, a thin smile curling at the corners of her mouth. 'Not as much as Ben does,' she said as the three of them erupted into laughter. But not Ben. Ben sat with the group, but was not feeling particularly part of the group, as much as he wanted to.

'Surely it doesn't hurt not to push these things?' Ben asked.

The laughter continued over his concerns and he sank back into himself, retreating to picking at the small shells dotted through the sand by his feet.

5

Summer 1995

S adie stepped out into the unlit hallway. The lamp from her bedside table bled out onto the wooden floor. Sadie shut the door quickly behind her, snuffing out the light. The wooden boards were cool under her feet, despite the warm, summer weather. Her feet padded to Tabitha's door that stood ajar next to her own room. She peered around the thin slither of warm, dim light to see her friend fast asleep, book in hand, with her own lamp still on. Tabitha's mouth hung open, hair splayed onto the pillows. Comfortable in the knowledge that she was out cold, Sadie pressed on down to the other end of the hallway.

The telephone stood ominously on the small wooden table. Sadie eyed the contraption with caution. It had given her so much bad, weird, life-changing news in the last twenty-four hours. What sounds and voices lay at the other end for her this time?

A small piece of paper fell from her scrunched-up palm onto the top of the wooden table, revealing two numbers etched in pencil between the lines. The first belonged to her parents, her family home. The second number belonged to someone whom Sadie hadn't spoken to for five years, someone she had hoped she'd never speak to again. She laid the paper flat on the table, stretching it out so she could see each digit in the dim light. Her left hand moved to grip the receiver as her right hovered over the numbers. The tip of her index finger pressed the first button, collapsing the white plastic disc into the space beneath it. The rest of the numbers followed, slowly, and Sadie lifted the receiver to her ear. She held her breath and chewed her bottom lip as the dial tone faded, replaced by a shrill ringing. It was late, maybe the person on the other end of the phone wouldn't pick up. There was a chance that they didn't even live in the same place anymore. Sadie didn't know what she might find on the other end of the phone line. A family? A husband? Anyone could answer. In a way, she hoped that anyone did. The ring sang in her ear for the tenth time. How many times was it supposed to ring before giving up? A gaping chasm hung between tones and, on the eleventh ring, someone picked up.

A croak, a voice breaking through a few hours of sleep to reach the outside world. 'Hello?' the person on the other end said.

'Hi,' Sadie replied, her heart dropping as she knew exactly who this person was. She'd hoped the person she needed to speak to wouldn't be there. That way she'd have a perfect excuse to delay even further. With any luck, she'd never have to speak to them ever again.

And yet, they answered. Sleepy, woken from a peaceful slumber, by someone they no doubt wanted nothing to do with.

'Sorry, who is this?' the person answered, shaking off the deep coating of sleep from their voice with every word.

Sadie stayed quiet, just for a minute. She strained her ears in the hopes that she might hear a child in the background, a husband calling out for his wife to come back to bed, asking her what's wrong, who's that on the phone? A dog barking, a cat scratching at the back door to be let out. Anything. But she heard nothing. Only silence, and the voice of a very old friend echoing through the phone lines, a hundred miles from where she stood now.

'Hello?' the person pressed, frustration apparent in their voice.

'Hi, sorry Callie --' Sadie stumbled, her tongue getting in the way of her words. 'It's Sadie.'

Callie drew in a deep breath. 'What do you want?'

Her tone was defensive, but Sadie knew she wasn't really angry or upset; perhaps more confused than anything else. Sadie's fingers made their way up to the space between her collarbones and she pressed into the skin. Her heart beat frantically underneath her muscles and bones, the deep red muscle expanding and contracting, fluttering under the pressure of her new found reality.

'He's come home,' she whispered. She knew she wouldn't need to say much more to Callie; she knew her old friend would know exactly what she meant, but she carried on talking anyway. 'He turned up on the doorstep of my parent's house, as if nothing had happened.' There was no answer. 'Ben's home, Callie.'

'That's not possible,' Callie responded. 'He can't be home. We saw him —', she stopped, unable to say the final words.

'I know. I don't understand it either, but I've spoken to him, Callie. He sounds exactly the same.'

'There's got to be some kind of misunderstanding, Sadie. Has your Mum got confused? She's not been well, you know. She might be losing her memory a bit, or, I don't know. There's got to be a sensible explanation for this.'

'I spoke to him Callie. I spoke to my brother. It was definitely him. What do we do?'

'How should I know?,' Callie hissed, the anger fizzing under the surface. Sadie remembered her old friend's temper, remembered how it had affected them as kids - but she'd never seen it as a problem until she was far enough away from it to get some real perspective. 'I can tell you one thing you can do for a start,' Callie grunted. 'Keep quiet. No one has to know anything, understand?'

Sadie nodded, mumbling her agreement.

'Reckon you can warn Vedat?'

The name stung Sadie. 'I can try,' she responded. 'Do you know where he is now? Did he move away?' *Did he escape, like I did?* she thought and hoped to herself.

'Nope. Still here in Rose Bay, still working with his dad in the garage, still a few doors down from me. Neither of us had the luxury of leaving this behind, Sadie. Not like you did.'

Embarrassment clambered up Sadie's face. Despite the darkness of the hallway, she knew the red had flushed up and settled on her cheeks. She forgot how much of this Callie blamed on her. But she blamed Callie just as much, so it seemed only fair.

'I'll try to ring him,' she said.

'Be careful then. He's way more fragile than he used to be,' Callie spat.

Sadie was unsure what that meant.

'Are you coming home then?' Callie asked.

Sadie knew this question was coming. She knew she ought to go home, but the further away she was, the further away her problems were. But she knew she had to go, sooner rather than later. She relented. 'Yes, I'll be heading home first thing in the morning.'

'Right. Don't try to contact me when you're back. I want nothing else to do with this, do you understand? Leave me out of it.'

'I can't do that, Callie —', Sadie started.

'—you can, and you will.' Callie slammed the phone down into its cradle, leaving Sadie listening to her own panting breaths.

CALLIE STOOD by the phone in her tiny home. The bristles of the doormat prickled her bare feet, the corners of the mat peeling up from the lino covered floor. Its colour had faded to grey from the light that flooded through the window. She looked around her house, suddenly livid at the peeling wallpaper, and the patches of damp that surrounded the outer corners, at the old, balding carpets and rusting kitchen. Sadie escaped, but she left her old best friend here to fend for herself, alone.

Callie stomped back to her bedroom, her dressing gown hanging open in the humid evening air. She dragged open her wardrobe door, grabbing then flinging shoes from the bottom of the cupboard and dragging them onto the floor.

She knew it was in here somewhere, that she'd find it if she looked hard enough. She'd not seen it in years but she could never bring herself to get rid of it. After everything that happened, she held onto it.

And there it was, at the bottom of her wardrobe, in an old Kickers shoe box. It didn't look like much, but she knew it had more meaning than it let on. It was an old photograph of the three of them, of Callie, Sadie and Vedat, arms flung over each other's shoulders, grins spreading from ear to ear. They'd taken the photo on an old disposable camera that Vedat had found in his family home. The cardboard contraption had clunked as they swallowed up the last image on the film with their happy, young, innocent faces. They had taken the photo before their first trip over to the island.

SADIE WAS STILL STANDING by the telephone. Her eyes were glued to the receiver, her hand grasping the slip of paper with Callie's number scrawled on it. Calling Callie had been one thing. She knew it wouldn't be easy, but she felt she had a duty to let her know what was happening. It was clear that she hadn't been thrilled to hear from her old school friend. But Vedat? Vedat was another story. She'd cared for Callie but the ties had been severed so suddenly, so surely, that she knew there was no going back. But she cared for Vedat on another level. She was protective of him. And she missed him.

Her fingers flicked through the small address book that lived by the telephone. His number was in here somewhere, but it had been so long since she'd looked at it, so long since she'd considered trying to contact him. But there he was,

underneath her Aunt Vanessa. Vedat. She pictured him at the
same address he'd been at since they were kids. He floated in
front of her, sitting at their huge oak dining table making
model ships with his dad, trying and failing to keep the paint
to the sections they belonged to. He was always so eager to
follow the rules, to stay between the lines. She hoped he'd
kept hold of some of his innocence.

Her fingers flew over the number pad; she was suddenly
desperate to hear the familiar warm voice on the other end of
the line. It may have been years since she'd last spoken to
Vedat, but she remembered every inch of him like it was
yesterday. She imagined him rushing to the phone, warm
plush lips settled in that natural smile he wore so well. His jet
black hair swept to the side, his dark eyes nestled amongst
his olive skin. The dial tone made way for the shrill ringing.
And it kept on ringing. Ten times, eleven times, twelve times.
Sadie so desperately wanted him to answer that she hadn't
considered that he might not. The phone rang out and Sadie
was left holding the receiver to her ear. She tried again, the
numbers clacking and the dial tone disappearing into the
ether. Ringing once, five times, eight times, twelve times, and
dying again. Sadie dropped the phone back into the cradle;
the disappointment of hearing only the dial tone and the
endless ringing crushed her.

'He might have changed the number,' she mused. 'Maybe
Callie's wrong. Maybe he did move after all.'

'I'M GOING HOME TODAY,' Sadie said to Tabitha as she watched
her make tea the next morning.

'I think that's a great idea,' Tabitha said, turning to her
friend and smiling. Her eyes were warm but Sadie could see

the pity swirling deep within them. She hated people feeling sorry for her. She'd grown sick of it. It never helped, not in any situation.

The call to her mum earlier that morning had been short. Sadie explained she'd be coming home later that day, she'd get the train as soon as she could and make her way from the city to the small seaside town that she'd grown up in. Her mum had been ecstatic, as if her daughter was coming home for a holiday visit or a celebration of some kind- not to face her family after being absent for half a decade.

'Should I be feeling excited?' Sadie asked Tabitha, stirring her tea.

Tabitha turned to face her, placing her hand on her hip. She was wearing a wrist full of sparkly, multicoloured bangles that tinkled as they settled around her hand. 'I don't know, to be honest. It's not every day that this sort of thing happens.'

Sadie nodded, flinging the spoon into the sink with a loud clatter.

'You'll feel however you feel, Sadie.'

You'll feel however you feel. The only thing Sadie was sure of was how unsure of everything she felt. She'd packed her small suitcase late the night before, after her failed attempt to reach out to Vedat. She'd folded a few outfits worth of clothes and placed them into the bag, only to decide they were too put together, too thought out. She removed them, repacked them, worried about what her parents would think of her clothing. Of all the things her parents would be worrying about, what their daughter looked like was certainly not one of them. She grabbed a book for the journey and a spare couple of batteries for her Walkman and managed to get around three hours sleep in total before coming back into the kitchen this morning to find Tabitha bumbling around as if nothing was out of the ordinary. The whole time she'd forced herself to stay awake in the hopes that Vedat would call back, only of course he wouldn't recognise the number that called. And it was the early hours of the morning.

'You should eat something if you're travelling all the way back in one go,' Tabitha said, handing Sadie a plate of toast. She'd miss this caring nature she'd grown so used to. She definitely wasn't about to receive that from her mum.

'Thank you,' she replied, taking the plate and hoisting herself up onto the high bar stool. 'What would I do without you?'

'Starve?' Tabitha winked. 'You'd probably drink less wine though.'

Sadie grinned. She ran a hand through her choppy hair and bit down on the toasted bread. Her teeth left high ridges in the peanut butter, the salty sweetness lingering on her tongue. She couldn't delay this any longer.

'I better get going,' Sadie said, wiping the back of her hand across her mouth. She slipped away from the breakfast bar, shrugged on her denim jacket, and clasped the handle of her suitcase.

'Make sure you call me, okay?' Tabitha shouted from the doorstep as Sadie dragged the small, two-wheeled case behind her.

'I will, don't worry. I've left my parent's number by the phone, just in case,' she smiled.

Tabitha remained perched on the doorstep waving, one hand on her hip, the other high in the air. Her fuchsia painted lips curved into a smile, but the concern never left her eyes. Even at the growing distance, that was all that Sadie could see.

6

Summer 1995

The train that would soon be carrying Sadie home was old, much older than the ones that thrust her closer to the centre of the heaving city every morning for work. It stood at the platform expectantly, the brown and green exterior peeling due to age, curling away against the early afternoon sun. It was grand, in its own way. Grand, but past its time. It held the same charm and atmosphere of a seaside town; once prosperous but readily forgotten, for more exciting, far off landscapes, left to fend for itself against the rare British sun. She hadn't set foot on one of these trains in years and, dragging her case up onto the small step, she was immediately reminded why.

The train was empty but for a few older couples looking to get away to the countryside for some fresh air, for some peace and quiet. But peace and quiet were the last things that Sadie wanted. They were why she came to the city in the first place. The silence of the countryside was oppressive and concerning, unnerving even. In the silence of her tiny home-town, there was no escaping your own thoughts. The most awful things that had ever happened in her life happened between the loudest noises. They happened in the silence, in the space between what people said, the gaps that nestled between the bustle of life, the lulls between the action. It's when things stopped, that's when there was trouble. She didn't trust places that were too quiet. And her family home was virtually mute.

She fumbled in her pocket to retrieve her train ticket, eyeing the details to find her seat number. She hovered around the carriage in search of her assigned seat, despite the emptiness of every bay. There was no need for the precau-tion, but it was far easier to abide by these rules than break them.

She was alone in the carriage, save for one older gentleman who was sitting towards the door. He was reading a broadsheet, holding it high over his face so only his legs jutted out from underneath like a comical child's toy. Sadie shrugged off her jacket and placed a styrofoam cup of too-milk tea down on the rickety old table in front of her. She slid into the small space, her case tucked away above her head. The train juddered to life moments later, sliding away from the platform, away from the hustle and bustle and noise of the city, and towards the stillness of the countryside. Great.

Sadie leant her head on her hand and settled her eyes on the fast changing landscape that flicked by outside the train window. The skyscrapers, office buildings, restaurants and busy streets lined with shoppers all soon slipped away into the past, as the train dragged her begrudgingly closer to home. She squinted, concentrating on minuscule details as they whizzed past, colours smudging together in a blur behind the glass. Every time she found something to concentrate on - a multicoloured balcony, a vintage car - her eyes jolted back in front of her with the growing speed of the locomotive.

A few minutes into the journey it began to rain. It hadn't rained in almost two weeks; the country was experiencing a dryer than usual summer so far. The ground opened up, grateful for the water as it cascaded from the sky. The water came down with conviction, cathartic and heavy, thrumming against the side of the carriage as the train rattled through the thinning suburbs. Despite the rain, the heat still held its claws on the landscape. The combination of heat, the cooling precipitation, and the fan whirring on the inside of the carriage caused the windows to steam, concealing the outside world and trapping Sadie inside the train, blind. Condensation ran down the inside of the window. Sadie caught the droplet on her fingertip, surprised by its chill, and traced a line through its trajectory down the side of the glass plane. Within a few minutes, the summer shower had passed, the windows cleared and the sky returned to a rich shade of blue. The clouds parted, drifting lazily across the sky. It was like it had never happened.

A handful of minutes passed in this same state. Sadie simply staring out of the window, watching the world go by, realising and accepting how little control she had over any of it. Anything that had happened or anything she had decided to do in her life had been as a reaction to something far bigger than herself. At the time, she wondered if she'd ever truly had free will. When she moved to the city, she convinced herself that it was in search of opportunity and positivity, but the reality was it was in reaction to the disappearance of her brother. She could no longer face the streets of her hometown, the old, weather-beaten dog-eared posters that her parents refused to remove from every outdoor surface. Her brother had disappeared and yet, in a way, he was everywhere.

Her parents had given up the facade shortly before Sadie's move. They held onto their marriage with both hands so tightly and for so long that it damaged both of them irreparably. They could no longer look at each other without their minds flitting back to Ben, arguing about what one or the other could have done to prevent his disappearance. What more they could have done to keep him safe. And Sadie was done with the negativity and the constant weight of guilt that followed her around, her very own dark cloud filled with the tears of her family, her friends, herself.

She wore that guilt around her neck, over her back like a sack full of bricks. It forced her own personality and independence inside of her and she lost herself in Ben's disappearance.

Sadie rummaged in her bag to find a magazine to pass the time. It was a lengthy train journey and she could use a vapid distraction, but after a few minutes of flitting between hollow articles about weight loss and body transformations, she gave up. There were very few things, she assumed, that would have the power to distract her from how she was feeling. She threw the magazine onto the chair next to her, the high-gloss cover laying in stark contrast to the deep green and reddish-brown padded upholstery.

She plunged her hand into her bag again, pulling out her headphones and Walkman. She found comfort in the ritual of choosing a CD from the small collection she'd grabbed from her shelf, from unwinding the headphones and clicking the disc into the frame. The headphones nestled her ears, the foam now holding a constant dent from the shape of her head. She clicked play, the first track filling her ears. Nope, she mumbled, jabbing the skip button in search of the song she was after. *Track eleven, found it.* She closed her eyes, leaning her head back against the old, worn headrest, and let the warm twang of guitar fill her ears. It might have been an old song, but it did something to her when she listened to it. So she listened four times in a row before nodding off in her chair, her neck tipping towards her lap.

She was back in the office, sitting at the front desk, working away on some mindless task that Graham had ordered her to do. No one else was around; all her teammates had already left for the day. It was dark outside - the kind of dark that's more blue than black. The moon was bright and partially hidden by light smudges of clouds. Stars dotted the sky and a light mist was settling around the city, lacing its smoky trails between the buildings and cars. Sadie's fingers felt heavy around the pen she was gripping, the weight of the Parker anchoring her hand into place in the jotter in front of her.

There was something breathing a short distance behind her, its breath moist and warm against the back of her neck. She didn't feel scared of it, she'd learned not to be. She turned her head to lay her eyes on it but once she'd turned, she found that it was no longer there. She could have laughed; of course it wouldn't be there, of course. She knew what it was. She'd learned the hard way but now she knew exactly what she ought to have seen when she turned around. So why, then, when she rotated in her chair for dramatic effect, where her eyes met with nothing more than the wooden cupboard door and the exit from the office?

Her eyes narrowed, squinting at the door in case it had slipped between the cupboard and her manager's office, but it was nowhere. Maybe she wanted to see it; maybe it was never there. Giving up, she turned back to her desk, half expecting, half hoping whatever it was to come flying at her from underneath her desk. But again, there was nothing unusual there either. She slid a large calculator from the back of the desk and rested it next to the ledger in front of her. Her fingers bounced off the keys, the clacking echoing in the empty foyer, reverberating off the windows and tall fake plants. The numbers swam in front of her eyes, sums and tallies and subtractions to tie the month end together. She worked until she felt the need for a break, but when she tried to stand she found that she was unable. Her legs were heavy and leaden, her feet welded to the carpet underneath the desk. Her back lifted away from the chair and fell again with a thud. She momentarily questioned the odd situation, but before she could question it too deeply she found that her fingers were bouncing off the keys of the old calculator again, looping on and off the buttons in an over-pronounced arc. She continued to work, no longer out of choice but compulsion. Her fingers flew across the numbers and formulas, blurring in front of her eyes, forming nonsensical sums and calculations. Even when she took her attention away from her hand, it carried on dancing across the buttons, tapping from one number to another, entering and adding and subtracting. There was no rhyme or reason, no sense of logic to what was happening. The screen on the calculator remained blank, seemingly hiding whatever she was doing. The small glass rectangle reflected her face back to her. She only saw herself staring back, looking far more frantic than she felt. Somehow the bashing of the buttons increased in speed, her nails catching under the keys and on the corners of the buttons. She winced as chunks of nail broke off and flicked across the table top. She kept going.

As she stared at the tiny, black-grey screen, she saw it. She knew she would. An odd wave of relief passed over her and she grinned the tiniest smile.

'You were hiding from me,' she whispered to the desk, 'but I knew you'd come out eventually. I've missed you, in a way.' The grin tickled the corners of her lips and excitement prickled across her arms. How could she say she'd missed it? Then the fear settled into her shoulders, creeping around her throat and into her heart; the realisation that this thing that she'd not seen for years had made its way back to her, that it knew how to reach her. It was behind her now, close enough for her to feel its breath on her skin, its damp, heavy breath coating her neck in a light, wet layer. Its current form was a tiny bit bigger than Sadie's own body. It stood motionless behind her, its tendrils snaking out like an out of focus shadow. Sadie's breathing slowed. A light film of sweat coated her palms. Four tendrils snaked away from the creature's body, curling like fingers over her shoulder and clenching her upper body. Upon contacting her blouse, the smoky tendrils solidified and formed long nails, polished to a high jet-black shine. The sharp tips threatened to pierce through the material, millimetres from her skin. Sadie held her breath as the tendrils moved from hands to a full arm, to a

torso that was pulling itself around onto her torso. There was
no face where you imagined one would be; there was no face
at all. Inky black ropes of smoke and muscle entwined
together in knots, coiling and curling across the figure's
outline. There was no mouth, no nose, no ears or expressions. But there were eyes. Deep amber eyes, the yellow-gold
of fire, full of orange and umber swirls and spirals. Eyes like
fossils that hinted at the existence of something much older,
something that had survived an unimaginable amount of
things and times and histories. They were much bigger than
you'd imagine the eyes of something this size - around the
size of a pair of suspended tennis balls.

It let out a low gurgle, the vibration shuddering in Sadie's
eardrums. Her hands had left the calculator now. They'd
drifted to grip the arms of the desk chair, holding on for the
inanimate object to somehow save her. Her torso clenched,
her stomach pulled in tight towards her spine and she
listened to it as it continued to grumble under its breath.
Phlegm rattled in its throat as it growled. Its other hand, or
paw, made its way over to Sadie's left shoulder, fingers curling
around her arm. It remained like this for a few minutes,
motionless. Both of its hands worked their way towards her
chest, fingers spreading out flat to feel the thud of her heartbeat. Its growling subsided, replaced by an eerie guttural
clicking, so low in register that it vibrated through her chest
cavity and out the top of her head. It was moving again,
slowly but definitely changing position. The fingers were
curling around Sadie's throat, not to strangle but to threaten,
to tease, to show that it was capable of ending it all in a heartbeat. It lowered its head to nestle into Sadie's neck, its long
onyx black tongue slithering between its pointed teeth and
licking her ashy flesh. Sadie held her breath. The rough

texture of the creature's tongue grated against her skin. The pointed tip of the tongue traced her jawline, behind her ear and out towards the back of her neck leaving a silvery trace of saliva behind it.

Sadie knew exactly what was coming next for she'd lived through it once already. She braced herself. The thing, the creature, the shadow - it whispered her name in a low, rasping moan, dragging out the vowels and hissing the syllables shut with a snap. It took a breath in, the cool air rushing past the skin on Sadie's neck. She looked back at the tiny calculator screen, desperate for a distraction, but instead found another viewpoint on her situation. Her eyes made contact with the glassy amber spheres in the tiny monitor. The creature screeched, throwing its head back and lunging its razor sharp teeth into her chest.

Sadie threw herself forward, her body bouncing off the chair in front of her.

'Oh Jesus Christ,' she panted, running her hands over the top of her chest. It had been such a long time since she'd had a nightmare that vivid and, despite learning how to calm herself during them, this one caught her off-guard. Sweat dripped in tiny beads down her neck, dancing across her chest. She ran her fingers over the moisture. Her hands trembled as she held her palms in front of her face.

'It's only sweat,' she breathed, startled by the volume of her voice. Relief seeped from her pores.

She unscrewed the cap from her water bottle. The calming sensation of the cooling liquid slowed her breathing but her panic was still on the verge of tipping her over. Her palm rested on her chest, stilling when she found her heartbeat, pounding against her ribcage. The gentleman hiding behind his broadsheet glared over the top of the pinkish coloured paper at her, quick to retreat behind his papery fortress when she made eye contact with him.

'God, how embarrassing,' she mumbled, jostling her headphones back over her head and clicking back to the one song that was sure to calm her nerves.

7

Summer 1995

The air tasted different in the countryside. People say the air, or lack of, in the big city makes you appreciate the freshness of the country and the sea all that much more. The space allows you to breathe, reconnect, stretch out, and relax. But to Sadie, the fresh, clean air violated her airways. It was too cool, too fresh, too pure; it couldn't be trusted. And the cooler evening air hit her hard as she stepped off the train and onto the rural platform. Even the concrete felt different to what she was used to. There were no ticket guards, no hoards of people, no families on their way to London Zoo or Madame Tussauds. There weren't even ticket barriers to prevent people from just getting on and off unannounced. This freer, more relaxed concept had become alien to her.

Sadie dragged her small case from the train platform,

down the cobbled ramp, and onto the main road of the town she grew up in. She faced down the long road towards her family home and took a deep breath in. She slipped on her headphones again, slotting her No Doubt album into the empty round space, and clicked play, hopeful that the batteries would last the half-hour walk home. Gwen's voice filled her ears but failed to bring her the joy that she normally felt. The music had an odd, sour taste on this side of the train tracks.

The commute, if you could call it that, took her past multiple sites from her childhood. She walked past them, lugging her suitcase, careful not to jolt the CD in the silver player so as not to make it jump and skip through the track. Her school, where she met Callie and Vedat and became almost surgically attached to them. The Sixth Form College that all three of them went to together. The library, where Sadie first dreamt of studying law. The church and the grave-yard and the small cluster of shops and the green grocer's and the swimming pool that hadn't seen a lick of paint since the 1970s. It was all still here. Exactly as she'd left it. She walked past the old pub that lost its charm and appeal the second she became old enough to actually go in. And the hill overlooking the beach, where they'd had that first conversa-tion, that jokey, jovial chat. The whole town had remained completely still since her leaving, almost waiting for permis-sion to age. Everything had become frozen in time, stuck between the second and the minute hand, not changing in case she came back to check on it.

She walked towards her driveway, her knuckles white against the suitcase handle. Her heart threatened to burst from her chest, the anxiety taking over her pulse. Her breathing came in ragged, uncontrolled inhalations and, more than once, she considered sitting down on the low wall that circled her house to steady herself. As she considered this for the third time she saw him, standing in the window. A thin white hand curled around the off-white netted curtains, a large green eye under a heavy brow and wispy lashes peering, slicing into Sadie's mind. He was exactly how she remembered him. Exactly the same. Only inexplicably different.

She stopped dead in her tracks and stared. His eyes bore down on her, his expression unwavering and empty. He didn't look sad. He didn't look happy. She didn't know what she had expected him to look like, but it wasn't this. His eyes were darting around, trying to focus on something outside the house. It was only when she followed his gaze that she registered the press crowding the pavement, the boom mics with their familiar fluffy heads, cameras slung over shoulders, and reporters checking notes and chatting. They didn't notice her at first. She wasn't who they were after. The presence of the news stations on her doorstep threw her memory back to Ben's disappearance. The awkward interviews, the intrusive questioning, the disregard for any of her family's feelings. She felt immediately protective of her old home and marched up to the gate waiting at the bottom of the path.

'Excuse me, are you here to see the Pickett family? Did you know Ben?' one reporter asked, making moves to step towards her. Another reporter grabbed his shoulder, pushing past, and shouted. 'That's the sister. That's Sadie, the older one.' The press moved behind her in a pulsating mob.

'I'm not talking to you, sorry,' she mumbled, walking past them and unlatching the small wooden gate.

'Just a quick question please, Miss Pickett?' a tall gentleman asked, outstretching his hand to get her to wait.

Sadie brushed past, ignoring his advances. The familiar erratic thrum of her heart echoed through her chest.

'I can't talk to you.' She turned to close the gate behind her, confident that the gaggle of reporters wouldn't have the gall to try to follow her up the path. She was right. They stopped outside the fencing of her family's front garden, still shoving their microphones in her general direction, barking questions at her. Keeping her head down, Sadie turned and began to walk up the path to her family home. It grew longer with every step she took, the shingled pavement stretching like a lengthy promenade. Every time she convinced a foot to step forward, the path reached further away, taunting her. The reporters continued to shout, their voices blurring into an incomprehensible mass of noise.

She placed an unsteady hand on the green painted door and wrapped her nervous fingers around the brass knocker. The metal handle was heavier than she remembered and she drove it back down with a thud. There was no answer, not straight away. She knew Ben was right inside, so why wasn't he coming over to let her in? She knocked again and placed her ear closer to the door. Behind her, the wave of reporters continued to buzz, a resilient chatter with the odd question breaking through.

'Don't answer it, Ben,' her dad's voice shouted across the hall. 'You stay there, I'll get it.'

Sadie risked a turn of her head to glance at the bottom of the path. The reporters jumped at their chance. Bright lights flashed as they snapped Sadie's photograph. The flashes and clicks of the cameras crescendoed, tightening their grip around the little space that Sadie had on the doorstep.

A bolt slid from inside the house, followed by the rattle of a chain and the twist of a key-lock and, finally, the door inched open, her dad cowering behind it. He pushed it open half a foot or so. The brass chain hung limp in the gap between the wall and the door. Her dad's face peered at her from the slither of the hallway, the chain cutting off his forehead. His nostrils flared and he pursed his lips, unwilling to say the first word to break the silence.

'Hi Dad,' Sadie said, peering in. 'It's good to see you.'

The man on the other side of the door didn't react in any way to her attempts at normalcy. He ruffled a weathered hand through his greying hair and unhooked the chain, standing aside. He refused to open the door any wider than a couple of feet and watched Sadie as she struggled to squeeze herself and her case into the house. She heaved her belongings over the step, rolling the case to the foot of the stairs and turned to her dad. Guilt washed over her face so freely, she wondered if it had been there the whole time she'd been away from Rose Bay.

His large, calloused hands pushed against the door, closing out the flashing and the shouting of the reporters. He was wearing a rusty coloured checkered shirt and dark jeans, the uniform she remembered from her childhood.

'Have they been out there long?' she asked, unbuttoning her jacket and laying it over her arm.

He nodded, motioning for her to hand it over and laying it across the bannister. 'They haven't left since they heard he'd come home.'

'They've been out there the whole time?' she said, the disbelief clear in her tone.

He nodded, his lips forming a pursed straight line. 'They seem to change shifts every now and again, but there is always a crowd of them. One of the Police Officers will go and chat to them every now and again, asking them to leave.'

Sadie frowned, her throat tightening. She rubbed her hands down the fronts of her jeans, unable to find the words to respond to her dad.

'One of the officers, Jillian, her name is. She's not here at the moment, but she'll be back later. She's been around a lot, talking to us, talking to Ben.'

Of course, Sadie thought. *Of course there'd be someone here to talk to Ben.* 'Right,' she nodded, glancing back to the front door. An empty sensation churned in the pit of her stomach.

'How was the journey home?'

Sadie smiled, a small curve in her lips but a smile all the same. 'It was fine, really. Old people getting in the way a bit, weird countryside trains and air that's too fresh. People walk a lot slower here, you know.'

'I'm glad you came home,' he said, holding his arms out and welcoming her in for a hug. It was only awkward at first, his big arms clasping rigidly across her back. He wasn't known for being the most affectionate, but he had his moments. 'There's someone who's desperate to see you.' He smiled, moving away from her and walking towards the living room.

Sadie shivered. The air in the room vibrated with energy and tension. She tried her best to replicate the shape of his grin and hoped more than anything that he wouldn't question the validity of her expression. He moved back to her, placing his hand on her back and nudging her towards the living room. Sadie's feet filled with lead, but she complied with her dad's directions, dragging her frozen torso behind him. An unnatural stillness settled over her shoulders as she fought the urge to bolt back down the garden path.

And there he was.

He looked older, slimmer, more tired than she placed him in her memories. But besides that, nothing had changed.

He stood around five foot eight inches tall, a couple of inches taller than her. The skin that clung to his cheekbones was grey and verging on translucent; he'd lost a considerable amount of weight. His hair had taken on a coppery tone; that wave she knew well causing the ends to curl up and kink around his face and behind his ears. The definition around his jaw had darkened and it hit her how old he must be now, how many years they had lost. Everything about him seemed the same, but so different in so many ways. Her eyes crawled over his skin until they lay still at the top of his head. His eyes seemed different. They were the same colour and of course the same shape, but there was something different about them. The blue of his irises had watered out and softened, the edges diluting and trickling into the whites of his eyes, like a stream seeping into the river bank. The longer she stared, the more bizarre they seemed. They were his, they were the same in many ways, but they were empty. She couldn't bring herself to step any closer to her younger brother, so she remained where she was, observing him from a distance. Her intrigue held her to the spot, studying him like some kind of near-extinct creature.

'Hi Sadie,' he said, expressionless. 'It's been a while.' *A while?*

'Yes, I suppose it has,' she replied, not breaking eye contact. His eyes, she thought, there's something wrong with his eyes. Her body stiffened as she continued to look at him. 'How have you been?' The question was too normal, too natural.

'Oh, you know. Not so bad. Getting used to it.' He held the

link between her eyes as if there were a thin wire that connected their pupils together.

'Sure,' Sadie replied, her reply stunted and unnatural. She looked at her brother with more than confusion. He wasn't registering how unusual the situation was. He wasn't understanding the weight of it at all.

'Gonna watch TV,' he said, turning and walking back to the living room. He flopped heavily onto the sofa. 'You joining?'

You joining? That's how he used to talk to her, never quite in full sentences. The same mannerisms, the same heavy fall into the cushiony sofa. She paused. 'No, I don't think I will for now. I need to walk about, stretch my legs a bit more after the train journey.'

'Okay,' Ben said, mirroring his sister's own forced casual tone. He swung back towards the TV set.

Sadie stared at the back of his head for a while, wondering if that would give her any answers. His hair was exactly the same to her as the day he disappeared: shaggy, uncontrollable, tendrils of warm red-brown hanging down in the back. She assumed her mum made him have it cut as soon as he arrived home; that's the sort of thing she would do. She'd be desperate to put things back to normal and forget the last five years of heartache. Of course staring at the back of his head presented nothing in the way of discerning his behaviour and she walked through to the kitchen to find her dad making coffee.

She closed the door behind her and leant against the work surface, watching her dad spoon in the dark brown granules and stir each mug. His free hand tapped against the granite worktop, his fingertips thrumming the solid slab. The spoon dropped into the sink and he handed Sadie her old mug from the days when she still lived in Rose Bay. She answered the gesture with a small but warm grin, and looked up into her dad's eyes for the first time since arriving home.

'You look exhausted, Dad.'

He nodded, pursing his lips and closing his eyes. 'I am,' he answered, bringing his hand up to his chin and brushing it over the greying stubble. He'd never had a beard, not in all the time Sadie could remember. He'd always made the effort to be completely clean shaven, but now the stubble dusted his face and neck. Grey semicircles weighed his eyes down and his cheeks looked gaunt. He wasn't tired, he was completely defeated.

Sadie sipped the hot coffee. 'How did he get home, Dad?'

There was a gaping pause, a lengthy time of Sadie waiting for her dad to respond and him returning the silence by staring at the floor between his feet.

'We don't know,' he murmured.

Sadie frowned. 'What do you mean, "we don't know?"'

He shuffled his feet, grabbing a cloth to wipe down the already spotless work surface. 'He arrived at the door, as if nothing happened.'

A cold wave spread through Sadie's body, a similar sensation to when her mother told her about Ben's reappearance all those nights before.

'I don't understand,' she said.

'Neither do I, Sadie.' He chewed his lower lip and met her eye again. He still had the cloth in his right hand, clenching the damp fabric between his fingers. 'The day before yesterday, I came home from work. It was quite late, I'd worked overtime again,' he started, ringing the fabric between his hands. 'I came in, got showered and there was a knock at the door. I assumed it was a neighbour or a sales person or something, at that time in the evening I didn't know who it could be. I didn't bother using the peephole to check, because I never do - why would I?' He took a swig of coffee. 'So I opened the door and he was just standing there, asking to come home.'

'Asking to come home?'

'Mhmm,' he mumbled. 'I opened the door and I — I just stared at him. I couldn't bring myself to say anything. He looked almost the same as the day he disappeared. Older, of course, but his eyes were so desperate, so tired. What was I supposed to say? I let him in. And the second he was in the house - in our house - I grabbed him and he clung onto my shoulder and I sobbed.' Her dad's eyes welled, all the grief and pain of the last five years finally allowed out of his chest.

Silence swelled between the two of them. The TV murmured in the background as Ben flicked from channel to channel. Sadie could see him sprawled across the sofa, exactly how he used to. Nothing had changed and yet everything was different.

'I don't understand,' Sadie whispered.

'Neither do I.' He waited to speak again, pulling at the edges of the dishcloth, separating the white fibres and dropping them onto the countertop. 'He came back. He was on the doorstep. Scruffy looking, skinnier and taller than when he left, but he looks the same. He came back and walked in and...picked up where he left off.'

''Where's Mum?'

'Gone to get food. She's celebrating, I think. It's odd, Sadie. Your mum seems happy but — it's not right. None of this is right.'

Sadie nodded, reaching over to her dad and slipping the cloth from between his hands. He ran a hand over his grey peppered chin and down onto his neck. 'I'm worried about him, Sadie.'

'Of course, we all are,' she said, placing her hand on top of his. 'I am too. Has he seen a doctor or anything?'

'Not yet,' her dad answered. 'He will, though. The Police are speaking to him a lot but he doesn't seem to be remembering anything. He's acting like nothing is out of the ordinary, like it was always the plan for him to come back five years later. And your mum is being really protective of him, which I of course understand but...it's not right, Sadie. I don't know.'

Sadie couldn't bring herself to respond. Her eyes locked onto the windowsill, staring at a dusty vase and half-used bottle of Fairy liquid. She lost herself for a moment in the shine of the white tiles, the clusters of dust that clung to the lip of the empty vase. None of this made any sense.

'Have you spoken to him properly?' she asked, not removing her eyes from the window ledge. The volume of her voice shocked her, but she pressed on. 'Have you asked him what happened? Where he's been? Who he was with?'

'Of course I have, Sadie,' her dad replied, frowning at the sudden change in his daughter's tone of voice. 'I've tried. We've tried,' he corrected. 'He doesn't remember anything. I don't know if it's PTSD or stress or repressed memories or what. I don't know. We need to give him time.'

'Give him time?' Ben's voice broke through Sadie and her dad's back and forth. He had heard the discussion getting louder in the kitchen and had wandered through. Neither of them knew how long he'd been standing there, how long he'd been leaning against the doorframe, watching them.

'Oh, it's nothing Ben. We're just having a chat.'

Sadie threw her dad a glare but swallowed the look of

confusion before Ben could register it. Her dad returned the expression, chewing on his lower lip.

'Right,' Ben nodded, grabbing a glass from the cupboard and filling it with cold water from the fridge. He left the kitchen without a word and returned to his position on the sofa.

'I don't know what's going on, but this isn't right, Dad,' Sadie hissed. 'He knows where everything is, he looks the same, he hasn't even changed the way he talks.'

Her dad's eyes dropped to the floor again. He'd clearly had these thoughts himself but hadn't vocalised them. 'He's not talking, Sadie. He doesn't remember much of what has happened to him.'

'Fine, I know,' she relented, frustration tipping into her voice. 'I'm gonna go and try to talk to him.'

Her dad grabbed her shoulder, his face pleading with her. 'Okay, but — be slow. Please.'

'I will, don't worry.' She shrugged free from his arm and walked through to the living room.

Ben was sitting on the sofa, his legs curled up underneath him. He was nudging the remote, flying through the handful of channels over and over, too quickly to see what was going on in each one. His vacant eyes hovered somewhere past the screen as the images blurred into a smear of colour. He finally let the screen sit on one image, his eye-line glued and unwavering. His fingers picked at the buttons, pulling and tugging at the tiny spheres of rubber.

Sadie lowered herself into the armchair next to her brother. She eased herself amongst the cushions, careful not to make any sudden movements or disturb him. She approached Ben as an animal tamer would a lethal creature - one step at a time and holding her breath. She watched him for a while, as his eyes slurred from the remote that he was still fiddling with back up to the screen. He didn't seem to be taking in any information from the screen, instead staring off into the top corners and watching the colours as they flickered and wavered between frames.

He shrugged, the question falling unanswered from his sloped shoulders.

'Anything good?'

He shrugged again, an isolated movement that didn't even seem to rock his body.

Sadie sat back in silence and studied him for a while longer. At this distance she could see the fine lines and darkened circles underneath his eyes, the beginnings of facial hair along his jawline. His skin was an odd shade of grey, washed out amongst the coral peach of the sofa. He looked up, registered that she was staring. Sadie blushed and turned away but he shrugged again. He didn't seem to mind. He sat motionless, a concrete cast of himself, staring in the direction of the television set. His eyes were utterly still now, not focusing on anything that was going on. She recognised the t-shirt he was wearing and, after a few minutes of pondering its origin, realised it was one of her old sports shirts. She felt an odd twinge at the realisation.

'Nice top,' she grinned. He used to steal her things all the time when they were growing up. Most of the time he only did it to see if he was able to sneak it past her.

He looked at her briefly and nodded. Was there a hint of a grin there? They sat in silence for a while longer, Sadie searching for ways to start a conversation, Ben continuing to stare into the far corner of the television set.

'Ben.' He looked up at her. 'How did you get home?'

His eyes closed for a second, nostrils flaring as he took a

breath in. 'I've told you already,' he whispered. 'I've told you all already.'

'No, Ben, you haven't. You haven't told us anything.'

'Yes,' he said, 'I did. I told you. I walked home.' His tone was steady. Rehearsed, even.

'But, walked from where? Where have you been?' Sadie's questioning sped up, the volume in her voice climbing. She needed to know.

'I've not been far,' he replied.

'That doesn't answer my question, Ben. You've been gone for so long,' Sadie pleaded, leaning out of her chair to try to catch his eye away from the television.

He turned to face her again. 'Well, I haven't really,' he paused. 'I've been right here the whole time.'

8

Summer 1990

'Ben, stop teasing your sister.'

'I'm not,' Ben wailed, throwing his arms up in the air.

'Don't make me come over there,' Patrick said, his bushy eyebrows raised high up onto his forehead. 'I wasn't born yesterday, kiddo.'

'Eurgh, don't call me that, it's lame.'

Patrick laughed, turning his back on his quarrelling children to head back to his shed. Ben waited, watching the back of his dad's head retreat into the garden. He rolled up another piece of paper, slotting it into the elastic band that he'd pocketed from school and pinged it at the back of Sadie's head.

'Ben! Come on!' she bellowed, fishing the tiny ball from inside her ponytail. 'I'm trying to work. Sod off already.'

'You're not busy,' Ben said, rolling more paper between his fingers. 'You're writing notes. Who are they for?' He leant over from his side of the sofa to peer at what his older sister was writing.

'Hey, no!' she squealed, throwing her torso over the scraps of paper and shoving her brother away.

'Oh, are they for a boy?' he teased, knowing full well who they were for. He threw his mouth open and slapped his palm to the side of his face. 'Let me see!'

'No way!'

'I won't tell anyone, especially not *you know who*.'

'Shut up Ben! They're not even for Vedat,' Sadie yelled, screwing the bits of paper up and cramming them into her jeans pockets.

'Oh, I was right then?' Ben folded his arms across his puffed out chest and smirked, the twinkle of mischief glistening in his eyes. 'Don't you think you're a bit old for love letters?'

'That's it,' she screeched, stepping up from her seat and storming off to her room.

Patrick peered back into the kitchen-diner, his back leaning against the outside wall by the patio doors. Juggling the need to be a responsible parent whilst not outwardly finding his two children's behaviour amusing had become a constant struggle.

'That was not very nice, Benjamin,' he said, leaning into his son's full name.

'Oh come on, she's seventeen! She's a bit old for love letters, don't you think?'

'Not my place to say. Go and apologise to your sister, please.'

'You are joking —'

'No, I'm not. Go on. I'm going to carry on working. If I can hear you two yelling at each other from the bottom of the garden, I won't be impressed. Got it?'

Ben sighed. 'Whatever,' he mumbled, walking up the stairs at a snail's pace. When he got to his sister's bedroom, he waited outside. The door was ajar and he could see her laying, face down amongst the cushions and stuffed toys that she still had. The letters were jutting out from underneath her pillow. He nudged the door.

'Sorry, Sadie,' he lilted.

'Mhmm. Sure.'

'Well, I suppose I'm not really sorry. But Dad told me to come and apologise.'

Sadie rolled onto her back and sat up. 'Thanks for your honesty, I guess.' A small grin plucked at the corner of Sadie's lips as she eyed her brother, tall and full of attitude, standing in her doorway.

'In all seriousness though, you should give up with the letter thing. It's a bit weird.'

Sadie glared at him, but the tension had all-but melted away.

'Have you ever considered talking to him?' Ben asked. 'Like, with actual words? From your mouth?'

'And when did you become so wise?'

'Just now,' he smiled. 'But really, you should just talk to the guy. It's a lot less weird than sending someone a love letter.'

'I don't know that I'm happy taking love advice from a twelve year old, but thanks for trying.'

Ben mimed being sick on the floor, holding his back and

dry heaving onto the carpet. 'Love,' he mimed, 'who was talking about ... love,' he wailed, chucking his head back and poking his tongue out as far as he could. He stumbled into her room, holding onto his stomach and laughing at his own joke.

'Hysterical,' she groaned, pushing the pieces of paper further under her pillow.

Ben wandered over to her chest of drawers and started moving her old stuffed toys around. 'Why do you still have these, anyway?' he asked.

She shrugged, making the universal noise for "I don't know." She pulled the end of her long ponytail to the front of her chest and started playing with the ends of her hair.

'Oh blimey,' Ben mumbled, leaning closer to the bedroom window. 'Has Dad got the radio on that loud again?'

Sadie shuffled to the end of the bed, closer to her brother. Their dad often had the cassette player blaring whilst he was working away on some DIY project in his shed, forgetting that there were other people in the house, well - the neighbourhood - that may not fancy listening to his choice of seventies rock. Again. Only this time it wasn't rock. The usual bouncy riffs of *Boston* were not floating to their ears across the lawn. Actually, it wasn't even the cassette player that Patrick had on, it was the radio.

'Unusual of Dad to care much for the local news,' Sadie thought out loud, leaning across Ben and nudging the window open. 'What's going on?'

The two of them leant across the desk and listened. The gentle breeze carried the stern voice of the news reporter to them. Something about a lost girl over on the island. Some appeal to keep looking for her.

'Oh,' Sadie realised. 'It's about that girl, can't remember

her name. She went missing ages ago when she was on some family holiday or something.'

'Hmm, who wants to come on holiday here?'

'That's hardly the point, Ben,' she said, frowning at her younger brother again. 'Shut up and listen for a sec.'

The siblings levered their heads closer to the garden to get a good earful of the radio programme. They soon learned that the girl went missing on a family holiday back in 1986 with her mum, dad and older sister. She disappeared on the tiny island off the coast of Rose Bay after her family stopped over there to see if they could spot some of the fabled birds and plants. Technically they were trespassing by being on the island, but that didn't go any further to explaining how someone could disappear on a space that you could lap in forty minutes. The girl had simply vanished. The coast guard assumed that she'd fallen somewhere, into the water on the other side of the island and drifted out into the channel, drowning. But no body had ever been recovered. A later theory was that she had fallen, but somewhere on the island. She'd tripped and injured herself and become trapped some-where, but that seemed unlikely given the size of the land. Other theories began to emerge, theories that the vast majority of people shrugged off as hearsay, as horror stories and myths. Theories that sounded unbelievable, even to the children living in Rose Bay.

'Oh, it's the four year anniversary. That makes sense,' Sadie said, her eyes still glued to the entrance of her dad's shed at the bottom of the garden. 'I wonder what happened to her.'

There was no answer from her brother. Sadie turned to see what he was up to, but found that he'd slipped from the room moments ago and returned to his own across the hall.

'Oh wow, well that was rude,' she muttered, fetching the pieces of paper from under her pillow. She thumbed through the scraps adorned with her loopy handwriting, any thoughts of the young girl still missing on the tiny island dissipating and soon forgotten.

9

Summer 1995

'Dad, something is seriously wrong here.'

Sadie had left her brother on the sofa and retreated back to the safety of the kitchen. She'd hoped her dad would have more to say on the topic. Her fingertips kept hovering back up to her throat, drifting towards her arteries to check her pulse, an obsession she was sure she'd never shake. Blood coursed below the surface of her skin, but the second she removed her hand she convinced herself it was going to stop again. Often she'd manage to convince herself in the short time between beats, that her heart had given out altogether. Setting foot in her old family home flicked a switch in her chest, intensifying the anxiety she normally felt. She held her shaking hand high up by her clavicle towards the base of her neck to feel the thud of her heart.

Her dad placed a large hand on her shoulder. 'I know, but I don't know what to say to you. You know as much about this as I do.'

'I'm going to take my things upstairs. I need to get out of these clothes, okay?'

The staircase leading up to the first floor was spotless. The soles of her Converse squeaked across the polished wooden floor, throwing her mind back to when she was a teenager and all those times she snuck back into the house hours after curfew, her shoes and footsteps threatening to unveil her location; they often did. The hall hadn't changed one bit. The wallpaper, the picture rail, the lacy net curtains, everything was all still there. All neat, all tidy - like a museum, preserved from her younger years. Her childhood, her old life, everything before Ben went missing was locked in this space like a vacuum. Not an inch had changed. The curtains were the same, the tiny family ornaments that crowded the window sills were the same, the fading, bleeding, bleached images of family members past were exactly the same. Not a thing had moved.

She ascended the stairs, her breath held in a capsule in her chest, her torso rigid. Her fingertips brushed the handrail. Memories flooded back of her standing on the top step using the wooden bar to steady herself at the realisation that her brother may never be coming home. She shuddered.

At the top of the landing sat the old window-seat, by far Sadie's favourite area growing up. It was a small seat, big enough for one person to curl up in, surrounded by the over-plump, overfilled cushions and the worn, crocheted blanket that her grandma had made all those years ago. She'd climb into the small space as a child with her favourite book or fairytale, clamber under the multicoloured blanket, and read until sleep took over. On numerous occasions her dad would come home from a late shift to find her curled up like a pretzel, book still in hand, fast asleep. He'd carry her off to bed, lifting the book from between her delicate fingers. Those memories seemed so far away, as if they belonged to someone else.

The door to her room was closed; she wondered when the last time was that either of her parents had delved inside. The door handle creaked under the weight of her arm. She stood in the hallway, mouth agape. Her room had not changed one bit. She had not been home in over four years, and nothing in her room had moved. Light pink wallpaper still stretched across all four walls, the same cushions and stuffed toys sat at the foot of her bed. The same fairy lights wrapped around her bed frame. She'd begged her parents for those lights for what seemed like years. Her room held so much history and the space that was once her haven now held an odd, stale sentiment.

She dropped onto the mattress, sinking into the thick duvet. Her hands spread out to feel the quilt cover, remembering its familiar texture and the warmth that emanated from under it. She nestled her fingers between the fluffy fibres of a cushion she had received for her sixteenth birthday. How strange it was to think that there may be particles of dust, flakes of memory still amongst the tassels from the day her brother left their family.

Her fingers spread amongst the soft fabric and she remembered the day Ben disappeared. She had been sitting on her bed cross legged, reading a magazine with one of those weird flowchart shaped quizzes in - how to choose the best haircut for your face shape or something equally vapid. She'd found those things fascinating as a teenager. Her back leant against the wall, her neck beginning to ache as she craned it down to focus on the words, when her mum came padding up the stairs in her slippers.

'What time is Ben due home?' An innocent question. He was almost a teenager, a popular one at that, and was often out with his friends in the evenings. He almost always came home on time, though. Unlike his sister.

'Not sure. Where did you say he was?' Sadie didn't move her eyes from the pages of her glossy magazine, her knuckles grasping the slippery paper, knuckles white with tension.

'He said he was going to Jamie's, but would be back for dinner. Maybe I'll give Jamie's mum a call.'

And her mum had left the room. Nothing unusual, nothing to write home about.

Sadie imagined her mum standing there now, pictured her leaving with her peach slippers scuffling across the floor in the way they used to.

She recalled how her mum had walked into the hallway to use the upstairs phone and perched on the window seat. She held the phone to her ear, her fingers twisting the cable and knotting it in on itself, a habit Sadie would mimic years later. The memory of her mum drifted back into the room, ringing her hands, the worry creeping through her eyes and resting in the delicate lines that were strung across her face.

'He's not with Jamie,' she said.

'Well, he must be with a different friend then. What about Samuel?'

'No, Samuel's away on holiday,' her mum said, shaking her head. Her eyes drifted around the room, in search of what Sadie didn't know.

'Jake? He spends a lot of time with Jake these days,' Sadie offered, still fixated on the silly quiz in front of her. She'd only given her mum an ounce of her attention. God, how she wished she'd given her more now.

'Yes, Jake,' her mum thought out loud, her teeth biting into her bottom lip. 'He could be with Jake. I'll try his mum,' she said, shuffling away and resuming her position in the window seat, her legs drawn together, feet twitching.

Another few minutes passed, another muffled conversation, words swallowed by an abundance of pillows and upholstery and velvet curtains. Another set of footsteps brought her mum back to her bedroom door.

'Jake hasn't seen him at all today.' Her mum's voice floated into the room.

'He's probably just wandering around again,' Sadie replied, flicking through the shiny magazine pages. 'Playing with the shop owner's dog or something. We really ought to get our own dog, then he'll stop obsessing over that mangy thing.'

'No,' her mum said, shaking her head. 'Jake's mum said he was due to come round and play with Jake today. They were meant to have lunch at their house, she'd bought sausage rolls and flapjacks.' She began to pace around the room, much to Sadie's annoyance. 'He never showed up.'

It was at that stage that Sadie finally put down whatever she was reading and paid attention to her mum. Ben was young and popular, but he was a good kid. He was a proper Mummy's boy and hated breaking the rules. If Ben was meant to have lunch with Jake, he would have had it. Sadie swallowed a growing ball of worry.

'Maybe we've got mixed up - he probably did tell you this morning who he was with. Have you spoken to Dad?'

'No, not yet,' her mum said, leaving the room. Sadie got up to follow and the memory faded.

The hours that followed that short conversation were, as cliche as it may have sounded, a complete blur. At some point her grandparents came round to comfort her mum, her dad left the house to search for Ben and within an hour or so the police had arrived to file a missing person's report. Everything went from a normal mundane Saturday evening to an utter state of panic in a matter of hours. Someone had picked up Sadie's life and all its characters on a plate and spun the whole thing on its axes, tipping the balance just enough to throw the whole thing into an unrecognisable parallel universe. A parallel universe where the police became a standard fixture, where tears and blank hollow stares replaced any other acceptable emotion and where hiding away from the outside world became the only thing her and her family could do.

Sadie brought herself back to the present day, her fingers gripping the cushion, still laced between the fibres of the light pink fluff. Her hands were clammy, fingers pulling on the loose strands. There was so much energy flitting through her limbs, buzzing to the surface of her skin. She couldn't sit still any longer. How could this have happened so long ago but feel so fresh in her mind? The thought that her brother was sitting a floor below her, after all this time, made her feel sick.

She dragged her small suitcase onto the bed, unzipping it in one satisfying sweep. The contents spilled out in no particular order. She'd not bothered to fold anything in her rush to leave, so her clothes tumbled from the silver capsule onto her duvet.

Her hands trembled as she took each item, refolded it and placed it back onto the bed, concentrating as best she could on the mundanity of the task. She could put it all away, she supposed. Each item could go back into its old home, where her clothes and belongings used to live. The wooden handle of the chest of drawers felt alien under her palm as she pulled on it, revealing an almost empty drawer. There were none of her old clothes in there, like she'd imagined there might be. But there was a small fabric pouch tucked away in one corner, bursting with dried lavender. The smell reminded her so much of her mum, the floral notes tickling her nose but calming her mind. Her mum had started leaving lavender pouches and potpourri around her room when Sadie had started to feel anxious or couldn't sleep. It helped, for a while. Until the smell became suffocating. Until her mum hid it in every corner of the house. Until the lavender that had started off so well-meaning began to serve no other purpose than to remind her of the anxiety that was inches away from taking over. She lifted the embroidered pocket from the drawer, turning it over in her hand. Her mum always meant well.

Her clothes slotted into the first couple of empty drawers, and Sadie zipped the suitcase, sliding it under her old bed. She felt the urge to check all of the drawers then, to see what remnants and artefacts from her childhood were hiding there. She slid the drawers from their frame one at a time, revealing nothing but more pouches of lavender. That was, until she got to the last drawer. It slid from the frame, but was definitely not empty. The bottom of the drawer was coated in a mixture of things from her teenage years; a couple of old Smash Hits magazines, a folded poster of an old boy band obsession, a stretchy choker that she'd nagged her mum for months and then only worn once because it was itchy. And hiding in the very back corner, amongst the colourful debris, was a folded piece of blush pink letter paper. It wiggled free and, despite there not being one of the embroidered pouches in this particular drawer, it still managed to smell of lavender. Sadie unfolded it, spying the familiar loopy handwriting she used to have as a seventeen year old. It was her letter to Vedat, the one that Ben had berated her for writing. She'd written it with the intention of giving it to Vedat before they left for university, only everything had gone south very quickly from that day onwards. Things had changed. She never gave the letter to him and they'd gone their separate ways without either sharing so much as a backward glance.

It wasn't a love letter, as such. Not in the respect that Ben had suggested. They'd been friends for a long time, Sadie, Vedat and Callie. And the three of them were preparing to move off in very different directions. It felt like such a big time in their lives. She wanted to give each of her friends something to remember her by, but mostly she felt she needed to let Vedat know how she felt before they all split up and only saw each other in the summer.

She held the letter for a few minutes longer, reminiscing how much easier it was to be a teenager, before everything went wrong, before they were forced to grow up so quickly. She'd scrawled his telephone number down before leaving her home in London with the hopes that she'd be able to steal a few minutes to try and call him again. Of course, until recently, she never did.

'No, I've got no comment to make,' a voice came from the downstairs hallway. 'Leave me and my family alone!'

Sadie slipped the letter into her back pocket and jogged downstairs. The familiar voice of Allison, her mum, filled the bottom of the house as she continued to yell at reporters that had tried their luck and followed her up the garden path.

'I won't be talking to any of you,' Allison yelled.

'Mrs Pickett, can you let us know if Ben is home?' one asked.

'Mrs Pickett, is your son speaking about what happened to him? Was he abducted?'

'Should we be concerned for the other children of Rose Bay? Don't you think you've got a responsibility for them?'

'Can we just have a quick word?' another shouted over the din of reporters.

Allison wrestled her way into her own home, squeezing through the door with bags of food shopping. Camera flashes exploded around her head and burst into the hallway. Sadie hopped down the last few stairs and pushed the door shut forcefully behind her mum, who was leaning against the wall.

'I am not ever going to get used to that,' she said under her breath.

'Allison.' Patrick burst from the kitchen and rushed over to his wife. 'Are you okay? They really shouldn't be coming up the garden path, they said they wouldn't.'

'Well they're clearly not very good at taking directions,' Allison replied. 'Thanks for coming out and rescuing me,' she spat, pushing her way past her family and into the kitchen.

'That's not fair, I didn't realise.' Patrick followed his wife through the hallway. 'I did offer to go out and get food, you didn't need to go.'

'Yes but I wanted to, didn't I? I needed to not be here for a few minutes.'

'Oh, with me, you mean?'

'Oh come off it, Patrick. Are you really making this all about you right now?' Allison bit back.

'Well it is, isn't it? You want to be angry at me for something.'

Sadie stepped back and watched her parents bicker, their voices creeping up to be heard by the reporters outside. She tiptoed into the corner of the kitchen, trying to get one of her parent's attention, but they continued to argue.

'They can hear you, you know,' she hissed, jabbing a finger towards the front door.

'Yes, I'm sure they can. Would have been nice for some support, Patrick,' Allison jeered.

Sadie met her dad's eye and raised an eyebrow. Not now, it said. Now is not the time.

Sadie's parents had stuck together through everything following Ben's disappearance, despite the general consensus that they were going to end up getting divorced. A happy marriage can only withstand so much, and on the face of it Allison and Patrick were unwilling to let their long relationship crumble when their son went missing and their daughter left home. Sadie often wondered whether that was the right decision for the both of them, but it was their decision and they stuck to it.

Patrick hovered around the kitchen, slotting cups and plates into cupboards, opening doors and shuffling them around. Allison leant heavily against the doorframe, watching him fuss over things that didn't warrant fussing over. Sadie craned her neck, trying to catch her mum's line of sight.

'Mum,' Sadie said, finally catching her attention. 'Are you alright?'

'Yes, why wouldn't I be?' she replied, running some hot water and washing the mugs that Sadie and her dad had used earlier that afternoon.

Because your son has reappeared after five years of being missing, Sadie thought. But instead of pushing her, she said, 'it's okay if you're not.'

'I am fine,' she asserted. 'I've got my family back together. I've got everything I've ever wanted.' She flashed a grin and continued to bustle around the kitchen space.

Is no one going to say anything? No one's going to register how weird this is? Sadie mused, tempted to let her thoughts slip out of her head to see how her parents would react. Her dad slipped back into the garden, presumably to hide in his shed to save being yelled at by her mum again, or being caught in the crossfire of any impending confrontation.

'Do you want to help me cook dinner, or are you going to stand there?'

Sadie blinked, shocked at her mum's directness. She picked up a knife and started peeling the potatoes that were left by the sink. She gripped the short knife, running the blade under the muddied skins and pulled, the peel curling and dropping onto the chopping board below her arms. The peels fell to the board, their contact audible against the silent backdrop of the kitchen. Sadie's heart thudded in her ears; she hoped her mum would break the silence, but she remained zipped up and stoic. Sadie was rigid with tension.

'Journey okay?' her mum finally asked.

Sadie had to stop herself from rolling her eyes at the unimaginative question. Did everyone in this household have to ask her that before engaging her in further conversation? Was this her parent's equivalent to talking about the weather?

'Yes, fine,' she answered, placing the peeled, pale potatoes in a saucepan of clear water.

When she was much younger, conversation had flown freely between her and her mum. They'd had shared interests, liked similar things; her mum had always been what her friends referred to as a 'cool mum'. But as the years stretched and Sadie became older, the differences between the two of them gaped out in front of them, a huge, empty cavernous space that neither of them knew how to fill. It widened every year and resulted in numerous lengthy awkward silences.

As Sadie continued to peel the potatoes, her mind wandered back to Vedat. The phone number she'd scrawled on a scrap of paper before leaving London burned a hole in her pocket. She wondered if he'd returned her call to the flat, if it might be worth ringing Tabitha to double check. Thinking of Tabitha sent a strange sensation down her spine; how could her life exist like this but also as it had with Tabitha at the same time? Was it possible that these two scenarios were playing out side by side?

Her family had been close to Vedat's family, but things had changed when Sadie upped and left a few months after her 18th birthday. She'd burned those bridges. And now she was back, and alone, she longed to repair them.

'Mum, does Vedat still live locally?'

Allison glanced up from chopping vegetables. 'Your Vedat?' she asked.

Sadie's heart panged at the colloquialism. 'Yes. Does he still live down Victoria Road? Or did he leave?'

'No, I think he's still there. Still in with his parents. Same house,' she replied, her voice muffled into her chest.

He was still here, fifteen minutes down the road. 'I'm going to go out for a quick walk. What time do I need to be back for dinner?' Sadie blushed, dropping the knife.

Allison glanced at her watch, at the pan of potatoes and back again. She shrugged. 'An hour should be fine,' she responded.

Sadie slid the last of the potato peel into the bin. 'I'll be back then.'

'Go out the back door,' her mum added. 'Much easier to avoid the newspapers that way.'

Sadie nodded and slipped out into the garden, past her dad's shed and out onto the back road.

VEDAT'S FAMILY home stood on the corner of Victoria Road, a few minutes from the school and the library. It was bigger than Sadie's family house and had an imposing air about it, with black iron gates encasing the front garden and a large white garage hiding Vedat's dad's car collection. The outside of the house reminded Sadie of a wedding cake; smooth, white royal icing coating the exterior walls, curling gates and hedges trimmed to interesting shapes and the driveway arching up to the garage doors.

The familiar metal latch on the gate opened, rust fraying and peeling in the corners making it harder to push on the hinges. Sadie's Converse ground into the gravel with a crunch as she made her way up to the front door. It had been years since she'd done this, but it all felt so familiar. She jabbed her finger into the doorbell and waited for the faint sound of the chiming in the hallway. She could hear movement in the house, rustling and rushing to get to the door. A few seconds passed and the door was pulled open by none other than her old best friend from school.

'Hi,' she said, feet firmly on the doorstep. Sadie's knees shook.

'What are you doing here?' he responded, the question as much running through his eyes as the uncertainty in his voice.

'I,' Sadie started, taken aback by his abruptness. 'Ben's come back.'

A quick nod. 'I know, we noticed the news vans all over the road.' Vedat looked down at Sadie. 'That doesn't explain why you're here though.'

'Vedat,' she said, shocked by his coldness. 'We need to talk.'

'No, no we don't,' he affirmed, moving to close the door.

Sadie jumped up and placed herself in the way. 'We need to talk,' she hissed through clenched teeth.

'There's nothing to say, Sadie. I want nothing to do with this.' Vedat forced the door closed against Sadie's body, pushing her back out onto the doorstep to stare at the solid wooden slab. She turned to walk away, still hoping that as her back turned he'd have a change of heart and come out after her. Sadie glanced over her shoulder, but he didn't resurface.

Sadie returned to her home through the back roads that wound behind Vedat's home and her own. She slipped back through the gate behind her dad's shed to find her family hovering around in the kitchen waiting for her mum to place dinner on the table. She hid outside to watch them from a distance. Her mum was busying over the stove, her dad was laying cutlery down around the table mats and her brother, Ben, was waiting in the corner, staring. It didn't look all that unusual, from a distance. It was a normal family, going about their normal business on a normal Sunday afternoon. Only, the closer you looked the more the cracks made themselves apparent. Allison was fussing over everything that bit too much, worrying about every last detail. Patrick was finding anything to keep himself busy, but refused to talk, worried about saying the wrong thing and resorting to saying nothing instead. And Ben. Well, Ben stood, statuesque, emotionless.

His complexion was more of a greyish tinge than earlier and the skin hung limp from his cheekbones. Her eyes remained on him for a handful of minutes; in that time, it seemed like he didn't move at all. His limbs were straight by his side, even his fingers outstretched like those of a toy. Then he flinched, the way an animal does when it dreams. A quick twitch that made Sadie jump and catch herself as she stared at her more than unusual family situation. His eyes contacted hers, locked on. What was that expression?

Sadie's skin crawled as she made her way back into the kitchen through the garden door.

'Did you see him?' Allison asked.

'What?'

'Did you see Vedat?'

'Erm, no. He wasn't in.'

'Yes he was,' Ben said.

Sadie looked up, frowning at her brother.

'He was in, he just didn't want to see you. That's right, isn't it?'

Her frown deepened. 'What? Why would you say that?'

'Because it's true, isn't it? You went over to see him, he wouldn't let you in. He's got no interest in you and your silly little love letters anymore.' He said it matter of factly, his voice dry and flat. It wasn't spiteful, but he knew the power in his words. He knew the impact they would have, he had to.

'Ben,' Patrick interjected.

'It's fine,' Sadie said. 'He's not wrong.'

'What happened between you and Vedat? You used to be thick as thieves, you two.'

'I don't know,' Sadie said. 'We got older I guess.'

'Right, move over everyone, dinner's ready,' Allison beamed, placing the meals down on the mats on the table.

Everyone slid into their seats, the same ones they would have sat in five years ago. An unsettling sense of uneasiness sloshed around in Sadie's stomach and she wondered how much her family were feeling it too. Here they were, sitting around the table eating Sunday lunch as if everything was normal, as if nothing at all had happened in the last five years. But of course, that wasn't true, something *had* happened. Something that should have prevented any of this from being possible.

The scent of roast chicken wafted up from the plates, inviting yet somehow unsettling. Warm gravy, crisped potatoes, fresh vegetables. It should all have been so appetising and yet Sadie couldn't settle the lapping of waves in the pit of her stomach.

'Can you pass the salt please, Ben?' Allison said, holding her hand out for the little ceramic shaker. Ben passed it to her wordlessly. 'Thank you, darling,' she replied.

Sadie cocked an eyebrow, glancing over at her dad who was wearing much the same expression on his tired face. Keeping this up was beginning to exhaust her.

'There's extra gravy if you like,' Allison declared to the table. No one answered, instead focusing intently on their own plate of food. Sadie scooped up a piece of meat and slid it into her mouth. She chewed on it as if it were made of glass, as if too sudden a movement would throw the balance of the whole table off. The table, which was made up exactly how she remembered as a child all those years ago. Her family, sitting in their assigned chairs, chewing and swallowing and making all the right moves in all the right places. Sadie eased her cutlery down beside her plate. Even her breaths were shorter than normal, her expressions muted and stunted. Allison cast a glance at Patrick who was moving the food around his place, studying it. Ben had hardly touched any food before he rested his own cutlery down. No one said a thing. The food was there, the people were there, the actions were there, but there was no feeling. No "mms" of appreciation, no full mouths nodding thanks to Allison for cooking, no small talk about the day or the week ahead. Nothing but an awkward, acted out play.

'I'm not sure I can do this,' Sadie croaked. It was one of those things that she'd meant to say but the thought had slipped out of her mind and onto her tongue, and before she knew it she'd laid it out for inspection by each member of her family.

'Can't do what, dear?' her mum asked, her voice sickly sweet. 'Oh, you're not going vegetarian again? You didn't mention —,'

'No, no it's not that. I can't do this. I can't pretend everything is normal. I can't sit here, eating dinner, making small talk.'

'Well, what do you suggest?' Allison placed her own cutlery down now, her hands holding steady over the top of the silverware. 'You've got to eat.'

'Well yes, but...Mum, can't you see? This isn't right. This isn't natural. We can't just pick up where we left off.'

'And why not?'

'Well,' Sadie responded but her words trailed off. In reality, she didn't know the answer, she just knew it wasn't what they were attempting to do right now.

'Go on, I'm waiting,' her mum pressed, the familiar thread of impatience coming through in her voice.

'It's like the Stepford Wives or something. We're all sitting here, having a lovely Sunday lunch, you're trying to get us all to chat away and have a wonderful old time, like — like nothing's happened. We're all here having a good old catch up over dinner with... with someone we assumed was dead!'

A heavy cloth of silence settled over the table. Sadie placed both hands on her knees, her face flushing red, heat creeping up her neck. 'Oh shit,' she mumbled. 'I - I'm sorry.'

'No, you're right,' Patrick said. 'But you're also wrong. There's no way any of us can possibly know the best way to deal with this situation, but yelling at each other isn't it, Sadie.'

She nodded, willing her shoulders to curl in on her body and slide under the table. She looked up at her mum, who hadn't moved or spoken since her outburst. She kept her eyes glued to the table setting in front of her, but Sadie could see the tendons flinching and clenching in her jaw. Tears began to brim in her eyes and slip down her cheeks onto the plate.

'Mum,' Sadie said, placing her hand out to hold her mum's own. Allison flinched, rubbing her hand over her face. 'I think we'll call it a night,' she mumbled, moving over to the kitchen. 'I'm going to have a bath.'

10

Summer 1995

The house was quiet. Allison and Patrick had both gone to bed without saying another word to Sadie, as if her coming home was what had caused the tension and the blow up over dinner, not the fact that her brother had reappeared after five years of being A.W.O.L. Allison fussed over Ben: straightening his hair despite him having nowhere to go, running her hands over his face to check he was still real, constantly asking him if he was okay, if he needed more food, if he needed some fresh air. Allison's behaviour was cloying, suffocating. Sadie could only imagine how Ben was feeling.

Only that was the thing. Ben didn't seem to be feeling anything at all. He was quiet and stoic and unbending; it was unsettling. At times, Sadie wondered if he was actually real. If she were to run her own hands over his face, would he be there? Would his skin be cold and lifeless, a statue of alabaster and marble?

Sadie had paced around her room willing the hours to slip by, exhausted but unwilling to sleep. She did not want to get into her childhood bed, under the pink covers that looked as if they hadn't been changed since she left for London. Eventually she peeled them back, knocking numerous stuffed toys onto the floor. The sheets were stiff with cold, the uninviting chill passing through her body. The glass eyes of her childhood toys glinted in the darkness, taunting her. She had been so excited to leave this town, this house, her bed. Being back in it felt like a curse, a cruel joke dragging her backwards and down into a strange museum of the belongings of her youth. The bed was stale, the room cold, the items she'd felt nostalgia for had lost their meaning. Everything tasted sour.

Sadie's ears twinged in the darkness. The house had been silent for what felt like hours, but now there were clear footsteps walking across the landing. Someone getting up to use the bathroom, she thought, forcing her ears and heartbeat to calm. But there it was again. Pacing. The footsteps were heavy outside her door and unmistakably pacing back and forth. She slid her legs out of the covers and into her slippers, tiptoeing towards the bedroom door. There was the unmistakable hint of a draft trickling in from around the doorframe. The door handle relented under her palm, the door itself creaking only slightly against the hinges. Ben was on the landing, wearing a pair of their dad's jogging trousers. Sadie's heart twinged at the realisation that, of course, none of his clothes from before would fit him now. All those lost years, gone forever. God knows how he'd spent them.

'Ben,' she whispered, her voice thunderous in the otherwise silent hallway. 'What are you doing?' She expected him to brush her off again, to ignore the question or to act like his behaviour was anything but odd. But he didn't. As he looked up at her, she realised he'd been crying. His eyes were wet and shimmering in the low moonlight that broke in through the gap in the curtains, his cheeks were red and his fist was full of sodden tissues.

'I can't sleep,' he said, pulling at the tissues and dropping tiny pieces of white to the floor like snow.

'Do you want to chat?' Sadie felt a tug in her chest. She yearned to hold her brother, but she was so unsure of what he needed, of what he wanted from her. But Ben nodded, and Sadie motioned towards the staircase. The two of them tiptoed down and crept through to the kitchen. 'I don't remember how to sleep in a bed,' he said, his body flopped forward onto the dining table. 'It feels wrong,' he continued. 'The warmth. The toys from when I was a kid. Everything.'

Sadie nodded, more aware of how Ben was feeling than he realised. 'You look exhausted,' she said, taking a seat in the chair opposite him. 'Did you manage to sleep at all?'

Ben rested his head in his hands. 'An hour or so.' His skin was sallow and grey and it was only now that Sadie realised his hands. Before, he was too far away for her to notice, but now, up close, she could see much more. Scars lined his fingers and curled around his nails. What caused them, Sadie did not know, but there were hundreds of them etched all over his fingers. Ben realised she was looking, studying, and pulled his hands from the table, burying them in his lap.

'Sorry,' she said, embarrassed that she'd been staring.

'It's fine,' he shook his head. 'I don't know how to do any of this anymore.' He closed his eyes. 'Conversations. Acting normal. Emotions.'

'I can't pretend to know how you're feeling, Ben. None of us can. Mum wants to carry on as if nothing's happened, Dad's just, well, I don't know. There's not a handbook on how to deal with this.'

Ben nodded, closing his eyes again and taking a deep breath. 'I'm so tired,' he repeated.

'We could sleep down here? On the sofas if you like? To be honest I'm finding being back in my room weird too. Like some kind of strange shrine to my childhood, you know?'

Ben nodded in agreement. 'I'd like that.'

Ben stepped out in front of his sister, his body wavering with fatigue.

Breath caught in Sadie's throat at the sight of the back of his head, as if she were seeing him in 3D for the first time. As if seeing all of him made this all that much more real. He shouldn't be home. He couldn't be.

'Ben,' Sadie asked as they walked through to the living room and spread out on the sofas. 'Where have you been all this time?'

Ben closed up at the mention of his whereabouts. He drew his legs towards his chest and wrapped his arms tight around his knees.

'Sorry, I —,' Sadie said, leaning closer to her brother. 'I shouldn't have asked. I'm sorry. I don't want to upset you.'

'It's okay.' Ben rocked himself gently on the sofa, his chin leaning on his hands. His breathing came in quick, short gasps as Sadie recognised the beginnings of a panic attack.

'Hey,' she whispered, jumping from the sofa and kneeling in front of her brother. Her hands rested on top of his and she gently rubbed the back of his palms, desperate to calm him and ground him. 'Hey, look at me,' she said. 'Breathe. Breathe, Ben. In. Out. You're okay,' she assured him. His body continued to rock back and forth but his breathing began to even out. 'Ben, it's okay. Open your eyes.'

Ben's legs started to shake and jitter, his body no longer rocking but virtually vibrating on the sofa. Sadie continued to rub the back of his hands, willing him to calm down and desperate for him to not wake their parents. 'Open your eyes, Ben. Everything is okay.'

'It's not,' he whispered. His eyes opened, the flesh parting to reveal glistening amber eyes. Sadie flinched and threw her body back from Ben's knees. She scurried back towards the window, an icy chill clenching her chest. The fiery orange hue swallowed the whites of his eyes, embers and flames twisting amongst the spheres.

'Ben?' she uttered.

He clenched his jaw, tendons pulsing, nostrils flaring. His eyes darted from each wall in the room, trying to settle on something but failing. Sadie watched, mouth agape, as his eyes attempted to cling to something. to focus on something, anything. But the something always wriggled free, leaving his eyes to flit wildly from side to side.

'Ben,' Sadie whispered again, nervously laying her hand on her brother's knee.

The muscle in his thigh twinged under her touch, but she kept it there. His eyes continued darting from side to side in search of something that Sadie couldn't see.

'I...I can't see,' he said, panic clutching at his voice. 'Why can't I see?' his breathing started to pick up pace again, his chest rising and falling in quick succession.

'Breathe,' she whispered, dragging the vowels of the word out and praying that whatever was happening to Ben would pass. 'Just breathe.'

He nodded, clenching his eyes closed against the orange

spheres. Tears flooded down his cheeks, dripping off the end
of his chin. Sadie leant forward and held his head to her
chest, rocking his body and stroking the back of his head. 'It's
okay, Ben.'

Minutes passed. Ben's tears dried up and the pair stilled,
staying in a tight hug that neither was willing to let go of.
Sadie leant back, her hands under her brother's chin. She
swept away the last of the tears. His eyes opened, and they
were just that - his eyes.

'You okay?' she asked.

Ben nodded and collapsed back onto the sofa. 'I need to
sleep,' he whispered. She watched as he closed his eyes. His
breathing deepened and evened out, his chest rising and falling. His mouth fell open and he began to snore, purring into
the cushions on the back of the sofa.

Once she was satisfied that Ben had fallen into a deep
sleep, Sadie lay sideways on the other sofa, stretched out
amongst the cushions with her feet curled in at the end.
She'd seen those eyes so many times, but never at that close
proximity- and never belonging to someone whom they
really ought not to. She tried to sleep but every time she
closed her eyes, she saw them again. They wrenched themselves into the darkness behind her eyelids. Glowing spheres
of amber, those eyes of fire. She was desperate to sleep but
those eyes wouldn't let her.

SADIE LAY ON THE SOFA, her feet hanging off the edge, toes
brushing the plush carpet. Her eyes were heavy and the
early signs of a headache pulsed in her temples. The sun
began to pierce through the curtains into the living room
and Sadie knew, with the arrival of daylight, that she'd be

unlikely to get any more sleep than the couple of hours she struggled through already. Her parent's shuffling footsteps echoed down the stairs as the house came back to life. She glanced over at Ben. He was still sound asleep, curled up on the sofa and taking up as little room as he possibly could. After the events of last night, he went out like a light and didn't make a sound for hours. There were a few moments where Sadie considered checking his pulse to check he was still alive, appeased only by the gentle rise and fall of his chest.

'Morning,' a voice came from the stairs. Sadie turned her head and spun around on the sofa.

'Hi Dad,' she yawned, holding her hair back off her face.

'You both okay?'

'Mhmm,' she nodded, her eyes drifting between open and closed. 'Ben's still sparko,' she said, getting to her feet and following her dad through to the kitchen.

'Coffee?' he asked.

'Oh God, yes. Please.' Sadie's body flopped against the wall, the concrete frame all that was holding her up off the floor.

'What are you both doing down here?' Sadie's stomach dropped off a cliff edge. There was no way she could tell her parents what had happened last night.

'Erm, I heard Ben creeping around on the landing last night,' she faltered. 'He couldn't sleep. He was struggling in his old bedroom, which I get. To be honest I feel the same way.' Sadie's words were broken by a huge yawn and she threw her hand over her face. 'So we stayed down here. He went off around midnight and hasn't stirred since.' She rubbed her hands over her red-rimmed eyes.

'Guessing you haven't slept too well?' Patrick asked, grinning. His face was kind, it always had been. This morning it was the same, but there was a hint of concern there too.

Sadie shook her head, stifling and swallowing another yawn. She was happy to receive the coffee in a steaming hot mug. 'Thank you,' she smiled. 'I'll be fine after some caffeine.' She raised her mug in front of her face. Her left cheek had a long imprint running along it, dented into her soft skin from the upholstery.

'Cheers,' he joked, clunking his mug against hers.

'Is Mum alright? After last night, I mean?'

'Hmm,' Patrick thought on the question whilst taking a swig of hot coffee. 'I don't know. She's taking the whole thing pretty hard, but in a very different way to us. All she's ever wanted is for her family to be back together, and now it's happened I don't think she knows quite how to process it.' Patrick took a seat at the kitchen table. 'When Ben first went missing, your mum didn't sleep at all. She ended up on medication to knock her out, then had to take pretty strong caffeine pills in the mornings in order to function. Him disappearing took a big part of her with him. We need to give her time.'

'I get it, it's fine,' Sadie nodded. And she did.

AT AROUND 11AM, the doorbell rang. The last Sadie knew, her parents didn't actually have a doorbell, so the shrill ringing came as quite the surprise. Patrick shuffled to the door and flicked open the peephole. Since the press had taken camp in the front garden, the family had become quite cautious about answering the door to anyone and everyone. To Sadie's surprise, her dad peered outside, turned his back and called her name.

'It's for you,' he said.

'What?'

'Vedat and Callie are here.'

'Both of them? Together?' Sadie asked. She'd imagined she might be able to talk to them both separately, but the idea of them being in the same space together - that didn't seem likely at all.

'Yep,' her dad said, moving away back into the living room.

Sadie moved over to the door, opening it enough to see her old school friends without letting the press get an eye full.

'Hi,' she said nervously.

'Hi Sadie,' they both said. Callie draped herself against the doorframe, her head tipped to the side. Vedat stood to her right, arms folded, back straight. His head shifted from Sadie back to the small, committed group of reporters that clustered at the bottom of the driveway.

A whole conversation passed between the three of them in silence. What are you doing here? Why didn't you answer my call? Why wouldn't you let me speak to you yesterday? What have we done? Can we fix it?

Instead of any of these questions, Sadie said, 'shall we go for a walk?'

'Erm yes, that's probably a good idea,' Vedat answered, shuffling his hands even further around his stomach.

'Sure,' Callie agreed.

'Wait here,' Sadie held her hand out, slipping her shoes on and sticking her head into the living room where her mum, dad and Ben were sitting. 'I'm going to go out for a while, I won't be long.' She slipped her dad's key off the hook and, after looking down the path to see a small gathering of news reporters, she motioned for Callie and Vedat to follow her through to the garden and out onto the back of the road. 'Probably best we go this way,' she said, slipping a jacket from the coat hook.

The three of them emerged onto the back of the road behind the house, having slipped through the garden gate.

'Honestly, those reporters have been there for hours. They must be bored. Or at least hungry.'

'They'll give up eventually,' Callie said, her voice confident, like she somehow had experience with this sort of thing.

Sadie swallowed her words and focussed on the sound of her shoes hitting the pavement. 'This is all very surreal,' she whispered to the tops of her converse. 'Ben being home, me being back, us being together.'

'Don't go thinking this is some kind of happy-clappy reunion, Sadie, because it's not,' Callie snapped.

'I know, I know,' she apologised, holding her hands up in surrender. Callie had always had an anger issue when they were children, but she didn't remember her being this bad. Looking at her, Sadie saw that Callie hadn't changed a great deal at all, but then she wasn't sure if she'd changed either. Her face looked older but the features were the same. The young, youthful button nose remained, slightly bent to the left as a result of the hockey game that led to the banning of the sport at their school. Her eyes were still the warm brown she remembered, though they were unmistakably more tired.

'Can we not argue already, please?' Vedat urged, walking at a distance from the other two on the path. 'Do we think this is a good idea?' he asked, motioning to the sea front. 'Is this where we ought to be going?'

'Where else do you suggest, V?' Callie asked, folding her arms and looking over her glasses at Vedat.

'Fine,' he mumbled, giving a tiny shake of his head and redirecting his gaze to the tops of his shoes.

A few more minutes passed as the three of them walked in fragmented silence, veering off the main road and down to the coastal path.

'What's he like?' Vedat asked, his voice quiet and sheepish.

Sadie took a deep breath in. She was unsure if telling both Vedat and Callie everything was the best idea. They'd find out either way. Easier to control the situation if she was in front of it, she supposed. 'He's odd, sort of like he never left, but in a way like he's not really come home either. I know that's not a very useful description. He's not himself,' Sadie said.

'Hmm,' Callie hummed under her breath. 'Does he... does he look the same?'

Sadie looked up to meet her eye. 'Well yeah, I suppose he does really - why wouldn't he?'

'Sadie, he's been gone for years,' Callie paused, hoping that Sadie would catch on to fill in the gaps. But she didn't. She continued to stare at her, unsure of what she was getting at. 'God knows where he's been, if he's eaten properly, if he's had access to clean clothes or water or what.' She paused. 'If he looks the same, that's surely odd to you?'

Sadie thought about her answer. Callie was right. Ben did look much the same.

They continued walking further along the road, grey clouds slowly drifting over the blue sky.

'Speaking of things never changing,' Vedat said, 'how do you feel about being back here? That's got to be weird, right?'

'Yes, I suppose it is,' Sadie answered. She had thought a lot about how little her hometown had changed. How the corner shop had remained the same with the same owner from her childhood, how the train station hadn't had a lick of paint, how the signs still proudly hung at the entrance of the village claiming that Rose Bay had won a prize in '84 for having the best flower display. 'It feels like the place has stood completely still,' she said. 'Does it feel that way for you?'

Vedat pondered his answer. 'I'm not so sure.' He buried his hands into his pockets, deep in thought. 'I mean, it's a bit different when you've been here all along. The changes can be so gradual that you don't realise they're even happening. But I guess it doesn't feel like the place has really changed since we were kids. Since we were at school, even.'

'The place is a mausoleum.'

'What?' Vedat stopped walking and faced Sadie.

'As in a tomb. A living, breathing tomb where time has stopped but the people inside are somehow still living.'

'Oh,' Vedat answered. 'Yeah, I guess so.'

'Sorry, I guess I was just thinking out loud,' Sadie mused. 'Where are we actually walking to?'

Callie stopped at the grassy edge and jerked her head over the ledge. 'For old time's sake?'

'I don't know...is now the time?' Vedat asked, stopping in his tracks as he watched Callie approach the overgrown track. The track was lined either side with lush green foliage and zig-zagged steeply until it deposited any walkers onto the shingle beach.

'If not now, when?' Without another word, Callie dropped down the small ledge and onto the track, walking at a fair speed away from Sadie and Vedat. The two of them hung back. Sadie wanted to follow but something made her feel reluctant to head down to the beach so soon.

'I don't know if I can yet,' Sadie whispered.

'It's alright, I'm not sure it's the best idea either,' said Vedat. 'But we can't let her go on her own.' He slipped his hand through Sadie's and stood toward the edge of the ledge, motioning for her to drop down first. Sadie hesitated. After a short internal battle, her feet lifted from the ground and dropped to the dry earth track below.

'What made you change your mind, V?'

'What?' Vedat looked around at Sadie. 'What do you mean?'

'Yesterday you shut the door in my face. Today, it's like that never happened. Why?'

'I don't know,' he shrugged. 'In honesty, I suppose it's because I know I can't abandon my friends.'

Callie's head flung round, catching the seriousness solidifying across Vedat's brow. Sadie blushed, her cheeks a deep red. She swallowed down the urge to cry, or to leave, and walked in silence a few steps away from the two people she grew up with. They couldn't have felt any further away at that moment if they'd tried.

The walk was exactly how she had remembered it; steep, unforgiving but beautifully scenic. The sea stretched out below them, a grey-tinged hue of blue, and the clouds sank in the sky to meet the horizon. She paused part way down to soak in the serenity of the area, closing her eyes in the cool breeze and taking a deep breath of salty air. The sea was still, its surface glassy. The old colour wheel that she remembered fondly from walks with her family still stood on the ledge. Copper coloured rust flaked around the pole of the wheel, but the circle itself was exactly as she had remembered it, each different shade of blue and green and grey with their own identities. The colours faded in and out of each other from a true deep blue, through to a lilac purple and misty sea-green. She gazed at the colour wheel, closing one eye so it seemed as if the sea began where the colour wheel left off. The disc creaked, the axis breaking off the rust that had been holding it in its place. Her hands moved around its surface to find the most closely matched colour with today's water and stopped at a greenish shade of blue. Almost perfect. Vedat came into focus in the corner of her eye. He was waving at her to come down the rest of the path, to get a move on. She gave one last look to the wheel and the warm memories of days out with her family and continued her descent. Callie had sped off in front of the other two and was already approaching the beach.

By the time she arrived on the shingled beach, Callie had given up standing and had sat amongst the stones. She was leaning back on her hands, reclining, holding her face up to the warm sun, the golden rays dripping over her neck. Sadie walked over and sat next to her, motioning for Vedat to join them. The water brushed against the shore, tiny shells and stones tumbling over one another and being pulled back under the water.

'Remember the first time we all came down here on our own?' Callie asked, throwing rocks towards the sea.

Of course she remembered. She didn't particularly want to speak about it, but there was no way she could scrape the vivid memory from her mind.

She nodded.

'Of course you do,' Callie said. 'After it happened, after Ben I mean, I came down here almost every day to look over to that island and wait for the day the sea gave him back to us.'

'Please stop, Callie,' Sadie interrupted. 'I can't, not now.'

'If not now, when, Sade?' Sadie flinched at the use of her old nickname. 'I came down here almost every - single - day. I still do come down most weeks. I sit and stare at that tiny island and wonder when he'll come back. And now he has come back.'

'Callie, come on,' Vedat urged, sensing Sadie's discomfort at the direction of the conversation.

'No, Vedat. Can't you see? He's come back. That must mean something, right? Sadie?'

'Callie, please,' Sadie begged, standing up from her position in the gravel. She looked up to the sky as the first drop of rain fell against her forehead. 'I'm going home. You're welcome to come and see him. But please, don't say anything, okay? Don't mention anything to him.'

'That's not how this can work, Sadie. We need to talk about this, don't you get it?'

'No, I guess I don't. Let's go, Vedat.' Sadie stood, making strides towards the track that would take them back up onto the main road. 'Are you coming or not?'

Callie shifted against the shingle and rose, following Sadie and Vedat back towards the greenery and away from the sea. Unlike Callie, Sadie hadn't been down to the sea or anywhere near it since that day. And she was finding it hard being anywhere near it today. The smell of it, the sound of it, the rushing of the water against the shore and the sound of the gulls circling high above in search of food only served to remind Sadie, to taunt her and haunt her. The salty scent lingered in the air, clinging to her nostrils. She once loved the sea, but was now on the verge of hating it.

They walked back to Sadie's house in silence. Droplets of rain tumbled above them, growing from tiny flecks of moisture to large spheres that tumbled and crashed overhead. Sadie wiped the water from her forehead and out of her eyes as they ascended. They emerged onto the main road a handful of minutes later, warm, damp and muggy in the evening heat.

The summer shower passed as quickly as it appeared and, by the time the three of them approached the path leading up to Sadie's home, the ground had all but dried up. Vedat stopped in his tracks.

'Sadie,' he said. 'Is that him, up there?'

Sadie followed his gaze up to her bedroom window. The old net curtains parted to reveal her brother's body and half of his face. His eyes glared straight ahead, motionless and cold.

'Yep, Sadie said, taking a breath in. 'See what I mean?'

'Yeah he's not changed a bit, has he?' Callie chimed in.

'He's a bit taller, maybe,' Vedat added. 'What's he doing up in your room?'

'I don't know,' Sadie shrugged. 'I guess Mum is probably up there too, so he's most likely with her I guess.' Sadie's answer didn't convince Callie or Vedat. In truth, it didn't convince her either.

Callie locked eyes with Ben and waved. He remained static, the only movement that of his blinking eyelids that drifted languidly up and down.

'I don't like this,' Callie said. 'I don't think I can come in.'

'Nope, I get that,' Vedat answered. 'But aren't you curious? Don't you want to know how he—.' His words trailed off as Sadie glared at him.

'Do you guys want to come up and see him? Because if

you do, I'd really rather you didn't lead in with an inquisition, okay?'

The other two nodded and followed behind as she approached the bottom of their driveway.

'Oh crap,' she hissed. 'We definitely should have gone round the back.'

The group of news reporters had thinned considerably, but there were still four of them standing outside a small van, chatting in hushed tones over notepads and fiddling with cameras.

'Can't fault their dedication I guess,' Callie grumbled.

'Just keep your heads down and walk quickly.'

Sadie unlatched the gate and marched, her steps confident, feet pounding purposefully into the pavement. She blocked out the questions that gushed from the reporters, words tumbling from their mouths and flying from their tiny jotter pads. *Ben...brother...kidnapped...family members...* The worlds slid off her shoulders; she ignored all of them.

The hallway was quiet. Sadie could make out her parent's hushed voices in the kitchen. She slid off her shoes and hung the spare key back on its hook by the door.

'Hi Sadie.'

'Jesus,' Callie gasped, 'talk about creep up on us. How are you, Ben?'

Ben had appeared at the top of the staircase, a loose t-shirt hanging limply off his bony frame. 'I'm okay, thank you. I didn't mean to scare you, sorry. How are you?'

Sadie watched the two of them talk. They'd never really spoken a great deal before the disappearance, so their exchange now was fractured, awkward. Vedat hovered by Sadie's side, peering around her at Ben like a frightened animal. A sickly green tinge speckled his cheeks. He looked as though he wanted to throw up, or pass out, or both.

'I'm not too bad, thanks, you know. The usual.'

'Mum and Dad are in the kitchen,' Ben added.

'I know, I can hear them. Have you guys eaten already?'

'No, we were waiting for you to come home,' Ben said, his voice lingering over the back end of the sentence. A pang of guilt fluttered through Sadie's tummy.

'What were you doing in my room?'

'Waiting,' he replied. Sadie nodded, accepting that she was unlikely to get much more out of him. He reached the bottom of the stairs and led the three of them through to the kitchen. Callie threw her a sideways glance as they pushed open the door.

11
_____

Summer 1990

urely it doesn't hurt not to push these things. That's what Ben had said. And the more they thought about it, the funnier it got.

'Can't believe we've only got a week of the holidays left. Again. How does this happen every year?'

'I know! Six weeks feels like a lifetime when it starts, but it goes by so quickly.'

'Gotta make the most of it, too, this is our last time all together,' Callie grinned.

The three friends were walking down to the beach, bottles of Scrumpy Jack cider and cheap Lambrini clinking around in the carrier bags suspended from their wrists, thoughtfully provided to them by Callie's older sister who was back from university. They reached their usual spot - the

shingle that spread from outside the sailing club. Of course
the club had long since closed and the lights had dimmed, so
by the time the three of them settled into the pebbles, they
were the only ones around for miles. The coast was empty.
They sat, popping the lids off the bottled cider as the sun
sank underneath the sea.

'Growing up is weird,' Vedat said. 'It's like there's an
unwritten rule that, once you're an adult, you're meant to
know what's going on. You know the rules, you know what
you're meant to be doing, so go make your own decisions.
Does anyone truly know what they're doing?'

'Nope,' answered Callie between frothy mouthfuls of
cider. 'No one knows and no one will ever know. Don't you
find that liberating?'

Vedat seemed to chew on this concept, whilst Sadie
responded. 'I guess so,' she said.

'We're nothing but tiny specks on the eye of the universe.
Nothing we do matters, in the grand scheme of things.'

'Oh great,' said Vedat, 'yes, much better.'

Sadie smirked at her two friends, watching them discuss
life's biggest questions. They were so opposite, but somehow
that made their friendship stronger. Sadie considered their
conversations quite the spectator sport, and took another sip
from her bottle.

'Well it ought to. Stop putting so much pressure on yourself, dummy.'

Sadie was giggling now. Not proper belly laughing, but
close enough.

'And what are you laughing for, miss "I'm studying law to
get my parents off my back?" You're as buggered as we are.'

'I have no idea what you're talking about,' Sadie tilted her
head up into the air, a knowing grin tugging at the corners of

her lips. 'I have a pure passion for law - it's what I was put on this Earth to do. If you haven't found your passion yet, that's your problem and I suggest you look a bit harder,' she smirked.

'Ha! Your passion, Sadie? If you had your way, you'd be reading books and hiding from the world for a living. To clarify, studying one of the world's most boring subjects is no one's passion, least of all yours,' Callie chided.

'Ah yes, and my passion is to become a middle manager in retail. I can't wait to get stuck into that for my entire life. There's nothing more fulfilling than tangled clothes hangers and dodgy Christmas shifts!'

They were all laughing now. That was how they'd gotten through life so far, and it wasn't likely to change any time soon.

The laughter increased with the growing stack of empty bottles. The more alcohol they consumed, the more they reminisced about past years at their school and childhoods.

'Remember that kid, what was his name? The one that told us all he had a dad that lived in China and drove a tank or something nuts?'

'Oh! That was the same kid that set fire to the roof of the music block - I wonder where he is now?'

More giggling. Reminiscing. More genuine wonderment at how some of the children in their year at school survived, or whether they would end up going to university or fleeing the country.

'Remember that kid that was suspended with some of the other boys for nicking one of the school canoes and trying to get over to the island on it?' Vedat was in hysterics, rolling around on the gravel and wiping the tears from his eyes.

'Oh God yes, what a weird day that was. I didn't even realise the school had canoes!' Sadie chimed in.

Callie sat bolt upright. 'We should do that now.'

'Sorry, do what now?' Sadie asked.

'That. We should take one of the school's canoes from the rowing club and see if we can make it over to the island.' She was up on her knees, trying to get the same level of enthusiasm for her old classmates but not succeeding. Vedat and Sadie stared disbelievingly at her.

'Not sure that's the best of ideas, Callie,' Vedat said. 'Trying to row a canoe with no experience and under the influence of,' he paused to check the now empty carrier bag, 'a lot of cider, might be one of the worst ideas you've had to date.' He was serious, but still smiling.

'Oh sorry, I didn't realise you were chicken,' Callie teased. Her brows jumped under the rim of her glasses, her eyes lighting up with the challenge of convincing her friends to live a little more on the wild side for a change.

'I don't know, Callie. I don't think it's a good idea either,' Sadie agreed. 'Have you ever actually rowed on open water and not just in a gym? It's quite different.'

'Well no, but there's a first time for everything. And you have! You're good at this rowing malarkey, you can captain us. Come on, where's your sense of adventure? What happened to our spontaneity and being carefree?'

Sadie looked over to Vedat, chewing her bottom lip. He looked nervous, most likely because he knew how often Callie got her way. In all fairness, Sadie was sorely tempted to run up, grab the red canoe that sat out the front of the rowing club, and launch herself at the glassy sea. He could see the look in her eye and shook his head almost imperceptibly.

'Callie, Sadie - this is a terrible idea and if either of you even consider running over to that canoe over there, I will be abandoning you. The sea is terrifying and I can't row. I'm happy to admire the water from here, but I'm not getting any closer, thank you very much. That's my last comment on the subject.'

'Oh, he's serious Sadie. Fancy being abandoned by your closest friend. Reckon we can cope without him?' Callie looked over at Sadie, that well known mischievous glint in her eye. She placed her hands slowly behind her back, moved her feet closer to her backside and jumped up, running off towards the rowing club.

Sadie looked over at Vedat who was shaking his head. 'You're such a parent,' she shouted, jumping up and sprinting after Callie.

'Oh for fucks sake, come on. I can't really leave the two of you - you'll drown!' Vedat shouted after them. 'Oh come on, don't make me do this!' He sat, pausing for a moment longer before giving in. 'Oh, for goodness sake,' he huffed, heaving himself up onto his feet and jogging after them.

Callie was way ahead, already only a few steps away from the cluster of small boats. She turned briefly towards Sadie and Vedat and shouted. 'How do we know which one is the school's one?'

'It'll have the emblem on, obviously.' Vedat responded.

'Oh, of course it will,' she nodded, pulling a canoe to the front of the club and heaving it down towards the shore. It was a dull red colour with patches of off-yellow and orange where the sun had bleached it and drained the dye from the plastic. Scratches lined the underside - the school's equipment was nothing if not well used. And there it was, on the nose of the boat. The school's emblem. A shield divided into three, the first section housing a long wave and the two below a squat wall resembling the perimeter of Rose Bay, and a quill. The oars that were propped up against the curved body of the boat fell to the ground with a clatter. Sadie grabbed hold of them both, throwing one over to Vedat and running towards the sea.

The canoe bobbed in the water, rocking as Callie clambered into the hollowed out body, followed by Sadie and a more begrudging Vedat.

'Are we actually doing this?'

'Oh come on now, Vedat, this is exactly the sort of thing you'd like to do. What if we find the witch, aye?' Callie was enjoying herself, taunting Vedat and smirking.

'That is not funny,' he replied, his face hardened by worry and anxiety. 'That's just a kid's story.'

'Oh is it? You are joking - you were well into those old stories. A little bit of you believes it, doesn't it? What about you, Sadie?'

'If we find her, I'll ask her for some tips on putting up with people like you lot as friends', Sadie joked, the laughter returning to the three of them as quickly as it had left. 'Now, who knows how to actually row this thing aside from me?'

Callie and Vedat grabbed hold of an oar each. Callie dug her paddle into the sand under the shallow water and pushed them away in the small red boat. The two of them struggled to get into a rhythm, the canoe hardly shifting from its starting position.

'Try rowing, would you Vedat?' Callie poked.

'Oh shush - it's not your fault we're not going anywhere. You're at a funny angle - we're going to end up going round in circles.'

Sadie gripped her sides, her arms crossed over her stomach as she folded in two. Tears streamed down her reddened face and she held her hand out to Vedat, ushering him to hand over the oar.

'Give it here,' she managed to say, between desperate gasps and belly laughs.

He handed it over, shoving it out in front of his body as if he was repulsed by its very existence. He folded his hands across his lap in mock defiance, seconds away from falling into fits of hysterics himself.

A couple of seconds later they were skidding across the surface of the water towards the small, tree-lined island, the oars splitting and folding the crystalline water in on itself. They made good headway, the boat skimming across the sea like a pond skater, the oars like the insect's limbs flinging its body towards their destination. The island wasn't far from the mainland. It sat, surrounded by water, expectant and proud and bursting with luscious green plants.

'Are we actually going to the island?' Vedat asked, his body leaning back in the boat. He'd now completely relaxed into the journey, basking in the last of the evening's warmth.

'Well I guess so. I won't have rowed all the way over there just to circle this thing around and head straight back.' Callie looked over to Sadie for reassurance.

Sadie shrugged, nodded. 'Sure.' In reality she was indifferent to getting out of the boat at all. 'Though we have run out of cider, so I guess we won't have a great deal to do.'

'We can explore a bit. See what all the fuss is about,' Callie replied, that mischievous glint back in her eye. She lifted an eyebrow and glared at Vedat as he nervously peered over his shoulder back to the mainland. 'I guess we've got our resident expert here to protect us, right Vedat?' She lifted her chin up, taunting him.

'What? Oh...yeah, sure,' he mumbled, turning his back to face his friends in the boat.

'You don't look too keen, Mr Ghost-hunter. Come on now, all those times talking about this as kids and itching to get over here, and now we're actually doing it. You must be intrigued at least?'

Vedat could only bring himself to nod. He'd gone from relaxed to concerned to fearful and back again, and now sat cross-legged at the end of the boat. His hands shuffled around in his lap.

'Nous somme arrive,' Callie said in her best Cockney-French accent, hopping out of the boat and planting her hands on her hips.

'Is that all you remember from French class?' Sadie teased, also turning to dig her own paddle into the dirt. They worked together to pull the boat up a bit closer, hopping out on the shallow shoreline. Vedat clambered out on shaky legs, the boat tipping and threatening to dump his feet into the cold water.

'Well, we made it,' Callie declared. 'After all these years, we finally made it.' They dragged the boat up onto the land, sticking the oars fin-first into the shore. Callie spun on her heels to face Vedat. 'Which way, boss?'

Vedat looked briefly to the edge of the island, craning his neck around the corners to save himself from having to actually move his feet. He puffed out his chest, clasping his hands behind his back, his teeth chewing into his bottom lip.

'How about we go this way?' Sadie offered, heading up over the shallow incline of sand and onto the grassy verge.

The island was small but well covered in thick, dense

forest and foliage. Sadie had never seen so many shades of green up this close - so many different kinds of fauna and trees and plants and so many birds. The island was bursting with life and colour. The three of them made their way into the trees, their happy relaxed nature returning to their strides and conversation.

Callie stormed off ahead, leaving Sadie and Vedat trudging along behind her. Their feet took them closer to the centre of the island, the undergrowth growing thicker with each passing step. The conversation flowed as they walked, the occasional pause to take in an odd looking flower or the shiny body of an unnervingly large beetle. Their steps continued, punctuated with comfortable laughter and warm smiles.

Sadie flicked her eyeline down to the beaten up Casio watch on her wrist. She squeezed the button on the side, illuminating the small screen in a garish green glow. 'Guys,' she said, 'we ought to think about heading back soon. It's getting kinda late.'

'What's the time?' Vedat asked, tilting his head to focus on the sky through the blanket of trees overhead.

'Nearly nine. The sun will set any minute now.'

Almost as if the sun was waiting for Sadie's permission, it slipped closer to the horizon. The sky began to lose its warmth, the saturation seeping below the shoreline. The three turned around to head back to the shore, and to the red boat that was waiting for them.

'Oh shit,' Vedat hissed under his breath. He'd slipped on a fallen branch or tree stump in the growing darkness, his hand shooting out in front of him to hold onto a nearby tree and break his fall. 'What the hell?'

'Everything okay?' Sadie turned back on herself to face

her friend. The sun had almost entirely slipped below the horizon, allowing the light of the moon to shine down through a clearing in the trees ahead.

'Yeah, I think so. I just tripped and stuck my hand in something sticky - probably just tree sap or something,' he said, wiping his hands on his jeans.

Sadie moved aside to let more light trickle in between the trees and froze. She threw her hand up to her face and puffed out her cheeks in an effort not to wretch.

'Callie,' she mumbled, causing her friend to pivot round and face Vedat.

'Oh God, what is that?'

Callie and Sadie were both standing aside from the light of the moon, eyes transfixed onto Vedat. They were staring at the tops of his thighs, where he'd dragged his hands moments earlier. He followed their line of sight.

'Oh Jesus, what the —,' Vedat shouted. His hands were covered in a gloopy red slime that he'd managed to spread all over his trousers.

The two moved closer to Vedat, careful not to stand in front of the light. 'It's probably just puss from a plant or tree, right?' Sadie offered, her face doing a terrible job at hiding her disgust.

'Oh yes, that well-known red puss,' Callie shot back, half in a trance, still staring at Vedat.

The light dripped around the forest, catching tree trunks and plants in its path. As Callie and Sadie approached Vedat, the moon's reflection shone on the tree closest to him, revealing a deep red, pulsating mass at the centre of the trunk. Sadie leant her head in closer towards it. The light caught the mass, and it glowed an eerie reddish pink. She frowned, trying to study the liquid.

'Guys, it's...I think it's kind of pulsing.'

'Pulsing as in...?'

'Pulsing as in, as in, well...with a heartbeat? It looks like it's being pumped from the inside of the tree.'

'Right,' Callie slurred, coming up behind Sadie. She bent her head around Vedat to get a closer look. 'Oh wow, that is disgusting.' Callie's eyes stretched wide, her nose inches from the red mass.

'What kind of plant would have that?' Vedat looked down to his trousers again. They were covered in a layer of plasma that had begun to harden, stiffening and sticking to his legs through the denim of his jeans. He scratched at the substance, shivering at the grinding of his fingernails against the scabs.

'Not a plant,' Sadie said. 'This is gonna sound mad but, guys, I think it's actually blood.'

'Oh God, Sadie, why did you have to say that?' Vedat was close to retching now. His hands were on his knees, face bent to the ground and eyes closed, as if shutting out the sight of the organ would stop it existing altogether.

'You're right, Sade.' Callie's face was inches from the red goo. 'Pass me that stick,' she said, pointing to the ground and holding her hand out. She didn't move her eyes from the recently acquired science experiment and waited for someone to pass her her chosen utensil.

'Well I don't think that's a good idea,' Vedat groaned, still bent double.

Sadie ignored him and handed over the large twig that rested by her feet. Callie jabbed the thin piece of branch into the pulsating mass and watched as it drooled more red liquid. Thick, deep brown-red liquid trickled down the side of the tree, pooling at the base of the trunk and dribbling into the grass. 'There's something else here,' Callie said, continuing her pseudo-scientific exploration with the tree branch, voice full of wonder. She shoved the stick deeper into the tree, wiggling it around and screwing her face up at the sound of an audible squelch. A few more twists of the stick, many more sludgy, wet sounds, and something fell from inside the tree. It hit the forest floor with a slap. The three of them stared at the mass that was now spreading and sticking to the ground.

Vedat groaned, holding his stomach. 'Is that what I think it is?' He staggered back.

'It depends,' Callie said. 'Do you think it's some kind of organ that inexplicably came from the inside of that tree?' Her words were full of sarcasm but the shaky timbre of her voice gave her away.

There was silence from the three of them as they stared at the red object at their feet. The surface of the thing rippled and fluttered. It was beating.

'I don't like this,' Sadie stammered. The moisture had evaporated from her mouth, leaving behind an acrid tang in her glands. She steadied herself against another tree and breathed loudly.

'I don't get it,' Callie exclaimed, moving forward with her stick at the ready.

'No! Don't keep doing that - we don't know what it is. And we definitely don't know why it's here. Probably best not to keep on prodding it like that.'

Callie looked up at Vedat, one eyebrow arched high on her forehead. She held eye contact with him, leant forward and rammed the stick deep into the organ. It rolled onto its other side, the sharp end of the stick perforating the outer layer. The stick dropped to the floor as red leaked out from the muscle from all angles. A sickly sweet, sticky smell rose from the ground, followed by a low hiss as the red sack emptied itself of blood. The scent altered from the sickly sweetness to a putrid, fermented aroma. Vedat threw his hand over his mouth, turned away from the group and emptied his stomach against the stump of another tree. The vomit sprayed out at all angles as he forced his hand over his mouth in a vain attempt to prevent the liquid from escaping.

'We should get out of here,' Sadie said, moving around the red sack and the pool that had now settled around it. She eyed the stick, now caked in dark tar and, as Callie rested her hand on Vedat's hunched shoulder, Sadie ducked and slipped the twig up her sleeve. 'Come on, let's go,' she repeated, marching off, far more confidently than she felt.

Callie brought up the rear, a hand still slung over Vedat's back. Sadie flicked her eye behind the group, eager to see if something was going to come and retrieve its lost organ, slinking out of the shadows to take it away. She didn't see anything. In a way, she was disappointed. She squinted behind her for some time, expecting, hoping, to see some animal lurch from within the trees, from between the bushes, and retrieve their hidden meal. There was nothing at all. No other sign of life.

They stumbled through the forest, the white light of the moon breaking in through gaps in the trees and dancing across the ground. Dark shadows stretched between the light, contorting the already menacing forest into twisted shapes. Finally, after what seemed like a considerably long time, the three of them fell out of the trees and back onto the edges of the island. The red boat was still there, the oars stuck upright in the sand. Waiting for them. Vedat hurried over to the water and dipped his hands in, splashing his face with the cool salty water to remove any trace of the vomit.

'Whatever that was, I don't fancy revisiting it,' Sadie murmured, stepping back into the canoe.

'Agreed,' Callie mumbled, shuffling into the boat and rummaging her hands into her pockets. Sadie sat quietly. The colour had flushed from her face. She rested a hand on her forearm, the sharp, solid outline of the twig pressing against her palm.

Callie and Sadie fetched the oars and began rowing. The only noise to break the quiet was the slicing of the blades through the gentle rippling water. The moon was fully up in the sky now, bright and clear and almost full save for a slither of darkness that curved around the left side. They'd rowed for a handful of minutes before Sadie broke the silence.

'Do you think...?' She didn't finish her sentence.

Callie met her eye. 'What? Do we think what?' Her tone was abrupt. Impatient.

'Do you think that could have been something to do with... you know?'

The other two didn't answer as quickly as Sadie would have liked. Callie would normally have jumped in with a sarcastic quip about how naive Sadie was, or how ridiculous she was being. Those were all stupid stories, right? Stupid tales spread by stupid children.

'I think it was a sick joke,' Vedat finally said. 'I think people go over there more than we think they do, and they left that there to scare anyone else that followed them over.' He sounded unconvinced. The others stared.

'You're right,' Sadie said, her fingertips hovering next to her leg.

The sky had hardened to a deep black. The stars shone,

pinpricks of light against their inky backdrop. An eerie grey light hovered across the canoe as it slid over the surface of the water. The island got smaller as they moved away, the details of the trees merging and slipping away from their view, but their rowing didn't slow.

Sadie took a loud gasp of air, sending her oar clattering into the bottom of the boat. Her fingers wrapped around the edge of the canoe, her knuckles white as she gripped and her body tense.

'What? What is it?' Vedat shouted. 'What's wrong?'

'I...I...,' she stammered.

'What? Say something, Sadie!'

But she couldn't. She couldn't say a word. She stared straight ahead of her, her eyes fixated on the shadows between the trees on the island. Vedat followed her gaze, just in time to see the fading glow of orange light. Or was it two lights? Or not a light at all. He made eye contact with them for a split second, and then they were snuffed out by something, a strong gust of wind that extinguished them as it passed.

'Sadie,' he whispered. 'What do you think that was?' His eyes fixed on the spot where the orange embers had been, where there was now nothing but a suffocating darkness.

'Nothing. It was nothing, you're both seeing things,' Callie said. 'We've had cider, the heart thing was weird, granted, and now we're knackered. Let's go back. Please.' She picked up Sadie's oar and pressed it back into her hands.

'Look at the water.' Sadie's voice floated from her throat. A jet black shadow seeped into the sea from what looked like the underside of the island. It bled from the trees, congealing the water as it made contact, making it harder and harder to row. They were only a few stretches from the shore of the mainland, and the blackness was travelling fast.

'Come on!' Callie yelled, frantically paddling and cajoling Sadie to do the same. They heaved against the black water, dragging the boat through the tide. The water had become thick and heavy, the consistency of treacle. Their arms flexed, muscles complaining and screaming against taut flesh. Despite the struggle, they managed to heave the boat back to the mainland.

Vedat was the first out. He flew from the plastic vessel and leapt onto the shore of the mainland, sprinting to safety back up by the rowing club. Sadie and Callie were close behind, dragging the canoe from the water and throwing it haphazardly back in the direction they found it. The shadow had stopped spreading and floated on top of the water, an onyx blanket drifting out to sea. It had ceased growing around three metres from the shoreline and now hovered in place, threatening to grow, to spread further, to reach and infect the beach. The underside of the canoe was stained a murky black; the oars spattered with strings of dark plasma.

'We should leave,' Sadie said between breaths, turning her back on the sea and jogging up the hill towards the safety of their homes. She rolled up her sleeves, shoving the fabric away from her clammy skin. She needed some air.

They marched wordlessly up the track, all three of them trying to process what they had seen and what it could possibly have meant. As they reached the top of the hill, they turned to face the island and the sea below them. It was completely normal, back to the standard shade of murky blue that they were used to seeing.

'We made it up,' Callie said, her voice strong and sure.

'What?'

'We made it up. We have had too much to drink, someone left that thing over there as a trick. The black water was all in our heads. We made it up.'

Sadie and Vedat didn't push her any further. It was clear that she was rationalising what had happened, desperate to find a logical reason for what they'd experienced. And in part, they were happy for some kind of explanation.

Even if they didn't believe it at all.

12

Summer 1995

Ben was sitting on the end of his sister's bed, leafing through an old book, one of her pillows resting on his lap. Sadie couldn't quite decide if his face looked peaceful, or simply devoid of any emotion that could give him away. His head was craning over the pages. He looked suddenly very old and forlorn, except for his smooth pink hands and cheeks. The words seemed to have a pull on his eyes, an anchor tugging his vision downwards. Sadie stood by the door watching him. Minutes passed and he didn't move a muscle. He didn't flick the page over, he didn't shuffle to get more comfortable; he was completely and utterly still. He could have passed for dead if not for the rise and fall of his small chest and the occasional flicker of his eyelids.

Sadie entered the room and sat next to him. The mattress depressed under her weight, causing him to lean towards her.

He didn't turn to face her, but she could have sworn his face softened as she joined him on the end of her bed.

'Ben?'

'Yes,' he answered, turning his face to meet her eyes.

'I want you to know that I'm going to stop asking you questions,' she said.

He squinted.

'I can't force you to talk to me, but I know something is wrong.'

He lowered his face to stare at the words on his lap again.

'And I know you need help, but you don't know how to tell me that yet. And that's okay. But when you're ready to speak to me, know that I'm here, and I'm ready to listen. I want to help you.' The steadiness in her voice wobbled.

The book held his attention, but something in the muscles in his body seemed to loosen and soften. He turned the page, laying his hands over the words as if he was able to absorb their meaning into his bloodstream. He turned to face Sadie and smiled. A small smile, but it was definitely there. For a brief second, Sadie saw him. Underneath the hardened shell of a boy that had been through something awful and something unspeakable, in that moment, she truly saw him.

'You can stay in here with me tonight, if you like?'

Ben nodded. He closed the book, laying it to his side. He reached his arms around Sadie, his torso relaxing. Sadie flinched, surprised by his sudden show of affection, but looped her own arms around his back. 'Thank you,' he mumbled into her shoulder. The familiar scent of the family's washing detergent pierced Sadie's conscience, the memories of the siblings dragging their heels to help their mum clip wet clothing onto the sagging line in the garden. So many memories attached to the smallest things, all clustered in their shared conscience and shared history. The first hug Sadie had had from her brother in five years. Her stomach swilled, a mixture of warmth, comfort and a peppering of worry that she still couldn't shake.

'Let's get some sleep,' she whispered back, and within minutes Ben's eyes were sealed shut, his chest rising and falling in a steady pattern. And all Sadie could do was watch.

SADIE MADE her way down the stairs. Her mum was sitting on the sofa, cross-legged, watching old repeats of some corny sitcom they used to enjoy as a family. The canned laughter echoed out of the tinny speakers, nudging her fake chuckles along. They were almost convincing. Sadie hadn't managed to have a real conversation with her mum since coming home, far longer than that in fact, and now was the time to put that right.

Sadie grabbed two glasses of lemonade from the kitchen and handed one to her mum, tear drops of condensation trickling down the edges.

'Thank you,' Allison said, cradling the drink between her palms, relishing the coolness of the iced drink against her clammy skin. 'I am glad you came home, you know.'

Sadie smiled and bowed her head. 'Me too.' She stared into the transparent liquid, willing it to reveal some words of wisdom or an answer to her many questions. 'Where's Dad?' she asked.

'Popped out for a walk.'

Sadie nodded. She got it: the need for fresh air, for clarity, even if it meant walking around the town on his own in search for it. 'Did the police come today?'

Allison winced. Her hands gripped the glass tighter,

fearful that any more force would smash it into her lap. She nodded.

'How's the investigation going?' Sadie's stomach clenched as she steered the conversation.

'Are they closer to having any answers at all?'

Her mum shook her head. 'No,' she exhaled. 'It's all so odd. He disappeared, vanished into thin air. And now he's back, as if he reappeared from the same air that took him in the first place.'

'Mhmm,' Sadie hummed, a light layer of sweat prickling her palms.

'They can't seem to figure anything out. And he's not saying much, which of course isn't helping. He needs to tell us what's happened so they can properly investigate.'

Sadie nodded. 'He'll open up when he's ready.' She hoped he would never be ready.

'Yes, I know. But it's been days now, Sadie, and he's still not even told us where he has been. Five years he's been gone, and we have no idea where he was. Was he being held? Who took him? How has he?' she choked, staring at the bubbles as they rose and fell in the glass. 'Was he taken? How has he survived, Sadie?'

Sadie placed her hand on her mum's knee, squeezing gently and edging closer. 'All that matters is he's back now. He's back, and we can rebuild.' Sadie's heart thudded, pounding in her chest cavity so forcefully that she thought for a moment that her mum might be able to hear it.

Allison's hand clasped her daughter's, the familiar shape of her wedding ring resting on the top of her palm. 'Did you hear about Gloyer's farm?' she asked.

'No. What's happened?' Sadie answered. Gloyer's farm perched at the top end of Rose Bay, its size imposing; the biggest farm in the county. The Gloyer family were essentially celebrities in the area.

'Well, they're saying a load of their crops were torched last night,' her mum answered.

'Torched? As in, burnt?' Didn't that happen before?'

'God yeah, but that was a long time ago,' Allison responded, running a finger around the top of her glass. 'Apparently a load of their fields went up last night and they only discovered it this morning. The whole place is covered in ash. I went by there earlier on my way home. It's totally obliterated.'

'Blimey,' Sadie replied, chewing on the news, and her lower lip. 'What do they reckon happened?'

'Not sure - probably some kids or something. But they never found out what happened last time either, so they're not holding out any hope for answers.'

'God, that's terrible,' Sadie swallowed, holding her own glass close to her stomach. It quivered as she tried to conceal her trembling hands, crystal clear lemonade bouncing between the glass walls.

Allison nodded in agreement, shifting up from the sofa and heading to the kitchen. 'I'll make us some lunch.'

Sadie stayed, perching on the sofa. The farm had been damaged before, five years earlier, on the eve of her brother's disappearance.

'WHO IS IT?' Sadie called through the door. She'd flipped the copper disc out of the way and leant her head closer

'You don't know me,' a woman's voice replied.

Encouraging, Sadie thought. 'Ok,' she murmured. 'What do you want?'

'I need to talk to you.'

'Are you from the newspapers? Can you be more specific?'

'I know what happened to your brother.'

Sadie stopped breathing. Her tongue swelled to fill her mouth. She leant her hand against the door to stop herself from toppling over.

'Come out here so I can talk to you,' the woman said, her face inches from the door, so close that Sadie could almost taste her musky perfume.

Sadie eased the door open and slid out onto the front doorstep. The woman was slight, her frame slender and shoulders sloping. She wore a long dust jacket, despite the warm weather, and flared light blue jeans. A tiny lightbulb flickered in Sadie's mind, an itch of recognition that she wasn't quite able to scratch. Her face was familiar. Her wide set deep brown eyes and honey-coloured hair had been present in Sadie's life before now.

'We can't talk here. We need to go somewhere else,' the woman said, leading Sadie down the garden path and unlatching the front gate as if it were her own. She buried her hands deep in her pockets and, as Sadie managed to get a closer look, she could see the dark purple circles hanging below her eyes. She didn't look old, exactly. Just fatigued. Exhausted.

The woman turned the corner of the unusually quiet road and motioned to a public bench. It was a spot Sadie frequented as a child, the inscription on the silver plaque welcoming her back, reading: for those who don't have a bench of their own.

'I'm Lorraine,' the woman said, sitting as far away from Sadie as possible. She would have folded herself up underneath the armrest if she could.

'Okay,' Sadie shrugged, her stomach churning with the sensation that she ought to know who this woman was. 'I'm Sadie, I guess.'

'Yes, I know who you are.'

Sadie raised an eyebrow and tilted her chin. Her mind was telling her that something about this whole exchange was off, that this woman was not the good kind, but for some reason that she couldn't work out, she remained seated. Her insides twisted. She waited for Lorraine, if that was even her real name, to continue talking, the vague familiarity of her features clawing at the back of Sadie's mind.

'Your name is Sadie. Your brother's name is Ben. Your mother's name is Allison and your father's name is Patrick.'

'Right,' Sadie said, shuffling further away from the woman, the rusting metal armrest digging into her side. 'Are you someone from the press? What is this?'

'No,' Lorraine answered, 'I'm definitely not from the press. The press won't talk to me anymore.'

Sadie raised an eyebrow and inspected this woman closer. She was slim and jittery, nervous. And oh so familiar. 'Go on then, who actually are you? Or are you not going to tell me?' Sadie's eyes widened in anticipation.

'My name is Lorraine. My daughter, Christine, went missing nine years ago on the island, just like your brother did. And I know what took her.'

13

Summer 1995

The moisture left Sadie's lips, seeping out of her throat and mouth. *Lorraine - of course.* She recognised her face from the newspapers, from the old news stories that were recycled all those years ago before Ben. From those times she'd spotted her in Rose Bay. From...

'The same thing that took my Christine, took your brother,' Lorraine interrupted Sadie's thoughts. 'But it let him back, or he escaped, or something.'

Sadie's heart raced. How much did this woman know?

'I saw the creature on the island. I saw it, its amber eyes and curling limbs, and it took my little girl right in front of my eyes. Why did it let your Ben go, but not my Christine? Do you know, Sadie?'

Sadie's mind raced. She had no idea why, or how, Ben had been able to escape. But since being home, things were becoming less and less clear. The boat, the trip to the island, Callie, Vedat, Ben, those amber eyes. Why did it let Ben go? Was he really able to escape from its clutches?

'You know something else, don't you?' Lorraine asked.

Sadie jerked her head back to meet Lorraine's gaze. 'What? No, no I don't know anything else,' she said, standing up and backing away from the woman. The sting of bile burned her throat.

Lorraine held her hand out to Sadie. 'Wait, don't go. You can help me, I know you can. You know how Ben came back. You know how he got to the island in the first place.'

Sadie's feet tripped over themselves as she stumbled backwards away from the bench.

'No,' she shouted at Lorraine. 'I can't help you. I'm sorry.'

'You can help me, you know something else!'

'I don't,' Sadie said, jogging away from the woman on the bench.

'You'll tell me eventually,' Lorraine called after her. Her thin voice hovered in the air, an ominous reminder that, perhaps, Sadie would relent what she knew. A reminder that Lorraine was not about to let this rest.

SADIE SLID her dad's key into the front door. Two voices she didn't recognise drifted into the hall. They weren't those of her parents, or of other family members that she had assumed would come over to witness the reappearance of her brother. They were professional voices, one male, one female. They weren't cold, exactly, but calm, collected, direct. She peered her head into the living room to see her family crammed together on the sofa, Ben in the middle and his parents squeezed in on either side. A police officer that she hadn't seen before sat in the armchair, and another leant against the chair. They held the full attention of the room, moving as one being, their body language eerily similar, trained.

'Ah, you must be Sadie,' the standing officer said, turning to look at her as she hovered in the doorway.

'Yes,' Sadie replied, 'sorry to interrupt, I'll just head upstairs and stay out of your way.'

'Oh no need to do that, Miss Pickett. You can come and join us. I'm sure Ben would like the extra support.'

Ben threw Sadie a glance beneath a frown, one she couldn't quite decipher.

'Okay,' she said tenuously, perching on the edge of a dining room chair, the polished wood digging into the backs of her thighs. The chair angled her to the edge of the group, signalling her position as the latecomer, the outlier.

'So Ben, you were saying that you walked home,' the officer glanced down at their notepad, flicking through a few pages, 'four days ago. Is that correct?'

'Yes,' he said, flat and emotionless. His eyes flicked up to meet his sister's. These weren't the officers she'd met earlier, these two were higher ups, power bubbling underneath their uniforms.

'And when you say "walked home", what do you mean exactly?' the other officer pressed, eyeing her partner's notes.

'Well,' Ben continued, 'I walked from the beach, to the house.'

'What part of the beach? Do you know why you were at the beach?'

Ben looked down at his hands. His fingers gripped his knuckles and he tugged at them nervously. 'Well, I was down at the Rowing Club.' He looked up at Sadie. Her stomach dropped at the mention of the rowing club, thoughts of dead fish and oil stained boats drifting to the forefront of her mind. The tendons in her feet jittered, the soles of her shoes bouncing up and down.

'And why were you there, Ben?'

'I don't know,' he answered, still looking in Sadie's direction.

'You don't know?' the officer pressed. 'What do you mean by that, Ben?'

'I mean, I don't know why I was there.'

'Okay,' the officer said, jotting more notes down in the tiny pad. 'Do you remember how you got to the Rowing Club?'

Ben shook his head. 'No, I...,' he stumbled over his words, 'I don't remember how I got there. I don't remember much, do I Mum?' He glared in the direction of his mother, eyes wide and glistening.

'Alright, alright,' Allison interjected, 'shall I get you some water, Ben? Can we take a minute please?' she asked the officers, standing up from the sofa and fussing over her son.

'Of course,' they replied, watching as Ben and his mum went off to the kitchen.

'Miss Pickett,' the officer turned his attention to Sadie as she sat, teetering on the edge of the dining table chair. 'I know you must have received lots of questions all those years ago, when your brother went missing. How was that for you?'

Odd question, Sadie thought. 'It wasn't the most fun experience, I'll be honest,' she said, embarrassed that she'd been so sarcastic. Her face flushed. 'Not something I'd like to go through again.' *And yet here we are.*

'No, of course not. I can only imagine how awful the whole thing was for a girl as young as you.'

What was that in their voice? What was hiding between those words?

'And you don't know anything about where your brother has been for these past five years?'

'No, of course I don't. Why would I?' Her voice was clipped, short.

'Oh, no reason,' the seated officer said, again looking through their notes. How many notes had they taken? The pad was tiny - there was hardly room on there for a handful of words.

Sadie looked down at her lap, averting her eye from the two officers. Her hands were slick with sweat and nerves as she struggled to answer questions that of course she did not know the answers to. Her dad remained quiet, statuesque on the far end of the sofa. The two officers rounded their bodies to face her more, their blazers and shirts moving as one entity and power.

'Where were you the night that Ben went missing?' one asked, though she didn't register which one it was; it didn't matter.

'I can't remember. It was such a long time ago. I was only a child.'

'Are these questions necessary?' her dad interjected. 'We've all answered these before. We've all lived that night over and over...', his words trailed off as the officer picked up where they left off.

'Of course, we just want to get as clear a picture of what happened to Ben as possible. You want to know what happened to him, don't you? You want to know where he's been?'

'Of course I do,' Sadie blubbed, turning to her dad to say

something, but he remained quiet, lips pursed and hands held in his lap.

'We're not trying to make you distressed, Miss Pickett. We just need to know if there is something that you might remember from when you were a child that will help us piece together what happened to your brother. You understand that, don't you?'

Sadie nodded. Her dad rested his hand on her knee.

'Good. Okay, so, the night your brother went missing. Where were you?'

Where was she? She could hardly remember. She'd answered these questions so many times before, and yet — 'I...,' she stammered, 'I was with my friends. We were celebrating the end of term at the school party.'

'Oh yes, the original file does mention that there was an end of year party and that you and your friends were there. For most of the evening.'

Sadie swallowed. 'We were there the whole evening,' she said. Her voice flopped out of her mouth as if it belonged to someone else.

'We have reports from some of the other students that you and your two friends, Vedat and Callie, left early. Do you remember why that was?'

Bile climbed up Sadie's throat, stinging her oesophagus. Her stomach twisted. 'No,' she said, the words coming from her mouth in a dry whisper.

'No, you didn't leave, or no you don't remember?'

Oh God. She paused. Which was it? Which one looked better on her? 'No, I don't remember.'

Okay,' the officer said again, flicking through the tiny pages of the ring bound jotter.

'According to our records, your brother was filed as missing at 11:30pm. Is that correct?'

Sadie didn't remember. Her eyes darted around the carpet by her feet.

'Your mother called it in after ringing around his friends' houses to see if he was there. You remember that, right?'

Sadie felt sick. 'Yes,' she nodded, 'I remember that.' Images of the glossy pink magazine flickered in her mind.

'Had you been drinking the night he disappeared?'

Sadie's eyes widened. What did that have to do with anything? 'I... I think I had a couple, yes.'

'Do you think that could have impaired your memory?' Were they trying to trip her up?

'What? No,' she stumbled, 'I definitely didn't have enough for that to happen.'

'So you should remember what happened then?' the officer pushed.

Sadie scratched at the backs of her hands, forcing her eye-line back up to the questioning officer. 'It was a long time ago.' She took a pronounced breath. 'It was a very upsetting experience. I think maybe I've blocked most of it out, you know?'

The officer didn't flinch. 'You were here when your mother contacted the police, correct?'

'Yes,' Sadie said, dragging the word out, biding her time, desperate for her heart to settle. Her hand drifted to her wrist and the settling thud of blood as it coursed under her fingertips.

'You'd been home, what, around thirty minutes or so?'

'Yes, I think so.' She didn't honestly remember. The night her brother went missing was a blur, a deep smudge in her memory. After he went missing, Sadie read up on other people's experiences of similar situations. Where they insisted that every minute detail of the event would be ingrained in their memories forever, Sadie couldn't bring herself to remember anything. She was unsure if it was buried deep within the ridges of her brain, or if she'd well and truly trained herself to forget all about that night. The last thing she remembered was staring at that quiz in her magazine, her eyes trained on the vapid words and colourful images. What hairstyle is best for my face? Or something equally as dull. She had that magazine glued to her lap for the whole evening —well, until her mum reported Ben missing. The glossy sheets of paper were cemented to the tops of her jeans, hiding the flakes of sand and dirt that had flicked up from the underside of the canoe.

'And what were you doing whilst you were home?'

'I was reading a magazine,' she said, her voice flat, remembering that quiz tumbling down the double page spread. The quiz that she never actually answered, she just stared at whilst her mum panicked and worried around her. Sadie should have been panicking too. Why wasn't she?

'So you came home from a party with your friends early to sit upstairs and read a magazine?'

'Yes,' she said, a dry prickling sensation clambering over her tongue.

'We have reports from some of the other students from that night that indicate that you, Vedat and Callie all left the party at 9pm that night. And you came home around thirty minutes before your mum called in Ben as a missing person, around 11pm. That means you were elsewhere for two hours, correct?'

Sadie looked around the room, as if the answer to the officers' questions was hiding in plain sight on the mantelpiece. The saliva had drained away from her mouth, an acidic tang hanging at the back of her throat. She needed some water.

'I think I went over Callie's house,' she mumbled, desperate for them to drop this line of inquiry.

'You think?' The officer's pen hovered over the pad, poised to cement whatever Sadie said next in truth; once her words were etched in ink, that'd be it.

'I honestly don't remember,' she panicked, the volume in her voice rising. 'As I said, that night was awful. I don't remember anything before Ben not coming home. Why are you asking me these questions?' she asked, her voice clipping the ends of her sentences.

'Oh, we're just trying to piece a clearer image together of when Ben went missing, where you all were, and where Ben has been for the past five years,' the standing officer said, as if their task was no mean feat. The officer sitting in the armchair hadn't said a word during the last few questions. He was furiously taking notes, scrawling in the tiny pad with a chewed off biro.

'I need to get some water,' Sadie said, standing from her seat and following her dad into the kitchen.

Allison and Ben walked back into the living room area as Sadie left.

'Are we done for today?' Allison asked the officers.

'Yes, we've got all we need for today,' the taller officer replied, their eyes flicking to their partner's. The officer that was still in the armchair flipped the notepad closed and slipped the pad of paper into his pocket. Sadie glared at it, as if it held a great power that she could gain if she were to get hold of it. 'We'll be back later on during the week. None of you are planning to go anywhere any time soon, are you? We may need to speak to you again. If we find anything in the meantime, we'll, of course, be in touch.'

'Thank you,' Allison said, shaking the hands of the two officers and seeing them to the door. Once they'd left, she turned to her daughter, her eyes squinting to get a closer look.

'Why were they intent on asking you all those awkward questions?' she said, tucking a loose strand of hair behind her ears.

'How am I supposed to know that?' Sadie barked.

'And you don't know anything else, do you? Other than what you told them five years ago?'

'Of course not!' Sadie shouted. 'Everything I know I told them back when Ben went missing. I don't know anything else now that I didn't know then,' she lied. Pushing past her parents, Sadie escaped the living room and ran upstairs, away from her parents, away from Ben, away from the questions and prying eyes. She hated being home, hated the sea air and the countryside where there was so little to hide behind. She suddenly yearned for the towering buildings of London, for Tabitha's friendly smile, for thousands of other people to slip between.

Instead, Sadie found herself back in her old childhood bedroom. The top drawer of her old dresser slid open, the soft wood relenting to her touch. She was looking for the magazine she'd read as a child, looking for the piece of her history that made it all feel more real. No sooner had she envisaged its plastic coated pages than it appeared, laying flat along the base of the drawer. Various other trinkets and snippets of her history piled on top of the glossy pages, hair bobbles, fraying lengths of ribbon, book marks. It slid out from underneath the debris, the colourful cover reminiscent of the era that it heralded from. A wide grinned, freckled teenager adorned the front, holding a locked diary, a vibrant pink scrunchie plonked on the top of her head. Sadie used to be desperate to look like those girls; colourful, vibrant, confident. She flipped the magazine over to look at the back. The back was always darker, less exciting. No one paid it much attention. But as Sadie turned the magazine over, her breath caught in her throat. Beige, crusted splatters of sand and dirt were mottled on the back page. How had it stayed there, stuck on the pages for all those years? Transferred from her jeans as she used the magazine to hide the lies that adorned the tops of the denim, that she was hiding from her mum. She wondered if she should get rid of the magazine now, if it would be obvious if she were to dispose of it. She'd spoken about it so much to her mum, and now to the police officers downstairs. She couldn't risk getting rid of it. But she could clean it. She grabbed a cucumber scented face wipe from her soap bag and scratched at the marks, watching as they came away onto the white cloth. *This wasn't a lie,* she thought to herself. She wasn't lying and this didn't prove that she was. This was just something that she had to do. The officers wouldn't understand otherwise.

14

Summer 1990

Sadie tiptoed out of her bedroom. A thick, humid darkness blanketed the house, one she didn't want to disturb with her own bedside lamp. Her feet touched the plush carpet in her bedroom, toes spreading amongst the soft fibres muffling her footsteps. She'd had a fair amount of practice at creeping around, sneaking home late at night. She'd learnt the noisiest spots of flooring, where the wooden boards creaked the loudest, where the old slats squealed in the darkness. She placed one foot in front of the other, rolling from heel to toe, until she was out in the middle of the hallway.

She slipped down the stairs, hopping across the steps from side to side to avoid the weakest spots that would alert her parents to her whereabouts. The downstairs of the house always seemed much darker than the upstairs. It held onto the black air, the small windows failing to catch any light from the moon or the many street lamps outside. She slid into the kitchen-diner, easing the door closed behind her.

The phone rang in the darkness, the alert shrill and piercing. Sadie only let it ring for one turn, her heart beating frantically as she grasped for the phone in the dark, desperate to suffocate the noise. The receiver was cold against her ear.

'Hello?' she whispered.

'Hi,' a female voice answered, quiet but stern.

'Is Vedat there too?'

'Yes,' Vedat answered, the line flickering between the three friends, the ropey connection struggling to hold onto their voices.

'Are you guys okay?'

They'd arranged to call each other in the early hours of the morning, away from prying ears and concerned parents. Sadie had wished the upstairs phone had a longer cord so she could drag it into her room, hiding under her duvet to whisper to her friends. It had been a long time since she had hidden away from her family to whisper to her friends, but something about their experience from the past few hours made her feel that hiding was necessary. Instead she'd had to tiptoe downstairs and hope that no one would realise she was out of bed.

'I guess,' Sadie answered. 'I feel odd.'

'Vedat?' Callie pressed.

'Yes, yes. I'm fine. Tired. And happy to never go over to that island again.'

The two of them waited for Callie to offer up her own thoughts about the evening, fully expecting her to say that they were overreacting, that there was nothing to worry about, that it was all in their heads. Instead, she remained uncharacteristically silent.

'Callie?' Sadie whispered. 'What's going on? Are you alright?'

Callie's breath could be heard over the phone, a deep breath in, a louder, whistling breath out. 'Yes, mostly. No, I mean, yes I'm okay. But I'm not that sure. Does that make sense?'

It did. They all felt it. They all felt fine, really, but they also felt like there was something innately wrong. Something they couldn't put their fingers on. Sadie felt strange, like she was out of place in a place that she'd always felt comfortable in. Like someone had borrowed her shoes for a day and worn them all wrong, rubbed down the soles so she could sense an unnatural amount of earth beneath her feet. Like someone had used her favourite pen and now, when she used it, she could still sense them in the ink cartridge, could feel the weight of their hand pushing against hers and changing the way she'd always written. It was an odd sensation, but it was definitely there.

'I feel like I've had the flu,' Sadie mumbled. 'My limbs feel heavy, my joints are stiff, my mind is foggy.'

Vedat groaned. 'Yeah, I know what you mean.'

Sadie's mind went back to the heart plummeting from inside the tree, dropping to the ground with a wet slap. Beating. Pumping, despite being far away from anything that could possibly require its circulation. And those eyes. The deep, orange embers aflame between the trees on the island.

'We need to go back.'

'What? Why would you suggest that?' Vedat hissed, the urge to shout straining behind his clenched jaw.

'Yeah sorry Callie, I'm with Vedat. Why on earth would we want to go back?'

'I don't know. I can't tell you why, it just feels like something I need to do. Will you come with me?'

'I don't know, Callie. I can't say I'm itching to go back,' Sadie answered.

'I need to go, Sadie. I can't explain it. I'll go on my own if I have to.'

'We can't let you go on your own,' Vedat said.

'Fine. But I'm thinking of going back now.'

'Now? Callie, it's 1am - if we sneak out and get caught, our parents will kill us.'

'Fine, I'll go on my own then. Bye —,'

'Wait!,' Sadie shouted, reigning her voice in and straining her ears to check that her family were still sound asleep. 'We can't let her go on her own, Vedat.'

'Fine,' Callie said, 'I'm on my way over to yours. Vedat, meet you there.' Callie hung up.

'Great,' Vedat whispered, his breath whistling through the gap in his front teeth. 'I don't like this, Sadie.'

'I know,' she agreed. 'But we can't let her go on her own. Are you coming over?'

'Yes,' he mumbled, hanging up. Sadie stood alone in the darkened kitchen, hoping that none of her family had stirred to hear what was going on. Going back to the island was the last thing she wanted to do, but she couldn't let her friends endanger themselves.

Callie and Vedat only lived a few minutes away from her house. Whilst she waited for her friends, she grabbed a string backpack and dropped in her dad's heavy duty torch. She fumbled around in the kitchen drawer in search of some spare batteries; she'd seen enough horror films to know that being back on that island without a source of light was the last thing she'd be stupid enough to do. There were also a couple of bottles of water in the fridge, which slid into the back next to the torch. She grabbed her trainers and the spare key from the hook, and slid out the front door, confident in the knowledge that there wouldn't be any journalists or news reporters out at this time of night. The door sighed closed behind her, the lock clicking shut. She walked in her socks to the bottom of the garden, sitting on the wall to tug on her converse and tussle with the long laces.

A few minutes passed, stretching out like hours in front of Sadie. The itch of sensibility tugged at the centre of her back, threatening to pull her back to the house. She could pretend that she'd never agreed to go back to the island with her friends, that she knew it was a ridiculous and dangerous idea. The temptation grappled with her conscience and somehow, despite the urge to retreat back to her bedroom, she remained seated on the low brick wall.

The moon was high and bright white in the dense black night sky. The air was unimaginably still, giving rise to the heavy humidity that clogged up the atmosphere. It was the clearest night Sadie had seen in a good few weeks. The stars shone against their onyx backdrop, pinpricks of light stabbing through like a pinhole camera.

'Where are you going?' a voice came from behind her.

'Oh Jesus, you scared me! Don't sneak up on me like that,' Sadie panted.

'You didn't answer my question.' Ben stood behind the wall, shoes on and hands planted on his hips.

'We're not going anywhere. Just for a walk, for some fresh air. Go to bed. Please.' Sadie held her voice still, the tones of panic teasing and threatening to tip her over.

'For a walk?' he repeated. 'Are you insane? It's gone one in the morning.'

'Thank you, Sherlock. Yes, I suppose it is late. But still, I'm going out for a walk.'

'What's in the bag?' he asked.

'Nothing,' Sadie answered, pulling the bag across her chest. 'Go to bed, Ben. Please.'

'Why should I?' Ben answered, his arms crossed over his torso, looking down his nose at his sister. 'Let me come with you, or I'm going upstairs right now and waking up Mum and Dad.'

'Oh come on, we're not ten anymore. Just go away.' Sadie nudged Ben on his shoulder, fighting the urge to shove him harder.

'Fine. I'll go and let them know.' Ben turned, jogging up the path back towards their front door.

'Wait!' Sadie shouted. 'You're not actually going to tell them, are you?'

'Yes,' Ben shrugged. 'Why wouldn't I? All you've got to do is let me come with you, or I will tell on you.'

Callie rounded the corner as Sadie and Ben were squabbling.

'Oh, hi Ben,' she said, looking towards Sadie, concern across her face. 'Everything alright?'

'Yes,' Ben said, before Sadie had the chance to say anything. Sadie rolled her eyes. 'Just chatting with Sadie about the plans for this walk of yours.'

Callie glared at her friend. Of all the times to not have telepathic powers, now was the worst. 'Oh she has, has she?'

'He's not coming,' Sadie assured Callie, throwing her own glance at her brother. 'He was just going back into the house, weren't you, Ben?'

'Oh yes, I was going back in to wake Mum and Dad up and tell them all about your sneaking out late at night. And the alcohol you've been getting Callie's sister to get for you. They'd love to hear about that.'

Sadie flushed. She couldn't let her parents hear about that, not after the last time they caught her and Callie drinking in the park. It did not go down well. She often wondered if her parents were ever children at all.

Callie let out a low breath. 'Let him come if he wants.'

'What?' Sadie rounded on her friend, disbelief spread across her face. 'He can't come. It might be dangerous.'

'Dangerous? Oh, now I'm definitely coming. That's decided.'

'Whatever,' Callie shrugged, hopping down from the low garden wall. 'Vedat said he'll meet us on the corner, by the way. Unless he has to ask Mummy and Daddy for permission as well, huh Sadie?'

Red hives rushed up Sadie's neck, planting themselves firmly on her cheeks. She didn't want to go back to the island at all, let alone have her younger brother tag along with them. God knows what he'd end up telling their parents.

'Where are we actually going?' Ben asked as they made their way down to the corner of the street.

'Down to the Rowing Club,' Callie announced. She led the way, as always.

'Why are we going there?' Ben asked, skipping to keep up with the two older girls.

'Just... no reason,' she answered. 'We just, well I just need to check something.'

'Well, that's weird. Whatever.'

Vedat was waiting on the corner of the main road, teetering on a low red-brick wall. He chewed on his fingers, the tell-tale sign that he was anxious. Sadie recognised it a mile off.

'Expecting someone?' Callie joked.

'Shh', Vedat hissed, holding his finger to his lips. 'I've been here ages. And keep your voice down, unless you want to broadcast what we're up to.' He drew his hand away from his face, burying it deep in his jacket pocket.

'Oh shush, you.' Callie prodded him in the ribs, strolling casually to the front of the group.

The group of four walked down to the beach. They followed the same route that Callie, Sadie and Vedat had taken earlier that evening, retracing their steps only now with Ben shuffling behind them. The walk down the side of the drop was harder to navigate in the pitch blackness, and, thankful for her earlier foresight, Sadie rummaged in her backpack for her dad's torch. The button crunched in the darkness, throwing a wide beam of cold white light across the path. The walk was surreal, like walking through a video game. Only a few steps in front of the group were illuminated by the torch's beam, the rest of their surroundings remaining submerged in a thick, tangible darkness.

'So when is one of you going to tell me what we're going down here for?' Ben was bringing up the rear, tailing the rest of the group, much like any other time he tried to wriggle his way into Sadie's circle of friends. His footsteps were weary in the darkness, the constant fear of tripping and falling down the side of the hill wedged in his brain.

'You already know,' Sadie called behind her.

Ben frowned and they continued walking in silence.

.   .   .

CALLIE SAW IT FIRST. Then Sadie, then Vedat. And finally Ben, though he had no idea of its relevance. The red canoe, nestled amongst the shingle in the same position that it had been before they'd taken it out onto the water. The oars were leaning up against the hollow body of the boat, the narrowed ends of plastic buried deep amongst the stones and shells, the school's emblem etched proud on its nose. It was fine and, at first, Ben didn't register what the others were so concerned about. But the more he squinted, the closer he got to the boat, the more he realised there was something not right.

The red of the boat gleamed in the white light of the torch, parts of the plastic bleached by long journeys in the sun and salty water. That was completely normal. The oars were completely normal. And the inside of the boat was completely normal. What wasn't quite normal was the belly of the canoe, which was stained a deep, dark black. An oil-like substance trickled up the side of the plastic, dripping from the top edge and floating in globules in the night air. The four of them stood a few feet away from the boat, mouths gaping in astonishment. Once the oily substance had slid upwards, against the pull of gravity, it floated in shiny spheres inches away from the boat itself.

'What the...?' Ben wasn't able to finish his sentence.

He walked closer, taking a knee around a foot away from the boat. The black goo that covered the underside of the boat continued to course upwards, defying gravity. Droplets of the deepest black hovered centimetres above the lip, vibrating in their suspended positions. Ben inched his face even closer, the other three merely standing by and watching him inspect the bizarre phenomenon. Each sphere floated, humming with energy. The colour was unlike any he'd ever seen. It was the kind of black that swallowed off all light round it, the deepest, darkest shadow any of them had ever witnessed. Sadie shone the torch onto one of the droplets, but it didn't reflect the light at all. The black swallowed the light, its surface flat, matt and totally unreflective.

'What am I looking at?' Ben asked, eyes transfixed on the globules. His voice travelled slowly from his lips, each word forming between his lips before he summoned the energy to release them into the atmosphere.

'We have no idea,' Vedat answered, his eyes locked onto the tar beads.

'I think you should move away a bit, Ben,' Sadie said, moving up towards him and placing a hand on his shoulder. He flinched as she made contact, as if her being there had pulled him from a trance. He turned to see her face bathed in the unnatural white light of the torch.

Callie shifted around the other side of the boat, her feet shuffling in the rocks and shingle. 'Guys,' she whispered, her voice cracking in the darkness. 'What is that?'

'What's what, Callie? We've already decided we've got no idea.' Vedat made his way over to Callie's side.

'In the boat.'

The four of them crowded around the nose of the canoe. Sadie lifted the torch, pouring light into the plastic shell. Each held their breath, each refused to talk and each refused to acknowledge what remained in the boat.

Ben turned to face his sister. 'I'm sorry,' he said. 'What is it exactly that I'm looking at? And why has it spooked you all so much?' Sadie remained quiet. Ben turned his head back to look inside the boat, wondering if there was something else hiding away in there that he'd missed. But there wasn't. There was nothing in the boat that could have been of interest.

Nothing except a branch, which appeared normal - broken off from a nearby tree. Though it was quite big and seemed to be dripping in the same substance that covered the belly of the boat. And actually, on closer inspection, it also seemed to be hovering a few inches from the plastic base. It, too, was vibrating in the same way that the droplets were, humming with an ethereal energy. Ben bent his knees, craning his neck to get a closer look at the twig. His nostrils flared as they registered a pungent, acrid scent of something that he didn't recognise. The fragrance carried the sensation of something that had fermented, or rotted, and the more he breathed it in to try and place it, the more his eyes watered until they were streaming down his face. He didn't flinch at the pain it was causing in his tear ducts. Instead, he continued to stare at the branch, leaning closer and closer towards it.

Sadie grabbed at her forearms, patted her hands across their emptiness. *It must have slipped out.* 'Don't touch it,' she gasped, her hand flinging out to grab her brother by the shoulder.

Ben jerked his eyes away, registering the stinging sensation in his eyes. He rubbed his sleeves across the wetness, blinking and squinting in an effort to flush out whatever he'd inhaled. He went to make some kind of sarcastic remark about how he wasn't going to touch it in the first place, but now she'd pulled him away, he wasn't that convinced he wouldn't have reached for it. And there was something in his sister's eyes, too, that made him keep his mouth shut. Fear. Actual fear, crawling around the corners of her irises. 'Okay,' he whispered, 'I won't. Don't worry.' He shrugged her hand from his shoulder and took a step back.

'It came back with me,' Callie uttered. 'I put it down on the island. I *threw* it when I saw —.'

'When you saw what?' Sadie's hands scratched around in her empty pockets. Her jaw clenched, grinding her teeth angrily in the back of her mouth.

'Erm,' Callie looked up at Sadie, but her friend was staring at the floor of the boat. 'There was an organ, or something,' Callie mumbled, the disbelief clear in her voice.

'Are you sure you didn't carry it back with you? By accident or something?' Ben asked.

Callie shook her head, fret lines carrying the doubt in her voice into her face.

'Ben might be right, Callie. We were all weirded out. You could have kept hold of it by accident.' The lie slipped easily from between Sadie's lips. She eyed Vedat, eager to know what he was thinking. The sensation of the branch tingled across her palm; she could almost feel its outline between her fingers.

'No,' Callie demanded. 'I literally threw the thing to the ground. I would have remembered carrying it back.'

'Back from where?' Ben asked.

'It's not that big,' Sadie said, ignoring her brother's questioning. 'You could easily have held onto it without even realising.'

'No! I'm telling you. You saw the heart, it hit the ground, I threw the stick, the end. I didn't pick it up. I didn't carry it back to the boat. I didn't bring it back here.'

'Maybe it wasn't...' Sadie's voice trailed off, jamming under her tongue.

'Maybe it wasn't what?' Callie's eyes widened, trained on Sadie.

'Nothing, nothing, sorry. Maybe you did just bring it back by accident, I'm sure it's fine either way. It's just a stupid stick, right? No harm done.'

'Guys,' Ben said, louder this time.

'Sadie, are you calling me a liar?'

'No of course not, I'm just saying it would have been easy to bring it back by mistake,' Sadie swallowed.

'Guys!' Ben yelled.

'What?' Callie bellowed back, finally taking her eyes off the hovering stick.

'Look.' Ben was pointing towards the water. There were a handful of fish bobbing only inches away from the dry shore. They were all upside down, dead, and floating, brushing up against the pebbled beach.

'It's just a few fish, Ben,' Sadie said. 'Fish die all the time. You live by the sea - it's not like you've never seen something like this before.'

'No,' he shook his head. 'Really look. Sadie, shine the torch over there.'

The group cast their eyes further into the water. Hundreds of fish bobbed up onto the surface, water frothing around their repelled carcasses. Their swollen bodies were buoyant, pinging up to the surface of the water at a comical rate. The sea was expelling them, forcing them to the surface and throwing them out of the depths. The group moved closer, Sadie's torch trained on the drifting animals as they skimmed the surface of the sea, bumping into each other ungracefully.

'Oh God, that is disgusting.'

Sadie grabbed an oar, ignorant to its splintered surface, and batted one of the fish that had padded up against the gravel. It rolled, flopping onto its side, revealing a glistening, tar stained body. It looked much like the underside of the canoe. They were riddled with black goo, emaciated from the inside out, discarded onto the stones. Swarms of deceased fish tumbled up onto the beach, their mouths falling slack, the thick dark tar oozing onto the rocks.

'Oh gross,' Sadie said, jabbing the belly of the fish with the flat of the oar. Its mouth dropped open. A steady stream of glossy black liquid flooded from its mouth, surrounding its carcass in a dark halo. A light mist lifted from the goo, drifting up into the atmosphere and carrying a familiar putrid stench with it.

'Oh no, not again', Vedat groaned, darting away from the smell, arms cradling his stomach.

Callie followed, jogging further up the hill, with Sadie and Ben behind her. 'Oh, that's awful.'

'That doesn't make any sense,' Sadie said. 'How can they smell that bad if they've only just died. That's revolting.'

The group moved away to the bottom of the hill and stared out to sea. The moon threw an eerie light over the bobbing bodies, lumps of rotting meat floating on the surface of the otherwise calm waters.

'So I assume you went over to the island then?'

'Yes, I suppose we did,' Callie answered. Like it was no big deal that they'd stolen private property and trespassed on what they'd always imagined to be some kind of haunted island.

'What made you do it?'

Callie shrugged, assuming the position of spokesperson for the group. In reality, none of them knew why they had done what they did. In part, it was probably due to the crowd mentality. Callie had made up her mind that she wanted to explore the island and wanted to see if her friends would go along with it. And they did. They all went over together. They were now all equally culpable for whatever they had done, whatever that could be.

'I thought you'd all agreed it was dumb, apart from Vedat?'

Vedat flinched at the mention of his name. 'For the record,' he said, turning to face Ben, 'I did, and still do, think it was a stupid thing to do. Even if none of the stories are true, which clearly they're not, what's the point in pushing these things? I've never been a fan. Just leave it be.'

Callie snorted under her breath.

'Look, we went over there to see what's what,' Callie said. 'Who didn't want to get over there as a kid? All those stories, all those rumours - we wanted a chance to see for ourselves before we were too old. And we did that, now we're back and that's the end of that.'

'So you didn't find anything then?' Ben seemed almost hopeful that they had, that there was some truth in the old stories and lively rumours.

'Nope, nada,' Callie lied. 'Of course we didn't find anything because there was simply nothing to be found. You need to stop listening to Vedat.' Sadie frowned, glancing up at Callie.

'So what did you mean when you were talking about some kind of organ? And the floating... thing? What was that? And the black stuff. I'm not an idiot.

Callie shifted, licking her lips and looking to Sadie and Vedat for support that was far from forthcoming.

She stood up, her knees locking straight. 'We should go home.'

'And ignore my questions, I take it?'

'Yes, Ben.'

The group turned their backs on the sea and made their way back up the path, onto the main road that led through the town. As they turned, Callie slid the branch up her sleeve, concealing the slender twig along the underside of her arm. The compulsion for her to take it pulled at her chest until she could no longer control it. And now a different compulsion, the compulsion to conceal and to hide it, tugged at her. She couldn't explain the desire, the necessity, to the others, so she hid it. It was easier that way. The thin branch sat snuggly between the fabric of her top and her skin, embedding its shape into her flesh like the blade of a knife.

As THEY TURNED and began their ascent up the side of the hill, Sadie let her eyes wander deep into the trees. There they were again. The deep glowing orange spheres of illuminated glass. She was no longer afraid of them, but she knew they weren't there to be amicable. She stared at the pulsating spheres of amber, at the fire held deep within them. The orbs were animated, plumes of smoke and flame circling and dancing in front of her eyes. She blinked, and turned away to make her way home with her friends, the outline of the stick clear to her under her friend's sleeve.

15

Summer 1995

Her body leant as the cushions on the sofa sank to the side. She eased open her eyes, her eyelids gluey with exhaustion. She glanced to her left to see Ben sitting cross-legged next to her. A dull ache settled behind her eyes, her mind heavy from the earlier questioning and all the unanswered questions from the last half a decade of her life.

'Hey, you okay?,' Sadie yawned, digging a finger around her eyes to scratch out the sleep.

'Mhmm,' Ben intoned. 'Earlier was awkward.'

'Yeah, you could say that.' Sadie ran her hands over her face, urging life back into her cheeks.

'I went to the island.'

'What?' Sadie whipped her head round to face her brother. 'When? Why?'

'I went to the island,' he repeated. 'For the last five years, I was on the island.'

Sadie's eyes widened, the pupils shrinking to pinpricks. 'Why?'

'I don't remember why. I don't think it was my choice.'

Sadie recalled the canoe, the red shiny plastic of the boat that she dragged out to sea with her friends. She shuddered.

'How did you get there, Ben?'

'I don't know,' he answered.

Sadie leant further back into the sofa, allowing herself to relax. 'You don't remember?'

'No,' Ben said, shaking his head and staring deep into his lap. 'I was at home, then out with friends, then everything went blurry and I woke up on the island.'

'Do you remember much of being on the island?'

He nodded. 'A bit. Not all of it. It comes back in bursts. I remember waking up on the grassy bank on the closest side of the island. I remember waking up and being completely alone. I remember the feeling of floating and rocking. I woke up totally isolated. And then she found me.'

'She?' Sadie's voice was a mixture of panic and confusion. *She*? 'Who do you mean, Ben?'

'The lady on the island, of course.' His tone hardened. The mention of this lady made his voice mature, the soft tones slipping away.

Sadie's eyes stretched impossibly wide. A cool film of sweat beaded at the back of her neck and she fought the urge to run.

'What did the lady on the island look like, Ben?'

'Oh, I don't know that I remember that,' he said, his voice bright and rhythmic, the higher end of his tone tinkling like a child's music box. 'She never let me look at her, not for too long. But she was kind. She helped me, I think.' His tone was confused, as was Sadie, the pitch lifting and dropping and circling back to cool and flat all in the space of a single sentence.

'Do you remember anything else about her? Did she give you somewhere to stay on the island? Did she say anything about, erm,' Sadie faltered over her words, 'did she look after you?' she corrected. Sadie leant forward, her torso teetering over her knees.

'Oh yes, she made sure I was okay.'

'So did she let you go? How did you get back?'

'I don't really know,' Ben said, retreating back into his reserved state, his head dipping towards his chest.

'What did she have you do on the island for five years?'

'I'm not sure.'

'Did she talk to you?'

'Of course, a little,' he relented.

'Ben, did she hurt you?'

He shot his gaze towards his sister. 'No, of course not,' he shouted. 'She never wanted to hurt me, she never wanted to hurt anyone. She wanted to look after me.'

Sadie recoiled at his shouting.

'We did things on the island together.'

'Like what?' Sadie asked, afraid of the answer.

'Well, we walked. And we talked. She told me about herself, said that not many people wanted to visit her anymore. Not many people believed she still existed. She was happy I was there for her.'

Sadie shuddered. The skin across the back of her neck raised and prickled, crawling with the idea that this 'lady', whatever she was, spent so much time with her brother.

'It didn't feel like five years when I was there. Five years?

Has it really been that long?' Ben stared at his hands, studying his fingertips and flexing his knuckles. 'Are you sure it was five years?' Sadie nodded. 'It definitely didn't feel that long. Anyway, she's let me come home now, so it's all fine I suppose.'

'What do you mean she's let you come home, Ben?'

'Well, she brought me back, of course.'

'She came here? From the island? The lady?'

'Yes,' he said, as if it was obvious.

Sadie swallowed, the phlegm tracing its way down her throat carrying beads of guilt and worry. 'Are you sure you can't tell me what this lady looks like?'

'Well,' Ben answered, visibly thinking and raising his chin to the ceiling. 'She looked kind of normal I suppose. Except, when she didn't. And, well... her eyes were different.'

Sadie's back straightened, her skin prickling. 'What do you mean?'

'Well, I never asked as I didn't know how to. But her eyes were quite strange.'

'In what way?' Sadie pressed her brother now, her voice becoming frantic. She was sure she knew the answer he was about to give her.

'They weren't a normal colour.'

'What colour were they, Ben?'

'I don't know how to describe them. They were kind of golden, an orange-y colour. Sort of yellow I guess.'

Sadie flopped back into the sofa, forcing herself to breathe. Her forefingers flew up to her throat to find the reassuring thud of her pulse. It raced under her fingertips and she counted it in her head. It needed to slow down, she needed to calm herself, but the pace of it was slipping out of control.

'She's okay, Sadie. Once you get to know her.'

Sadie flew up from the sofa and ran into the kitchen. She grabbed a glass from the draining board, shaking as she filled it with cold water from the tap. The clear liquid sloshed over the sides of the glass as she struggled to steady her hands. Ben walked up behind her and placed his hand on her shoulder.

'What's the matter?' he asked, nudging his sister to turn and face him.

Sadie couldn't answer. She couldn't tell Ben the truth, but she couldn't keep lying either.

'You've met her before, haven't you?'

Sadie's head jerked up to meet her brother's gaze. 'How do you know that?'

'It's written all over your face, Sadie,' Ben replied, his voice much cooler and flatter than before.

'I don't know what you mean.' Sadie brushed her brother off and moved back to the living room. She needed space, she needed time to think about what this could mean. She needed to talk to Callie and Vedat again.

'How did you actually get home, Ben? Really?' she asked again, her body leaning against the corner of the sofa.

'I told you. I walked.'

'On your own? How did you get back across the water?'

'How we always got across the water,' he said. 'But it had been so long since I'd been on the mainland that I had forgotten the way home, so she helped me.'

'Okay,' Sadie said, waiting for a further response.

'She helped me find my way here, back home.'

Sadie froze. The moisture that ran from her mouth and her eyes seemed to solidify, cementing themselves open. She found herself incapable of blinking and stared at her brother, wide eyed. A painful, swollen balloon of air trapped itself in her ribcage. 'When you say she walked you home... do you mean she literally walked you to the front door?'

'Yes, she was very helpful. She even knocked for me and waited until Mum answered the door, then she slipped away.'

She knows where we live.

'Did Mum see her?'

'Oh no, I don't think so,' he paused. 'Why? Would that have been a problem?'

Sadie frowned. 'Well yes, probably, Ben. We don't know who this woman is. We ought to tell the police about this.'

Ben mulled the idea over, chewing on his gum and ringing his hands in his lap. 'I don't think that's a good idea.'

'Why?'

'Well,' he paused, 'she wouldn't be very happy if I was to do that. And that would be bad for everyone, wouldn't it?'

16

Summer 1990

'Can you pass the milk please, Benjamin?'

'Only if you promise not to call me Benjamin again,' he smiled, leaning into the fridge and handing Sadie the glass bottle.

'Whatever, hand it over.'

They sat together at the table, eating breakfast, flicking through books and comics and chatting about the weekend. The sweet smell of Cheerios lingered in the air, the sugar seeping from the loops of cereal into the milk. Sadie always found it amusing to think back to when she and Ben were much younger. They never got on, never saw eye to eye as kids. Quite often they'd end up in physical altercations and their dad would be forced to separate them, kicking and screaming at each other over a broken toy or a cassette tape with its innards strung out across the floor. But then they seemed to grow up over night and pretty quickly they realised that they'd become good friends.

'Any plans for the weekend?' Sadie asked, rubbing a hand over her tired eyes.

Ben shook his head, his cheeks filled with cereal, milk bubbling in the corners of his mouth. He'd come back with her late last night, but there was not a single thing on his face that would give away how he felt.

'You're disgusting,' Sadie giggled, flinging a dry loop of cereal at her brother as it fell from the box onto the table. The breakfast table started in the kitchen but stretched out into the living room, giving them a slight view of the television set. Patrick sat on the sofa pretending to read the paper, his eyes peering over the top of the broadsheet to watch the news instead.

'You not hanging out with Jacob today?'

'Nope, he's on holiday at Camber Sands.'

'Oh,' she said, spooning another heap of Cheerios into her mouth, 'fair enough.'

They heard the newspaper ruffle from the sofa. Patrick had given up pretending to read the financial articles. The newspaper laid out beside him on the sofa, inner pages separated from their outer cover. His head rested on his hand and he was staring at the news programme, deep in thought.

'Ever think he knows what's going on outside of that TV?'

Sadie shrugged. 'I guess not. It's just his escape I guess.'

Sadie spooned the final few floating pieces of cereal into her mouth. Her ears honed in on something that was going on in the news. Something about fish, something else about birds. Some more about crops. She looked up to find Ben sat upright, his head tilted towards the TV set, his face quizzical.

'Did you hear that?' he asked.

'No...I'm not sure that I did. What was it?'

'They're talking about the fish, Sadie.' He stared at her, waiting for the information to sink in. The penny dropped. 'The fish from last night,' he added.

'What are they saying? I can't hear it,' Sadie said.

'Shh — hang on.' He held his hand out, urging his sister to be quiet. The two of them sat in silence, straining their ears to focus on the news reporter's voice.

'Sod this, I can't hear enough, or see anything,' Ben blurted, standing up and marching over to the sofa next to his dad. Patrick looked up, surprised to see his son sitting next to him.

'Oh, hello,' he said. 'Since when were you interested in the local news?'

'Very funny,' he mumbled.

Sadie followed Ben and perched on the arm of the sofa, much to her dad's annoyance. 'Chair,' he droned, conscious of the damage her sitting on the arm was doing to the settee. She threw him a glance and dramatically slid down onto the sofa cushions.

'What's got you two so interested all of a sudden?'

'Nothing,' Ben muttered.

'Erm,' Sadie considered, 'Ben's got a school project about... the sea and... ecosystems and things, right Ben?'

'Oh yeah, that one. I need to... do some research.'

'Oh,' his dad replied, happily accepting the reasoning. He lifted the paper back up over his face, continuing his facade of reading about the stock market.

Sadie and Ben stared at the programme. There was a news reporter standing down at the beach, her sandy coloured hair whipping in the breeze. She held one of those fuzzy microphones close to her face and was talking about the unusual circumstances that had seen so many people flock down to the seafront that morning. Behind her, people milled around, prodding the fish carcasses that lined the ground. The tip of the red canoe peered into the corner of the shot, its bottom stained an oily black.

The reporter walked over to an older gentleman in a checkered over-shirt and cap. She shoved the fluffy microphone in his face and waited for him to introduce himself.

'Jeff, from the rowing club,' he said in answer to the reporter's question. Sadie recognised him, probably just from wandering around the local area, or the local pub or something similar. The reporter pulled the microphone back under her chin.

'And can you tell us what happened this morning, Jeff?'

The microphone flung back towards his face. The reporter tucked her hair behind her ear and replaced her hand on her hip; she was clearly thrilled to have received the call for such an exciting job so early on a Saturday morning.

'Ah well, you see,' he started, 'I came down this morning, earlier than my normal mind, though I don't really remember why I came down earlier, I just had a feeling I suppose. Anyway, I came down to the rowing club first thing to get things set up - Saturday's a busy day for us y'see. So I came down, tired and not really paying too much attention, like. I opened up the rowing club, pottered around for a bit, cleared up and made a cuppa.'

'Yes,' she urged, desperate to hurry the conversation along.

'Oh yeah, sorry,' he stammered. 'And then I came outside to take a look at the conditions, because I need to fill out the board out front you know? I take that very seriously. We can't have people out on the water when it's not safe. Anyway, that's when I saw it.'

'Saw what, exactly, Mr...?'

'Blake. It's Mr Blake, but you can stick to Jeff if you like.' He paused. She was frowning at him over the top of the microphone. 'Oh sorry. So when I came out onto the beach, I saw hundreds and hundreds of dead fish. They'd washed up overnight, I reckon. Hundreds and hundreds of the things, their eyes all jammed open.'

'And have you seen anything like that before, Mr Blake?'

'Oh Jeff, please, you can call me Jeff.'

'Sure. Have you seen anything like this before, *Jeff*?'

'Well no, not like this. I've seen fish washed up before, of course. But not this many. And on top of that, it looks like there were some birds as well, further down the coast. Not so many, mind, just a handful. I guess the birds were going for the fish 'cause it looks like an easy dinner, you know? But then the fish are diseased or something, then it won't be long until the birds start dropping like flies too.'

'Yes, that does make sense. Well, thank you for that, Mr Blake,' the reporter said.

'No, thank you,' he said, shuffling back to join the people milling around in the background, his face beaming with pride after his debut television appearance.

The news reporter wandered over to a more official looking woman with a clipboard and pen tucked into her hair.

'Well folks,' she said, staring straight into the camera lens. 'Having spoken to a fair few people down by the sea today, it looks like there's been some kind of fish epidemic that has spread throughout these waters, affecting thousands, if not more, of our fish. We're being told to advise locals to stay away from the sea today whilst the clean-up operation takes place. For your own safety, please do follow this guidance and stay well clear. We'll be back with more information as soon as we have it.'

She turned away from the camera, and the screen cut away to the weather forecast.

Sadie turned to face her brother, who was still staring at the screen in disbelief. No one had noticed or paid any attention to the oil stained boat. No one had considered that there could be something else going on and for that, Sadie was incredibly thankful.

'Hmm,' Patrick mumbled from behind the wall of paper. 'I wonder what made that happen then? I seem to remember something similar happening before.'

'Really?' Sadie asked before she could stop herself.

'Yeah a few years back, maybe four or five years, something like that. Some kind of freak accident or disease blitzed through the waters for a week or so and then disappeared. Odd,' he mumbled, face still hidden behind the paper.

'Who knows?' Sadie mumbled.

'Either way, it's revolting,' Ben declared.

17

Summer 1995

Sadie sat cross-legged at the head of her bed, bolstered by the numerous cushions that she only understood now as an adult really were surplus to requirement, it wasn't just her dad being grumpy at spending more on pink fluffy soft furnishings. Her headphones nestled snugly over her ears, the raspy, distinct voice of Eddie Vedder filling her ears. There was something about this kind of music that got her in ways that nothing else could; she could listen to it on repeat for hours and never tire of it. She could hear her parents talking amongst the music, their words short and clipped. London felt a world away. Her eyes hovered between open and closed, the lids drifting somewhere in the middle of her irises. She watched as the handle of her bedroom door tilted downwards towards the floor, the door easing open. Ben peered around into her room.

'You okay?' she asked, slipping the headphones around her neck and jabbing the pause button on her Walkman. The CD clunked to a stop.

He nodded, taking a few steps closer to her bed. 'Actually, no,' he relented a second or so later.

'What's wrong, Ben?'

'It's happened again,' he whispered, his neck still bent towards the floor.

'What's happened again?' Sadie pressed, her heart hammering and the skin around her chest prickling in anticipation.

Ben turned his head to face her. He looked exhausted again, the grey skin around his eyes had darkened to an almost purple shade. 'The fish and the birds and the sea, and that feeling. Everything that happened before is happening again.'

'No, it can't be,' Sadie said, leaning closer to her brother and placing her hand on his knee. 'It can't happen again,' she whispered, knowing he was right, but knowing she couldn't afford for history to repeat itself.

'It is,' he said. His voice evened out, reverting to the emotionless and cold tone from earlier. 'It was on the news again, the same scientist down at the beach telling everyone how the fish have some rare disease that's causing them to bloat and die. And the birds are eating the fish and they're dying too. It's all connected, Sadie. It's all happening, all over again. Who knows how many times it has happened before this. The scientist said they're looking for patterns, Sadie. They know there's something connecting all of this too.'

Sadie stood up from the bed, her pulse thudding in her ears. 'It can't, Ben, it really can't.' Her palms prickled with sweat, her stomach churning noisily behind the rim of her jeans.

'Why not? I'm telling you it is,' he said. Something in his voice changed then, the tone dropped to become deeper and lower, his eyes locking onto hers and refusing to let go. 'I know it is happening again, Sadie. I know it,' he repeated.

'What does that even mean, Ben? How can you possibly know that?'

Ben held her gaze, watching as her eyes dropped from his. She swallowed, conscious that the action was visible to her brother, becoming aware of a newly formed pain in the back of her throat. 'We need to go and see it then.'

'Now you know that's not a good idea,' Ben said, his voice brimming with low energy. He tilted his head to look up at her, sitting like a small child on her bed, but his face was anything but the picture of innocence she remembered from their childhood. Purple rings circled his eyes, deepening his sockets and reaching up to his temples.

'You look unwell,' Sadie said, suddenly realising the truth behind what she was saying. 'Do you feel alright?'

'I feel fine, don't deflect, Sadie,' Ben said, his voice not registering her concern at all. 'What are we going to do?'

What did we do last time? Sadie thought, knowing the answer full well. The answer was there, from all those years ago. What they had to do the first time to fix things is exactly what they needed to do now, but she couldn't - they couldn't. There was no way.

'I don't know,' she whispered, collapsing onto her knees on the floor. She felt sick.

'You do know,' he answered.

She snapped her head back up to stare directly into his eyes again. How?

'We can't, Ben. No.' And that's when she realised. He knew far more about what had happened to him that he'd let on. He sat tall and rigid on the edge of the bed, watching as she collapsed in an emotional heap on the floor. She was crying at his feet and he wasn't reacting in any way at all, and that's how she knew. He knows everything.

'We're going to go out for a walk, Sadie, just around the village, round the back roads to give Ben some fresh air. Are you coming?' Sadie's mum had been possessed with the idea that Ben needed to get some fresh air for the last few hours. Ben hadn't seemed too bothered, but to appease his parents he relented and slid on a pair of their dad's old trainers, scuffing them across the floor and out of the back door.

'Oh, I don't think so Mum. I've got a bit of a headache coming on. I'll stay here.' She rubbed her fingers across her forehead, easing the tense skin over her skull.

'We won't be too long,' Allison called behind them.

Sadie pushed the door closed on her family, forcing out the tension and stress that had begun to percolate in her head. The pressure of the last few days lifted with their departure and Sadie took in a deep breath, allowing herself to relax. She waited, her ear held close to the door until she could no longer head her parents. Once she was confident they had gone, she padded through to the kitchen to use the phone.

Callie answered first, as always. Vedat joined the call a minute or so later, unsure why he was being called at all. Callie had seen the news, Vedat had made it a hard-fast rule since Ben's disappearance to hide from the TV set altogether.

'So the fish thing is happening again, right?' Callie asked.

'Yep,' Sadie said, wrapping the familiar phone cord around her fingers.

'It's exactly the same,' Callie mumbled, the sound of the news muttering away in the background. 'Like, identical. Bloated fish, weird goo, dead birds, hundreds and hundreds of the things all over the beach.'

'Yep,' Sadie repeated, tugging the cord around her finger until the end pulsed bright and red and swollen.

'What can we do?' Vedat asked. 'What do we need to do?'

'Well, there's always what we did last time,' Callie suggested.

'We can't,' Sadie gasped. 'None of this should be happening.' She grabbed the wall near the phone, panic close to pulling her under. She swallowed, a lump of anxiety, physical and sharp wedging itself in her throat.

'Well —,' Callie started, but her voice faltered.

'Well what?' Vedat pressed.

'Well I guess... you know. The creature let him come back, hell it sounds like it brought him back.'

'What are you getting at?'

'If it brought him back, it must want something, right? That was our end of the —'

'— no!' Sadie shouted, 'that's not what happened, Callie. It's not.'

'Okay, okay,' Callie eased. 'Look, I think we need to go and see what's going on. Regardless of what we decide to do, we need to see it for ourselves, don't you think? It might not be that bad, after all?'

'Okay,' Vedat said, waiting for Sadie to respond, but she remained quiet.

'Look, I'll come by tonight, after midnight okay? Vedat, meet me at Sadie's?'

'Fine,' he repeated, his nervousness trickling down the phone line.

'Sadie?'

'Sure,' Sadie finally replied, hanging up the phone.

IN THROUGH THE NOSE, three, four, out through the mouth, three four. Sadie's breath was steady, her inhalations controlled and her exhalation loud to remind her that it was there and all in working order.

'Flush out the negative thoughts and worries', she whispered in a whistling breath, imagining all her concerns lifting from beneath her ribcage. The events of the last couple of days were wearing her down, chipping away at her mindset, increasing the stress and pressure. No wonder her mum took to the wine so readily.

She placed her hands flat on the glass pane in front of her, splaying her fingers wide and focusing her weight onto each fingertip. The stretch of the skin between each digit felt good. Water cascaded from the shower head, pummelling her neck and spraying from her shoulders. Her mind was trained on each individual droplet, on each sphere of moisture as it connected with her skin. Breathing exercises had always been something that she'd try to practice regularly, and now it was helping her control her nerves and anxious temperament. She leant her head forward, face towards her toes and closed her eyes, imagining each and every droplet as it fell from the shower head and tumbled towards her body.

Everything was getting too much. The police visits were becoming more frequent, their questions harder to answer. She was getting tripped up by them much more easily. She pictured each question as a translucent piece of string, each crossing over the last to make an intricate web that threatened to trip her up should she answer any incorrectly. What if she'd answered something wrong already and hadn't even realised? What then? She had no way of knowing, and it was that helplessness that was threatening to overcome her. Even thinking about it now caused her heart to race. She jammed her forefinger and middle finger into the crevice beneath her throat, found her heartbeat and counted it aloud under her breath. *Control it, Sadie. Now is not the time to panic.* She tipped her head up into the stream of water, relishing the sensation of every drop as they bounced from her face and massaged her cheeks and tired eyes. Her long hair flowed down her back, washed away from her face by the powerful jet.

Ben had seemed to start warming up to her for a while. He seemed to be less inclined to end the conversation by staring at the floor, but he reverted back to his monotone state so easily. She was unsure what had changed, unsure what it was that decided which Ben she would be conversing with at which time. And she was still so unsure of just how much he remembered. A few times now he let on that he knew way more than he initially divulged, but then he'd revert back to not remembering how he even got home, let alone where he'd been held captive for the last five years, if he'd even been captive at all.

The cascading water had started to cool as the boiler ran out of steam. Sadie ran strawberry scented conditioner through the ends of her hair and rinsed it quickly under the waning flow. A few more moments to focus on the flow of the water and the meditative quality she had learned to enjoy so much. Maybe just a bit more, she thought, plucking the bottle back from the chrome basket that hung from the underside of the shower head. Her hands slipped over the plastic, struggling to keep hold of the shiny, soapy container, the saccharin scent of imitated berries hanging in the steamy air.

'Oh shit,' she muttered as the bottle fell to the shower floor, thudding and bouncing and hitting the top of her foot. She stooped to retrieve it, bending her stiffening knees. Her fingers curled around the bottle and she dropped it back into the basket. Water collected in the bottom of the shower. It rose a few millimetres at a time, covering her toes. Suds from her shower gel hung around the plug hole, sticking to something that had jammed itself there. Sadie ran her foot over the plug to see if there was something that needed loosening, some hair or product that had clogged. The ball of her foot ran over the ridged edges of the plug hole, the metal brushing against her skin. After a few attempts, she relented and, without turning the shower off, knelt to get a better view.

She brushed her fingertips over the ridged area again. Her fingers swept over a clump of matted hair that had wrapped itself around the spokes of the plug cover. She rubbed the hair between her fingertips to try to get purchase and began freeing it from the drain. It lifted, sliding from the hole easily, covered in the sweet smelling conditioner she had used only moments ago.

The hair slithered out in a golf ball size mass, long strands hanging from the clump in dark tendrils. She was the only one in the family that had hair of any considerable length. She drew a hand up to her scalp, tracing her fingers across her roots to feel for any missing patches. She stared at the hairball, placing it on the corner of the shower before turning to the drain. The water seemed to be flowing, happily sinking beneath the shower floor.

She stared into the drain and saw nothing but darkness.

Nothing except — wait, what was that? The water pounded the back of her head, cooling as the hot had all but run out. She reached her hand behind her, ceasing the flow of water, and returned her eye to the black hole in the corner of the white floor. There seemed to be something else down there after all. A lid or cap or something.

'How did that get down there?' she breathed, kneeling down on all fours, her knees slipping on the wet surface. She lowered her head closer to the hole. There was definitely something else down there. Something white, its surface glistening with moisture. How long had it been stuck, hidden under all that hair? She lifted the small grate out of the plug hole, placing it down next to the mass of hair and shower products. She could fit one finger down into the hole and rummaged around in the drain to loosen whatever it was that had become stuck down there. The tip of her finger made contact with something smooth. The surface of whatever it was depressed under the weight of her finger and she recoiled, whipping her hand back up from the floor of the shower.

'What the hell?' She lowered her head once more, levering her face inches from the opening in the floor. She stared into the dark hole, trying to focus on whatever it was that had found itself lodged in the pipes under the shower. And she saw it. A small sphere covered in an off-white, milky sheen. She strained her eyes, desperate to work out exactly what it was. Her brows furrowed deeper into her forehead, knotting together as she concentrated on the black space.

She lowered even closer to the floor. Her nose pressed into the white tiles of the shower cubicle, one cheek brushing against the textured floor. The plug hole was pushing into her eye socket, threatening to swallow her down the piping.

The milk white thing was wedged about four inches into the pipes. Even as her face and head blocked out any available light to the tube, the object somehow glistened.

It moved.

It rolled to one side and flickered back to the centre as if it were righting itself. Sadie's torso jerked, desperate to drag her body away from the unidentified object, but her head wouldn't allow it. Her face, her eyes, her neck refused to let her budge. Her body was cemented to the floor of the shower cubicle. Her lungs held onto her stale breath, burning her throat. Her eyes refused to let go of the object and she stared, desperate for it to reveal itself so she could breathe again. Maybe she'd made it up. Maybe it didn't move, and it was her nudging it that somehow made it spin to the side. She leant closer again.

'Oh my God,' she screamed, throwing herself towards the back of the shower and freeing her face from the plug. She threw her hand up over her mouth and suppressed the need to vomit. 'It's a fucking eye,' she gasped. Her whole body shook, the taste of acid rising in her throat, dancing sharply across her glands. 'How the hell did that get in there?'

Sadie willed herself to lean over the plug one last time.

'It can't be an eye, there's no way it could be.' She rubbed her hands into her own eyes, willing them to see what was really happening down there. 'I'm just tired, this isn't real,' she muttered to herself. 'This can't be real.'

But there it was, hovering in the darkness. Her eyes widened, locking in on the organ and refusing to budge. It blinked. Just once. The eye in the drain blinked. When it opened again it revealed a deep, amber iris full of flames and swirls. It blinked again, descending the pipes into complete darkness, and then it was gone. Sadie's breathing quickened.

She knew that eye. She knew where it came from, but not how it had come here.

'This can't be happening,' she repeated under her breath. 'This can't be happening.'

The last time she saw that eye, those colours glowing in the darkness, she lost her... no. That can't happen again. The fear of history repeating itself lodged in her chest. And Sadie gave into her body's instincts, vomiting onto the floor of the shower.

18

Summer 1990

The stick throbbed against Callie's arm. Each tiny bristle scratched and scraped against her skin as they walked, but she didn't care. She'd get home and take a closer look at it, but she wouldn't tell the others; they'd freak out, probably panic. They wouldn't understand why she had to take it with her. Hell, she didn't totally understand why she had to take it with her.

She dropped Sadie and Vedat off on their road and finished the journey to her house on her own. No one was likely to be home so she didn't feel the need to rush. And if they were home, they'd probably be blind drunk and she didn't really have the energy to deal with that. The stick somehow gave her confidence, in a weird way. She could feel the energy within it, pulsing through her arm, giving her power. Giving her the voice and strength she needed to survive this. She rounded the corner onto the road that held her family home, if that's what she could call it. The houses in this part of the town were much smaller than those that Sadie and Vedat lived in. The cars were much older, more beaten up and the houses were falling into disrepair. Callie had lived here all her life and she'd never known anything any different, not until she became friends with the two from the posher end of town. Her parents resented Sadie and Vedat for their money, so Callie kept them shielded from her home life as much as she possibly could. It wasn't that she was embarrassed of having less, or growing up in different conditions to those two, it was just that they had had so much more.

Her key slid into the door. She heaved the old wooden slab open and walked into the unlit hallway. The smell of booze and cigarettes hit her. They say your body gets used to certain smells, but for Callie the smell of her own home grew stronger every day.

Every light in her home was out. Just as she'd expected; no one was home. Her finger flicked against the landing light, illuminating the upstairs of her house and shining like a beacon towards her bedroom. Her room was her sanctuary. No one but her, and occasionally the cat, ventured in, and for that Callie was grateful. She slid off her beaten up Reeboks, digging her toes into her heels and shunting them into the corner by the door.

Her feet padded up the stairs, her toes aware of the ageing wooden slats peeking out from under the threadbare carpet.

She flopped onto the bed, the mattress sinking under her weight. Springs had been threatening to break free for a while now, so she'd become used to lying down on one side of the bed, her body curved around the protruding metal.

She slid off her hoody, careful not to damage the relic that had followed her home from the island. The stick was smaller than she remembered. The branch was fraying at the ends but the majority of its length was smooth. Almost too smooth. Too smooth to be made from any normal tree, or at least, any tree that Callie had seen before. Her fingers ran along the top of the wood. It really did have such an odd texture, like that of marble or stone. The more she looked at it and studied it, the more she realised she was not convinced that it was simply a twig.

She rolled it over in her hands. Her fingertips caught on something on the other side, some kind of indentation or engraving. On closer inspection she could see that it was a series of scratches, though the more she looked, the more she became sure that the scratches made some kind of pattern that ran the whole length of the stick and tumbled off the edge as if the author ran out of room. What the hell was this thing? She didn't know, and didn't have a clue how to find out. But for some reason, Callie felt the urge to hide the relic from the island. There was something about it that screamed out to be hidden, that urged to be concealed from the world, and she would abide by that desire. She lay the stick down on the pillow next to her head and drifted off to sleep.

BURNING. She could smell burning. Heavy and dry, catching in her nostrils and the back of her throat. She heard herself make a small cough, her consciousness floating above her body in its semi-wakened state. It wasn't loud enough to stir her, but it did worm its way into her subconscious. The smoke coiled up from around her head, snaking in beautiful grey patterns in the space above her face. Each trail laced between the next, smoky ribbons of charcoal and ash dancing inches away from her features. It wasn't clear what was burning. She was still asleep so didn't have the where-withal to open her eyes and assess the situation. But she knew it was happening, deep down. Behind her closed eyes, there were no dreams. Just Callie, unconscious. But every now and then a trail of bluish smoke weaved in front of her face, so she knew it was there.

It tugged on her concentration. She tried to hone in on where it was coming from, but it was no use. Then she tried to work out what was actually burning. It didn't smell like plastic. It was more like singed hair, or something charred. The smell intensified. The source of the burning was getting closer. The smoke thickened, polluting the air that Callie was breathing. It lay across her throat, a small blanket looping and knotting and tightening around her oesophagus. It was coarse but smooth and velvety, filling her airways.

She spluttered, this time waking herself. She sat up in bed, her head frantically turning from side to side. She could still smell the burning - it was happening outside of her dreams. The bedside lamp flickered to life as Callie leant over and thumbed the switch, accidentally knocking the light over in her haste. After she had righted the lamp, it became clear that the smoke was coming from the corner of her bed. The relic. The corner of the duvet had trailed over the stick, hiding it from her sight. As Callie lowered her torso to where she knew it was, she noticed that the corner of her white duvet had turned a golden-yellow colour.

Her fingertips pinched the corner of the duvet, edging it back to reveal a long, thin burn in the bedspread. The stick was cool to the touch, but the underside and where it had rested on the pillow were different shades of black, orange and gold, all intertwined. Flakes of ash crumbled from the bedding and fell into Callie's hands like filo pastry. The whole room smelled of singed hair. She plucked the stick from the fabric and placed it on the polished wood of her bedside cabinet. She needed to work out what this thing was. In the meantime, she knew she couldn't let it out of her sight. From that morning on, Callie would strap the stick to her forearm and hide it under layers of clothes which, in the summer heat, was easier said than done. She grabbed the stick, held it against her arm and taped it in place with micropore from the bathroom cabinet. There was real power in this inanimate object, she knew - she could feel it. It vibrated through her arm and gave her a sense of its power.

She needed to go back to the island to work out what this thing was.

SADIE JAMMED AT the rewind button on her Walkman, listening as the cassette tape clunked and clicked in protest. She rammed her finger into the plastic and depressed the button as far as she could push it. The foam headphones swallowed her ears as she listened intently for any sign that the cassette was behaving in the way it ought to be. She pushed the foam into her head. The sounds of the blood rushing between her arteries filled her ears like the crashing of waves. A gentle crackling crept from the device, crawling up the cables and into Sadie's senses. A low feedback hummed into the headphones. Sadie cranked up the volume to drown it out, but the louder she made the song, the louder the feedback became.

'What the...?' she mumbled, removing the headphones

from her hair and glaring at what she once considered to be a high-tech piece of kit. As she removed the headphones, the crackling petered out until it disappeared altogether.

'Fine,' she grumbled, slipping the headphones back on. 'Much better.' She leant her head back against her pillows.

The crackling and hissing started again, slipping itself between the lyrics of the latest track. Sadie sat up, pushing the earpieces closer to her ears and listened. It started off as a low crackle, the noise that tissue paper makes when you scrunch it up tight into a ball. The rustling and crunching increased, building in a crescendo the more Sadie concentrated on it. The more she focussed on the other thing hiding in the noise, the more clearly she could discern it; a voice.

Sadie clenched her jaw and listened on. She leant across to her bedside table and grabbed a notepad and pen, and began jotting down what she could hear between the static and white noise.

You've taken something that isn't yours...I'm going to need it back...

Sadie swallowed, her stomach clenching.

You came to my home, you stole from me, and you expect me to not be angry?

The bile in the pit of Sadie's gut swirled.

You've taken something that is mine, so now I'm going to need something of yours.

Silence. There was nothing else. Sadie stared at the hastily written scrawl. She jabbed the rewind button, waiting for the familiar whirring sound of the tape in reverse, but no such noise came.

'Is there nothing else?' she said, stabbing the rewind button and cranking the volume up as high as it would go. The tape crunched in the device. Sadie wrenched the player open, the innards of the tape spewing like dark brown intestines onto her bed.

'Shit,' she hissed, throwing the nest of liquorice tape down by her crossed ankles. A crackle came from the headphones again. She grabbed them, despite their no longer being anything for them to read and play, and shoved them back over her hair.

Until you give me something I want in return, I'll remain in your hometown.

'What is it? What could you want?' She scrawled the words down.

Until you give me someone for my family, I won't leave you alone. I'll only become worse, so bring me what it is I desire. Bring me someone for my family. If you don't, I won't leave you alone. Ask Lorraine.

'WE NEED TO GO BACK, don't we?'

Sadie, Vedat and Callie sat together on the wall that lined the beginning of the beach. They were crossed legged, staring out to sea and pondering the events of the last few days. Callie felt the twinge of wood pressing into her skin as she eyed up her friends, their faces gaunt and tired from sleepless nights of worry. The skin around Sadie's eyes had greyed, her lips dry and flaking as she idly picked at them with chewed fingernails.

The fish kept flooding in. No one knew where they were coming from, and no amount of scientific testing seemed to yield any answers. The fish didn't appear to have any kind of disease, but their bellies were stained black and swollen to three times their natural size. It was a wonder how their skin hadn't torn open along the seam. After a day or so, the stench began to waft up from their bloated carcasses. The breeze grabbed a hold of it at the corners, laying it like a sheet until it hung across all corners of the town. Somehow the first wave of bodies was the smallest.

With the hoards of fish came an insurmountable number of birds desperate to get their fill of such easy prey. And of course, with these eager, hungry birds came an equal amount of dead, disease riddled birds. They soon joined the fish that lined the beach, their bloated, bulging bodies too much for their twisted wings to keep in the air. Some of the birds managed to fly off before the disease tore through them and they collapsed further inland, inside the town. They fell from the sky, sacks of contaminated, cancerous aves. One fell from a great height above the children's play area at the local school, plummeting from the sky and crashing to the ground with an almighty crunch as its bones crumpled under the force.

The smell had cleared now, though the inhabitants of the town were unsure if it had dissipated or if they had simply gotten used to it. Either way, the three teenagers were unfazed by the newly familiar scent as they sat only meters away from the rolling waves, discussing their options.

'Did you hear about the school?' Callie said, picking up rocks and flinging them further towards the water.

'No...?' Vedat responded.

'Apparently,' Callie started, launching a small pebble at a bird who had started to peck at yet another bloated fish carcass, 'a small group of birds managed to fly all the way inland to the school. They reckon their hearts gave out as their bodies were right over the assembly hall and they plummeted through the ceiling. Some of the teachers thought the school was being bombed.'

'Oh wow, that's horrific,' Sadie replied, rubbing her hand up her arm, picking at the skin around her elbow. 'Were the kids okay?'

'Yeah, luckily it happened right after their lunch break, so there was no one left in the hall at all. Still, pretty scary, huh?'

'Hmm,' Vedat nodded, looking out to sea. He'd become quieter and more cerebral since this has all kicked off, more inward looking and far less willing to open up to his friends. His arms folded tightly over his torso. 'Could have so easily gone the other way,' he said, frowning.

'I guess,' Callie replied, pulling her sleeves down to her wrists.

'Why do you think we need to go back?' The question came from Vedat, whose face had all but lost its colour at the concept of jumping into the stolen canoe for a second time.

'I don't know,' Callie lied, her fingers tracing the outline of the branch against her sleeve. 'I know it sounds stupid, but it's just a feeling, you know? I really feel like we need to go back. What if the stories were true, Vedat? Those stories we told as kids. About the land dying and crawling back into the sea, about the creatures and the darkness and the things that hide in the trees. What if they were true? And what if we did something to upset something when we went over there the first time? That thing that fell out of the tree? We don't have a clue what that was.'

'I know what you mean,' Sadie replied. Vedat turned to look at her, shocked that she was in agreement. 'It's like an itch,' she continued, her own fingernails digging troughs in her irritated skin. 'An itch to go back. An itch you can't ignore. But an itch you know will bleed if you pick at it. I think it's a bad idea to go back. But I think we ought to.'

'Wait, what? Why? Why would you say that?' Vedat was on his feet, his hands trembling by his sides.

'Well isn't it clear? The thing wants us to go back. Whatever we did woke up something terrible over there. And now it's coming over here.'

'No, sorry Callie, that doesn't make things any clearer. We have no proof that it's come over here, we just know the fish and birds are affected but they would have been diseased over at the island, right? Their deaths don't mean that the... the... whatever. It doesn't mean that it's over here, does it?' His voice shook.

'Well, you asked for my opinion, so I gave it to you. We ought to go back and find whatever it is we've woken up.'

'I'm not convinced it's as serious as that, Callie,' he said. 'I'm not about to give in and accept all the silly stories we told as kids.'

'Vedat,' Sadie started, her eyes glistening. 'Don't you feel it too? Ever since coming back to the mainland, I've felt this itch that's telling me to go back, you know? Like an irritant, something odd feeling under my skin, like bugs or lice or tiny magnets dragging my attention to the island. Come on, you must know what I mean?'

Vedat shrugged, resigned to the power that his two friends had over him.

'We'll go back tonight,' Callie said, finishing the conversation.

Vedat's eyes widened. 'Really? Is that necessary? Why tonight? What's wrong with going early in the morning? In the, you know, daylight?'

'We can't risk getting caught, Vedat. You know that.'

'Great. Well fine. You two are clearly going to overpower

me. But just so you know, I think this is a bloody terrible idea.'

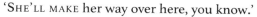

'SHE'LL MAKE her way over here, you know.'

'Oh God, you've got to stop creeping up on me like that.'

'I saw what you did,' the woman said, still following Sadie, unfazed by her outburst. 'Don't worry, no one would believe me if I told them.'

'I'm sorry, I don't know what you mean.' Sadie brushed off the woman's advances and sped up towards the entrance to her road. The sky over the island was darkening, deepening to a bruised shade of purple, peppered with fat grey clouds.

'You stole the canoe. I saw you do it.'

Sadie froze mid-step, her back towards the woman. *Keep walking,* she willed her feet. *Move!* 'We didn't steal anything,' she responded, cursing herself for opening up so easily.

'Yes, you did. But that's not the worst thing, is it?'

Sadie spun to face the woman. She was dressed in an oversized crocheted cardigan. Threads and strands of colourful wool trailed off the edges of the cape-like garment, swallowing the woman's small frame.

'My daughter went missing on that island, four years ago.'

Realisation dawned on Sadie. 'You're that girl's mother?' she whispered, stepping her feet back to gain some distance.

The woman nodded.

'What happened to your daughter?'

'Officially? No one knows. The police settled on her disappearing from the island, drowning and being washed out to sea. But is that what really happened?' The woman stared at Sadie. 'No, I know it isn't. Something took her, and I saw it over there with my own eyes. I've stayed here for years in the hopes that the island would give my little girl back.'

Sadie swallowed, a hard lump forming in the centre of her throat.

'I know you've been over there. And you've made it back. That will have annoyed her.'

'Annoyed who?' Sadie asked, her eyes wide.

'I don't know her name, I'm not sure anyone does. But she's over on that island, waiting for people to go over so she can make sure they never come back.'

'Sure.' Sadie edged away from the woman, her front teeth grinding together. She glanced up at the sky, suddenly eager to be back home.

'She'll know where to find you.'

'I think you should go, please,' Sadie urged, picking up the pace.

'It won't matter what you want,' the woman said, her eyes trained on Sadie's face. 'It won't matter what you need, or what you desire. Soon enough, she'll be here. You'll see.'

Sadie's feet picked up off the floor somewhere between a walk and a jog as she left the woman behind her. Her family home opened up in her view, the front door enticing her closer. She made her way over the threshold, risking a glance over her shoulder. The colourful shaggy cardigan was still in view, the hues blending and blurring together, curling up towards the woman's face like a cocoon. The woman hadn't moved. Sadie jammed the key into the front door, fumbling to get it to cooperate, and tumbled through into the hallway.

'Everything okay, Sadie?' Her dad was standing in the doorway of the kitchen just as Sadie fell through the opening, slamming the door behind her.

'Yep,' Sadie said in a quick, short expulsion of breath.

Her hands reached up to the brass disk covering the peep-hole, flinging the metal out of the way and pressing her eye deep into the convex lens. The woman was still standing there, still staring where Sadie had been moments ago. Even from the relative safety of her own home, Sadie could make out the solemn expression on her face. But it wasn't just solemn, there was something else crossing those eyes.

Patrick placed his hand on his daughter's shoulder.

'Dad! Blimey, give me some notice!' Sadie flinched and jumped to the side.

'Give you notice? I was just there? Come on, what's going on?'

'Nothing, Dad, I'm fine,' she lied, fighting the urge to press her eye against the lens again. Was the woman still standing there? The question burned through Sadie's body.

'It doesn't look like nothing.' Patrick pushed past, leaning his own face towards the peephole.

Sadie clenched, her entire body tense as her dad's back straightened. His shoulders grew rigid. He took a deep breath in.

'Ah, I see.' He pulled his head back from the door. 'That's Lorraine. What did she want?'

'Nothing, she didn't want anything. Wait,' Sadie paused. 'You know her?'

Patrick nodded. He pursed his lips but didn't offer anything further to explain who this woman was and what she wanted with Sadie.

Sadie frowned. 'She's not very well, is she?'

The tension and rigidity seeped from her dad's shoulders. 'No, that lady has, unfortunately, not been well for quite some time now.'

'Where are the rest of her family? She can't be here on her own, surely?'

Patrick ran a large hand over his face, the short stubble of hair grating like velcro against his palm. Sadie could see the inner workings of his money as he decided what his daughter needed to know, and what he could omit. He took a breath in, his hands falling by his side.

'She is here on her own, actually. Her youngest daughter went missing years ago on a family holiday, as I'm sure you've worked out already. Lorraine refused to leave Rose Bay, convinced that someone had taken her. The official statement was that she'd drowned or something similar, off the coast of the island. The dad and the older sister went home, and Lorraine stayed. I have no idea how much contact she has with them, but if her behaviour is anything to go by, I'd imagine she's very much alone.'

Sadie nodded, her eyes drifting to the floor. 'Do you think she's okay?'

The corners of Patrick's lips turned down. 'Well, physically yes, I suppose so. But in every other aspect of the word, I'd be pretty confident to say no. Just leave her be, alright Sade?'

'Of course,' Sadie nodded again, shrugging off her dad's hands and heading up to her bedroom.

Sadie couldn't shake the image of the woman at the end of the driveway, her multicoloured cardigan fraying in the wind. She wondered if she was still there, still standing where Sadie left her moments ago. The itch to look out of her window, to crane her neck around the corner of the building and see for herself was nagging at the back of her mind. But what could or would she do if she was still there? Sadie shrugged, the movement rippling down her body as she reached over to her nightstand and grabbed the closest book. Her eyes roamed the pages, recognising each word whilst not reading a single one.

There was a movement outside her bedroom door, the bright light of the hallway cut up by dark, lengthy shadows.

'Are you coming in?' she bellowed, not lifting her eyes from the book's pages.

The door opened, revealing her brother. Ben walked in, thumping next to her.

'Yes?' she joked, eyeing him under heavy eyelids. 'Can I help you?'

'What we saw, down on the beach...' he started. 'What was that, exactly?'

'I'd love to tell you, only I don't know to be honest.'

'Do you really not know? Only...', he stalled.

'Only what, Ben?' The book lowered to rest on Sadie's lap. 'What are you trying to say? Come on, spit it out?'

'Well, it's just,' he fumbled. 'You're a terrible liar and Vedat is even worse. Did you really go over to the island?'

'What makes you say that?'

'Well, nothing, really. But you are all really bad at lying and I guessed you'd done something stupid. I guess you just admitted it, really.' He didn't wear the face of someone who considered their actions a 'got-cha' moment; in fact, he didn't look smug at all. If anything, he looked concerned.

'We didn't go over there, don't worry.' Sadie's face reddened as she lifted the book back up over her eyes.

'Okay.' Ben shuffled, his toes turning inwards to face each other. 'So say hypothetically that you did. What would you hypothetically have seen?'

'Nothing Ben. We saw nothing.'

'So you did go then?'

'No, Ben - drop it.' Sadie's voice rose, but she still hid behind her paperback.

'So, you didn't go to the island?'

She nodded.

'And you didn't disturb something when you were over there?'

'No, Ben. What does that even mean?'

He ignored her question. 'And you aren't planning to go back over there with Vedat and Callie tonight?'

The book thudded to her lap, the pages clapping together and sending the bookmark tumbling to the floor. 'How do you know that?'

'You speak way too loudly on the phone. And you have to walk right past my bedroom door to get to the stairs, which creak more than you think by the way. The reason Mum and Dad don't hear is because they're basically deaf.'

Sadie bit down on the inside of her lip. 'You can't say anything, okay?'

Ben nodded. He sat for a while in silence as Sadie continued to leaf through the book. She stared at the words, eager for the distraction. Not a single character held her attention.

'What's Dad doing?' Ben asked, lifting off from the bed and stepping towards the window.

Sadie shrugged, placing the book back on the nightstand and stepping over the bookmark to join her brother.

'What is going on?' he mused, motioning for Sadie to look out of the window and follow his gaze. She traced Ben's line of sight until she found what had grabbed his attention.

'That,' he pointed. 'What is that?' He leaned his face close to the glass, his breath fogging up the thin pane.

He was staring at their dad's shed, the once deep coloured

wood panels of his pride and joy now a faded golden hue as they'd been bleached by the sun and salty sea air. His silhouette bled through the single window, sawing something, or connecting or fixing or breaking something as he so often did. But it wasn't their dad who was holding Ben's attention. The problem came from much lower down, below the shed. The golden coloured wood didn't hit the floor. It had a small gap of four inches or so where it had effectively been built on tiny stilts for one reason or another. And from that gap there appeared to be something. Waiting. Something the colour of coal, swilling and swirling around the base of the shed, directly under their dad's feet.

'Do we go and tell him?' Ben asked, eyes wide and mouth agape.

'I don't know,' Sadie answered. 'If we go and disturb it, then what?'

Neither of them knew. The darkness began to build, whipping itself into a frenzy of tangled shadows and matted vines. Writhing tendrils and smoking coils of soot lapped at the edges of the shed, pushing farther and farther towards their dad with every slither.

'That's it, I'm going down there,' Ben declared, pushing away from the window and launching himself down the stairs. Sadie followed, both siblings ignoring the need for shoes and throwing themselves into the garden. The outline of their dad could be seen clearly through the perspex window of the flat-pack shed, its shape watered down by the cloudy plastic.

'Okay, now what?'

'How the hell should I know?' Sadie hissed, teetering around the kitchen door.

'Well I don't know. I figured you might have some kind of

clue seeing as you quite clearly went over to the island. Have you seen this thing before?'

The *thing* coiled in a curled mass, tentacle-like ribbons licking the underside of the shed. It stirred in recognition of their arrival. Ben inched towards it, his arms locked by his side and unblinking eyes wide.

'Ben!' she hissed, 'what the hell are you doing?' Her hands curved around the doorframe, gripping the nearby brickwork as if the house were about to up and fly away.

'I don't know!' he responded without turning his head. His socked feet dragged him closer to the mass of smoke, heel toe, heel toe. 'I just know I can't stand there and do nothing.'

Sadie swallowed, her teeth crunching together. She followed, her feet sinking into the dewey blades of grass. The shadow seemed to register Ben's movement, flinching as he came closer to the door of the shed. A pair of warm, amber spheres rolled around amongst the smoke, seemingly free of any connection to the smoking tendrils. Ben kneeled and leant his head in closer.

'What the fuck are you doing?'

'I don't know,' he answered calmly, leaning and tilting his head to get a better look at the amber globes as they oscillated, suspended above the ground amongst the black smoke. 'Don't you think they're beautiful?'

'Are those... eyes? Looking at you?'

'I'm not sure.' Ben knelt on the damp ground, the light denim of his jeans drinking up the moisture and pigment of the freshly mowed lawn. His forearms lever his body inches away from the creature, easing himself closer.

'Ben! Don't get that close!' Sadie ran, her body suddenly free of the fear that solidified in her limbs. She slammed her hand down onto her brother's shoulder, the force causing him to flinch and fall towards the shed and the coiled creature.

Ben turned his face back to the creature, in time to see it recoil from his flinching movements. The amber eyes dulled, blinked and extinguished themselves, smoke swallowing the fire that burned seconds earlier. He watched as it shrunk down, coils folding in on themselves, concertinaing and disappearing underneath the wooden shed. He flung his head around to face Sadie.

'Well done!' Ben yelled. 'I was going to work out what it was! Or what it wanted.'

'Oh? And how were you planning on doing that, Ben? Bloody ask it?'

Ben clenched his jaw, his back teeth sliding and grinding together in annoyance. He pushed himself up from the ground, brushing the loose blades of grass from his knees. As he stood, he saw his dad still working away in his shed, doing whatever stereotypical things dads do in sheds. Patrick noticed his head bobbing above the window frame and peered out of the door.

'What do you two want?'

'Pleasant,' Sadie teased, her voice fumbling across the syllables. She flung Ben a look, searching for something to say to stall her dad's questioning.

'We came out because there was, erm,' Ben fumbled.

'Mum wants to know if you want a coffee,' Sadie interjected.

'Mum?' Patrick eyed his children from beneath his unruly brow, his arms clamped across his chest.

'Yes,' Ben responded, his voice tilting upwards at the end of the word.

Their dad frowned. 'Mum's not in.'

'Oh, er —,' Sadie stammered, throwing a glance at Ben for assistance that was apparently not forthcoming.

'Did you want a coffee then?' Ben threw in, his face lifting into an off-kilter smile.

Patrick squinted, his warm skin creasing around the corners of his eyes. 'Sure,' he said, 'that'd be nice, I suppose.'

'Great.' Ben route-marched to the kitchen, dragging his sister along with him.

19

Summer 1995

S adie's CD player was playing up again. It had been on the blink for a while now, but today it had seemingly gotten worse. She had little to no luck with technology. And the situation felt terribly reminiscent of one she'd lived through already.

She flicked off the music, silencing the thrum of the latest grunge single that droned through the wires. The singing relented, the guitars ceased, but she could still make out the shadow of a song resonating through the yellow cord. She held her breath, focusing on the wispy noise as it held onto the headphones like an imprint of the CDs that had spun around in the disc player. She'd been here before. There was the slightest hint of a tune, something she couldn't put her finger on. It was low in tone, like the deepest bass she'd ever experienced, groaning in her ears and across the tops of her teeth. She flicked the power button on the device, hoping that her action would silence the reflection of music in the electrical current. The power light faded out, taking with it the noise. She couldn't hear anything else initially, but then she found it, a tiny croak or crackle in the very corner of her ears.

Maybe darkness would help. If she dulled all of her other senses, that might allow her to hone in on her hearing only. She leant over from her bed, dragging the curtains across and extinguishing the light. She closed her eyes, just to be sure, slowed her breathing and began her search. A low hum began to fill her ears. A guttural, deep, gurgling sound. That couldn't be an impression of a previous track, the leftover residue of her favourite songs.

She squeezed her eyes tight, willing her conscience to focus more clearly on the sounds in her ears alone. Amongst her breathing, amongst the pulsating of her heartbeat, she could make it out: a growl. She could no longer mistake it. Phlegm rattling between teeth, saliva dripping from one layer of canines to the next. It drifted in and out of her mind's eye as her eyes clamped closed. The amber eyes she was becoming worryingly used to seeing flickered across her vision.

'Oh,' she gasped, her body flinging upright in her bed and her hand grappling with the headphones, tearing them away from her ears. Her breath caught in her throat and her eyes flew open. Ben was standing at her door, his body angled towards the window and eyes wide.

'Ben?'

His outline was clear in the doorway, the light filtering in from the landing. Sadie reached behind her and pulled open the heavy curtains, the daylight flooding back into her bedroom.

He moved towards her. 'She's here again.'

Sadie jumped off the bed, casting her Walkman aside and realising, as she did so, the music still rattling amongst the foamy earpieces. She could have sworn she'd turned that off. The concern shook from her face as she turned to look out of the window, knowing exactly what she would see. The dark shadow that still crept into her dreams from half a decade ago swirled underneath their dad's shed. It remained where it was, swirling and curling and coiling, the black folds of smoke swallowing any light that ventured near it. They knew from last time that it had no need to attack. Not yet.

'What do we do?' Ben asked, steadying himself on the dresser. He looked up at his older sister, concern smeared across his face. She could see it then, how young he still was, the naivety still lacing his eyes. He wanted to rely on her, he needed to. She was his older sister. It was her job to protect him. She didn't have time to battle with her past guilt, not now.

'We gather information. We don't go into this blind, not like last time.' She swallowed, grabbing her bag and Ben's hand and running from her room. They flew down the staircase two steps at a time, Sadie's hand tight around Ben's the whole way; she couldn't risk letting go of him, not again.

'Where are we going?'

'We need to see someone,' she replied, her breath ragged. It had taken her a long time to realise who it was that they would need to seek help from, but now she knew, it was as if it was a certainty all along.

'Who?'

Sadie turned to Ben, her face stern. 'Her name is Lorraine, and I think she can help us.'

'SADIE, we've been walking for twenty minutes now. Do you actually know where we can find this Lorraine woman?'

They'd been ambling along the main road for what felt like much longer. Sadie only revealed once they were out of the house that she did not, in fact, know where to find Lorraine. She'd considered running back and asking her dad, but she knew that would raise alarm bells and besides, she had no idea if he'd have a clue where to find this woman either. So she figured they'd just leave and walk and something would come to her eventually. Only, of course it didn't.

'What are we planning to do? Wander around until she magically appears?'

Sadie bit down hard on her lower lip. The reality of the situation was, yes, she had been hoping that Lorraine would just appear. She shook her head, stunned by her own naivety.

'Look, I don't know, okay? I know we need to see her, I just don't know exactly where she'll be.' Sadie gripped her brother's hand like a vice, dragging him behind her as she marched off ahead. 'How is it I've seen this woman around loads since coming home, and the second I actually need to see her, I have no idea where to find her?' Sadie grumbled, tugging at her brother's arm.

'Watch it, you're hurting me,' he complained, wrenching his hand away from her.

She winced, loosening her grip and failing to hide the hurt from her face. She couldn't risk hurting him, not now.

'This is hopeless,' Ben whined, beating the soles of his shoes into the concrete path. 'Oh, hey Sadie?' He lifted his gaze to meet hers. 'Did you ask Vedat and Callie to come along?'

Sadie followed her brother's pointing finger. Vedat and Callie were perched against the old wall that lined the top of the promenade. Callie was staring at the soles of her feet as Vedat apparently held a conversation with the side of her head. Sadie swallowed, chewing on her dry, stress-bitten lips. *Did she really want to involve them in this again?* Before she had a chance to answer the question in her head, Ben picked up the pace, yelling and waving to announce their arrival. 'Well, I suppose it makes sense to have them here,' she muttered, following in her brother's footsteps.

'So wait, let me get this straight. The creature has made its way back onto the mainland, and you think that Lorraine, basically the Miss Havisham of Rose Bay, is the best person to help us get rid of it?' Callie locked her arms over her chest.

'Actually, yes,' Sadie replied, holding her voice firm. 'I'm certain of it actually.'

'And you want us to come along and do what, exactly?' Vedat's eyeline wavered between Sadie's left cheek and the top of the wall. He couldn't bring himself to look her directly in the eye.

'Well, I'm not sure. But I think what happened five years ago has something major to do with why the creature is here now.'

'Right.' Vedat sounded anything but convinced of Sadie's theory.

'Well, I suppose we're in then.' Callie stood, motioning for Vedat to follow her.

'There is the slight issue that Sadie doesn't actually know where to look for Lorraine,' Ben added helpfully, still ambling along the top of the cliff edge and looking down to the shore.

'I, well... no, that is very much true...' Sadie conceded. 'But I'm sure she'll be around here somewhere. I swear I've seen her here multiple times since being home. She seems to be everywhere and nowhere all at once.'

'What was she wearing the last time you saw her?' Callie asked, peering her head over the ledge towards the shingled beach.

'Some kind of faded, multi-coloured cardigan thing.'

'Oh, well fingers crossed she missed wash day. If she's still wearing that, it shouldn't be too hard to find her.'

'Wait,' Sadie blurted, motioning over the fauna coated lip of land. She pointed, her arm outstretched, finger rigid. She was pointing to a woman in a familiar, crocheted cardigan, the corners of the knitted fabric lapping gently in the summer breeze. The woman was rummaging around in the shingle and pebbles, looking for something. 'That's her,' Sadie said, taking off at speed towards the coastal path that would deposit them onto the beach.

Ben hurried behind her, jogging to keep up as Sadie skipped down the path, hopping over tree roots and plants that had begun to crack through the pavement. 'We can't risk losing her, we might not be able to find her again!' she shouted to the others over her shoulder.

The group burst onto the promenade to find Lorraine in exactly the same position she had been in moments ago, studying and inspecting a handful of shells that she'd plucked from the stony beach. From a distance it appeared as if she hadn't moved a muscle, let alone considered running from the group.

'Sure glad we ran,' Callie puffed, her back bent and chest

heaving. 'Definitely looks like she was going to make a run for it.' Sadie glared, making her way over to the woman, each step deliberate and tenuous amongst the shingle, as if she knew if she moved too fast Lorraine would bolt. She transferred her weight from one foot to the other, praying that the movement didn't cause the pebbles and shells to cascade away from her.

'Lorraine?' Sadie approached, suddenly aware of a cluster of darkening clouds in the corner of her vision.

'I was wondering if you might try to find me again,' Lorraine answered, keeping her back to Sadie and Ben as she faced out to sea, towards the island. She was fiddling with a handful of tiny, pearlescent shells, rotating them between her fingers and letting them drop, one by one to the floor. The gentle sea breeze swept through the colourful fibres in her long cardigan, plucking them from the fabric and suspending them in the air. They stood on end like some kind of rare, exotic fur, the colours all eerily vibrant in the darkening sky.

'Do you know what's going on?' Sadie's voice floated out in front of her, the sound parting from her body.

'I have a theory.' Lorraine let her arms drop down to her side, the shells glittering as they dropped back amongst the fragments of rocks around her feet. 'I never stopped looking for Christine, you know?'

'Of course. Just like we never stopped searching for Ben,' Sadie answered, her voice breathy. Ben flinched in the corner of her eye.

'Yes, but Ben is different, isn't he?' Lorraine turned to face them, her fingers still outstretched and reaching for the ground, tapping nervously against her thighs. 'Ben is different. I'm assuming this is Ben?' she nodded towards him.

Ben nodded, his feet rooted firmly amongst the shingle.

Vedat and Callie had slid to the edge of the group, standing close together and doing nothing to hide their confusion.

'It's nice to meet you, Ben,' she said, walking over to him. She stretched out her hands, clasping his in hers. 'Ben is different,' she continued, her eyes locking onto his, 'because Ben came back.' She moved closer, her gaze glued to his face, studying him with the same intense look in her eyes as she had when she stared at the shells in her palms. Her skin was soft, but ridged with deep wrinkles, the same wrinkles that feathered the perimeter of her pale pink lips. 'Why did you come back Ben?'

Ben threw his gaze towards Sadie, his eyes wide and mouth pursed together. He was searching for support, for her to come over and protect him, but she didn't move. Vedat threw a glance towards Sadie, too, a glance that said *what does she know?*

Lorraine dropped Ben's hands, her fingers drifting up towards one half of a heart shaped pendant hanging from a gold chain around her neck. 'How is it,' Lorraine continued, 'that my baby girl, my youngest daughter, was taken from me over on that island and she never came back, but you - you managed to come home. Does that seem fair to you?'

Ben shook his head.

'And you all went over to the island together, is that right?' she said, glancing accusingly between the group. Ben shook his head, his brow furrowing in confusion as he watched the other three nod sombrely.

'And yet, only the three of you returned?'

There was no answer. Ben's eyes darted between them.

'Somehow there was a group of you, all there to protect one another, and yet one of you simply didn't return.' It wasn't a question so much as a statement, a statement that none of them knew how to respond to. 'Anyway,' Lorraine continued, looking towards Sadie and dropping Ben's other hand. 'I've got an idea. Want to hear it?'

This time Sadie looked over to Ben, her eyes wide with fear. He glanced away from her, shoulders slumping and torso curling in on itself. Lorraine lifted her eyebrows, waiting for an answer.

'Sure,' Sadie whispered, her voice cracking.

Lorraine shuffled away from Ben, nestling her hands into the pockets of the woollen cardigan. 'When Christine went missing, a part of me disintegrated, like ash at the end of a long cigarette. My personality broke up, dropped away from who I thought I was, and drifted around this town, into the air. My family and I remained in Rose Bay for weeks following her kidnapping - I refuse to call it a disappearance - that's not what it was. Weeks passed and no one saw a thing. There were search and rescue teams, helicopters, the coastguard went out every day and returned everyday empty handed. There were teams of people on that small island, enough to make it sink. And yet, we found nothing, for there was nothing to find.' Lorraine shifted the weight between her feet, glancing over to the island and back to Sadie and Ben on the shore of Rose Bay. 'And then it got to the point where Gavin and Mandy, my husband and my eldest daughter, went home. They couldn't see the sense in staying here any longer. Gavin needed to get back to work, and Mandy back to college. And they left. Only, well, I couldn't bring myself to leave. What if she came back? What if she reached out or tried to contact me? And besides, what used to be my home no longer felt like home at all, not without Christine there. I couldn't bring myself to leave.'

Sadie's chest tightened. She could so clearly imagine what this woman was feeling, she'd been there before.

'Anyway, I figured if I were to stay in Rose Bay, I would try to figure out what happened to my baby. I wanted to learn more about the island. The people of this town must know something, right? It took me a year to finally come across someone else who had lost someone. Apparently it takes quite a while to gain trust when you're known for being a hysterical and volatile woman; as if they could expect me to be anything less than that. Anyway, it was a gentleman on the other side of the town, behind Gloyer's farm. He lost a daughter, fifteen years or so ago, vanished into thin air. They'd always known children would take boats and row over to the island and nothing had ever come of it, until his girl rowed over there with her brother and only the brother came back. Then, a year later, I came across another family, right on the outskirts of town, almost in Minnis Bay. They recalled a family story of their Grandpa and Great Uncle going on a fishing trip, decades and decades ago now, and only their Grandpa came back with little to no recollection of what happened to his brother. He was so upset by the whole situation that he never spoke of him again. Now, you're not telling me there doesn't seem to be a pattern in there, are you?' Lorraine paused, looking between the group.

Sadie eyed Ben, wondering how much he was picking up. His head was tilted towards the floor, feet shuffling in the shingle. Both Callie and Vedat were listening intently, though Callie's face turned to a scowl the more she considered what Lorraine had to say.

'Go on,' Lorraine encouraged, eager for one of them to highlight the pattern.

'Erm,' Sadie started. 'It looks like young children are going over to the island, and not coming back?'

'Well, you're partly right,' Lorraine said, her tone taking on that of a young child's teacher. 'But if you look a little harder at the examples we've got, we can see that the children that went missing never went to the island on their own. They were always with family, or siblings, or a group of friends.' She eyed up Callie and Vedat who shuffled uncomfortably under the weight of her eyes. 'And somehow one of the siblings always ends up staying on the island. Do you think that's right, Sadie?'

Sadie felt her face flush. She hugged her hands tight across her lower abdomen, swallowing down bile and the urge to run to the sea and vomit. She nodded, a quick, sharp, silent nod.

Lorraine glared at Sadie, her eyes fixed on her reddening cheeks. Sadie felt her age melt away, as if with each second that Lorraine glared at her, she lost a year of experience and was merely a child being scolded by her elder. The knowledge that Lorraine held shone in her eyes. She intimidated Sadie.

'With the help of some of the other families that have been impacted by whatever has been happening over on the island, I managed to uncover that there may well be around seven or so families that lost children, siblings, loved ones, whoever, to whatever is over there, spread across the last 300 years or so.'

'I'm sorry,' Ben interrupted, stepping forward. 'Are you suggesting that this... *creature*... has been around since the 1600s?

'Potentially, I mean, I'm not certain. No one is. But it's certainly a theory. Anyway, with this new information and help from the families around the town, I managed to gain access to a lot of historical documents back in the earliest days of Rose Bay even being a town. And you know what I found?' Lorraine folded her arms, hanging back for one of the siblings to answer her.

'No? Okay,' Lorraine continued. 'I found two very high profile cases. Both women, both within ten years of each other towards the middle of the 1600s. The first was a woman known as Betty, though her name was likely Elizabeth. The story goes that she caught her husband cheating on her as she became older, the classic tale. He hit her, abused her, the usual awful situation that befell many women in those times. And effectively she'd decided she'd had enough and drove a knife through his chest, leaving him to bleed out on the floor of their home. She was hanged in the gallows that once stood in the middle of the town. There's evidence of an old tale that says her soul escaped her body and drifted over Rose Bay to haunt and taunt the citizens for the rest of its existence.'

'Hmm,' Sadie squinted her eyes, not convinced of this story.

'Why would she have targeted us? What would she have against a bunch of kids?' Callie asked, planting a quizzical hand on her hip.

'Well, those were my thoughts exactly. That's why I carried on digging. I don't believe our dear old Betty is the disgruntled creature on the island. There was another case, after all.'

The group watched Lorraine as she delved into great detail about these women who lived such an unfathomably long time ago that they felt almost fictional. She was an expressive talker, her hands flying around inches from her face and spreading tiny hairs of colourful wool into the air as they dislodged themselves from her cardigan.

'So, the other woman was a bit more interesting. Her name was Ada something or other, I forget her last name. She lived on the mainland towards town with her family, and, from what I could tell, she had a lot of siblings. She was the eldest of the children and so it fell on her to look after her youngest brothers and sisters when her father was out working on the farm and her mother was otherwise engaged doing housework or something or other. At the age of sixteen, that is, mind you. But sixteen back then made you an adult. The story goes that, one day she was looking after her middle sister Nora in the fields that backed onto their property. They didn't own the property, they weren't particularly rich, but they had access to it and as their dad worked for the farm, they were allowed to use it. Nora was a handful, a picky younger child of around the age of twelve at this point. Something happens between the siblings, a scrap or quarrel or something similar and Nora runs off into the woods. Ada obviously follows her and can't find her. The siblings and Ada search for Nora for hours, unsure of just how far she could have made it into the woods before any of them followed her. Some time later, the accounts of this are not all that detailed, Ada does find Nora, crumpled up like an old crisp packet at the bottom of a tree. Her foot is trapped, tangled in some old gnarled roots that caused her to trip, fall and smack her head at the base of the tree. She's dead.'

'Oh God, that's terrible,' Sadie uttered. 'But I don't understand - if Ada didn't do anything wrong, how does that lead us onto our creature on the island?'

'And how do you know so much detail about the family?' Callie added, her eyes high on her forehead.

Lorraine tilted her head. 'Of course I may have added some flourishes to the story,' she confessed, turning away from the accusatory glare of Callie and Vedat and focusing on Sadie. 'Well, she may not have done anything wrong, but her family blamed her and accused her of killing their youngest child, for not protecting her when she was left in charge of her wellbeing. The village, which was not the town of Rose Bay we know today, turned on Ada and shunned her, forcing her to leave. The folklore then goes that Ada fled to the island as she didn't know where else to go. The chances of a young girl making it over to that island in the mid 1600s and actually surviving for any length of time are pretty slim. So, that's the theory I'd put money on if I were a gambling woman. Ada's our creature. She hides out on the island, bitterly and maybe justly vengeful towards the town and her family that shunned her.'

'And you think, over 300 years later, that she's still over there?'

'I do.'

Ben shifted at the memories of Vedat recanting the stories on the beach, of Sadie and Callie refusing to believe them. Ben believed them the first time he heard them. He was just a child when he first heard them, so of course he'd let other people tell him they were nonsense, let other people convince him that he was naive and childish. It was odd to think that he'd been rightly concerned all along. 'The old stories we used to tell each other,' he whispered, 'what if they were rooted in some kind of truth? What if she just wants her siblings back?' Ben mumbled. An icy chill ran down his back and settled in his lower abdomen.

'What?' Callie blurted.

'She wants her family around her, right? That makes

sense I suppose. She wants to care for her siblings. If that's all you knew and you were shunned and destined to live entirely alone, you'd want your family around you too, right?'

Sadie nodded slowly, the realisation setting in that this theory could in fact have some weight to it. Ben leant back on his forearms, the weight of this new knowledge clearly weighing against his chest. He glanced at his sister.

'Ben, do you remember her saying anything about siblings when you were there with her? Did you see any other children, anything over there that might show us that Ada is our lady? Anything at all?'

'I don't know, I remember so little.'

'Well think about it,' Sadie said. 'Both of her victims were children, right? How old was Christine when she went missing, Lorraine?'

'She was coming up to her twelfth birthday,' Lorraine uttered, her face turned towards the island again.

'And I was twelve,' Ben said. 'And so was Nora. What if she was trying to replace her younger sister? Could that be possible?'

'God knows,' Sadie said, unsure of what constituted possible any more. 'I suppose it's as good a theory as any.'

'So do we have any idea what we need to do to, I don't know, get her to go away?'

'Nope, not a clue I'm afraid,' Lorraine said.

'Great.' Sadie leant back into her arms in the shingle, her head tilted up towards the sky. 'Think, think,' she repeated. 'There's got to be something that we know, something out there that can tell us or show us what we need to do.'

'What did you do the first time?'

'What do you mean, what did we do the first time? We didn't do anything, which is why Ben ended up being taken from us.' Sadie shot Callie a look before flicking her head back to the ground. She wasn't going to go over this, not again.

Lorraine nodded, an exaggerated arching movement where her chin almost made contact with her chest.

'But there is something else that's been itching my brain,' Sadie said. 'If Ada was banished and fled to the island, we can assume that's where she had to stay, right? All the old tales of the witch, whether they're made up or not, they normally come from some fact, right? If Ada was banished, as the old tale says, she shouldn't be able to make her way onto the mainland willy-nilly, she just shouldn't be able to do it.'

'Hmm,' Lorraine hummed, her hand resting on her chin and the bent forearm of her left arm that was angled across her chest. 'What's the only way someone can come back if they are banished or exiled?'

'If they break the rules,' Ben offered, shrugging his shoulders high up to his ears.

'What if they were invited back?'

'Yes. But how would we have invited her back?'

'Unsure, but maybe we have. Maybe we've done something to allow her safe passage back to the mainland.' Lorraine ran a hand over her chin, deep in thought.

'When I was in London, still living there, I saw the creature every now and then. But it wasn't in the same way as now, or back five years ago. It was like a watered down, transparent version, like an imprint or a memory or something. Like I could have been imagining it. But back here, back here is different. When I see it, I know it's there.'

'We need to find her,' Ben whispered.

'Are you mad? Why would we do that?'

'It's either that or have her dictate your lives for the rest of time,' Lorraine said, her tone flippant as if the concept wasn't really all that bad. 'To be honest I'm at the stage now where I just want to know what happened to my daughter. I neither care nor particularly want to find out what else this creature wants with Rose Bay. Rose Bay is not my town, but it has my daughter. This decision is on you, but I'll help whichever way you decide to go.'

'I understand that,' Sadie pondered, chewing her bottom lip.

'Okay, so we need to find the creature, or her, or whatever we're calling this thing, and work out how to re-banish her?' Callie moved closer to Sadie and Ben, readying herself to leave the beach. 'We can't just march over there and demand to see her, demand her to show herself.'

'No,' Ben said thoughtfully. 'I think she is on the mainland right now. We've seen the creature how many times in the past twenty-four hours? I really doubt she's gone back to the island, not now that she knows we know she's here. And, well...' he faltered, closing his mouth tightly around the last few words.

'And what?'

'Well, this is going to sound impossible but... I think I can sense her. I knew she was in the garden earlier,' he glanced at Sadie, 'and I knew she wanted something. I think I can sense that she is still on the mainland somewhere; I don't think she's gone back to the island. I mean, I can't pinpoint her location or anything, but I can feel that she's not far away.'

'I think I might know where to start looking,' Lorraine said, jumping up onto her feet and cajoling the others to join her. She tilted her head to look up at the coastal path that wrapped around the top of the beach. 'Let's think about this logically.'

'Logically?' Callie spat. 'I'm not so sure logic has much of a place in this conversation anymore to be quite honest.'

'Your sarcasm is indeed, very helpful.' Lorraine turned her back on Callie and focussed her attention back on Sadie and Ben. Callie jerked her chin out and went back to concentrating on her tightly folded arms. 'Where would she last have been? When she was over here, I mean, in her own era?'

'I guess, well... I'm not sure,' Ben mumbled. 'Did we have courts back then? Would she have had to go to court? For what happened with her sister, I mean?'

'Yes,' Sadie said, recalling her history lessons from her last years at school, her voice suddenly louder with her added confidence. 'We did have courts, but the court is no longer there. It's the library now.'

'Well, I for one think that the creature, or Ada, would likely still be around the last place she was naturally, before being kicked out of the town,' Lorraine said, standing from the shingle and speeding off to the bottom of the coastal path. 'So that's where we should start.'

The group walked at speed up the steep incline, thighs and calves burning by the time they emerged onto the top of the walk. The library was not far from the seafront and Lorraine led the group round the wide seaside roads that led into the centre of town.

Lorraine led, her feet pounding the pavement with increasing speed the closer they came to the library. Ben followed close behind her, constantly craning his neck and searching left to right for any sign of the creature's presence. Sadie was third, but only a few feet in front of her two friends. The colour had drained from Sadie's face and come to rest in hives across her throat and chest. She wanted to come face to face with the creature that took her brother no more than she wanted the hives to stay there for the rest of her life. And Callie and Vedat walked at the back of the group, whispering to each other and doing nothing to hide their concern.

A cool sweat settled across Sadie's back, clinging to her armpits. 'Do we actually know what we're looking for?' she called out from the back of the group. 'We don't know what form she'll be taking, right? We've got no way of knowing?'

'We'll cross that bridge when we get to it,' Lorraine called out, still speeding off in the direction of the centre of town.

The centre of Rose Bay was not dissimilar to most other seaside towns alongside this particular stretch of the coast. The buildings were a strange mixture of Victorian town-houses that had been converted to apartments, some fake Tudor style buildings with the exposed beams seemingly appliquéd onto the outside of the wall as an afterthought and a spattering of more modern apartment blocks and shops that had, in no way, been built to keep the character of the town in any way at all.

The group headed towards the library, one of the most traditional of all the buildings in the centre of town. The building itself was erected sometime in the 1800s, Sadie vaguely remembered from getting her local history badge at Girl Guides. It was made of sturdy, warm red brick, multiple windows gracing the front of the facade perfectly symmetrical to each other. It didn't look like a court building to Sadie, but then, of course, she only ever knew it as a library and hadn't actually set foot inside a court before. The door to the building was a new addition in a dark, forest green.

'What do we do, go in?' Ben asked, approaching the door and pushing into the building.

'Probably a good start,' Sadie replied, following her brother.

The library was quiet, as it normally was for an early Saturday afternoon. Freestanding shelves lined the floors, sectioned off into all the favourite genres and interests. A handful of people milled around, rummaging through the latest paperbacks and talking to the librarian. An elderly gentleman stood at the reception desk apparently arguing with the older librarian, presumably the manager, about a late book that he claimed had the incorrect date stamped on it. There was nothing out of the ordinary.

'Let's have a bit more of a look,' Sadie suggested, making her way between two tall shelves of paperbacks. The three of them walked between the books, their shoes scuffing against the well-worn carpet. The shelves protruded from the floor, reaching high up to the ceiling. The wooden structures blocked off the natural light, their angular shapes throwing dark, sharp shadows across the floor. Sadie squinted into the shadows, searching, almost urging, the tendrils of the smoky creature to appear.

'There's nothing here,' Ben said, shuffling past a pair of women rifling through the mystery section. 'This is a dead end.'

They searched the entire library, edging between bookcases and checking each and every corner twice over.

'Ben's right,' Lorraine said, 'there's nothing here.'

'Do we really think she'd come somewhere so public?' Sadie asked, leaning against a bookshelf. 'Would she be so brazen about it?'

'Maybe not,' Lorraine said, leading the group out of the library. The librarian stared at the small group as they left empty handed, her eyes wary but not concerned enough to address them.

The mid-afternoon sun was high in the sky as they stepped out into the courtyard in the centre of town. 'If I was a witch, where would I go,' Sadie uttered.

'Ah, that old chestnut,' Lorraine said. 'At least we can be lighthearted I suppose.'

They sat on an old wooden bench opposite a fountain, silence surrounding them as they thought in unison. The fountain was usually the target for young children dumping washing-up liquid, causing bubbles to expand and flow onto the concrete square. But today it seemed quiet, no washing up liquid, no young people making trouble, just a few families meandering around.

Sadie watched a young family buying buckets and spades from the shop across the road, the youngest boy swinging his colourful castle shaped bucket on the end of his arm. There was another child with them, presumably the older brother, who seemed less excited at the prospect of the colourful plastic but uncontrollably excited at the idea of jumping into the cold sea. Sadie always found it amusing that there were families that even bought those buckets and spades. There was so little sand down at the beach, the majority of it was hidden under layers and layers of shingle. Sadie's heart panged as she watched the young family interact with each other, laughing and smiling on their day out.

'The forest,' Ben said, breaking Sadie's train of thought. 'Where she lost her sister. She'll be in the forest.'

'Oh, of course,' Lorraine agreed, standing from the bench and immediately making a beeline for the edge of the square that took you towards the outskirts of the town. 'We can get in through Gloyer's Farm.'

20

Summer 1990

'I fail to see why we have to go back,' Vedat whined for the fourth or fifth time that afternoon. 'What exactly are we going to gain?'

'Look,' Sadie replied, 'you don't have to if you don't want to. Feel free to stay here. Me and Callie are more than capable of looking after ourselves.'

Callie ran a hand over her arm. The branch pressed against her soft skin. Having it held there had been almost unbearable over the last day or so. The inanimate object seemed to heat up and drastically cool down again whenever it pleased, leaving a line of tiny welts and grazes up and down her forearm and a growing discomfort in the base of her elbow. 'Is Ben meant to be coming?'

'What?' Sadie glanced over her shoulder and up the

driveway. 'No, no he isn't,' she said, marching back up the path towards the door and her brother.

'You can't stop me,' he said, before she had a chance to reach him. 'I'm either coming with you, or you're not going either.'

Sadie dragged her hand over her face, her palm sliding over her features. She let out a sigh. 'I don't think it's a good idea for you to come.'

'And I don't think it's a good idea to go at all. I could always go and tell Mum and Dad,' Ben teased, turning his body back towards the front door as if threatening to march back up the path and tell them everything. 'Do you think they'd like to know how you keep stealing things and trespassing? And potentially awakening spirits in order to bring terror to our hometown?' He twisted his face into a mock expression of shock.

'Oh stop it, Ben,' Sadie retorted, folding her arms across her chest. 'Please, just go back indoors. You can't come with us.'

'You can't possibly believe that, Ben?' Vedat asked. He was standing at the very bottom of the path behind the small, black metal gate, scuffing the toe of his once-white Converse into the gravelly pavement. His hands hovered in front of his chest, pulling the toggles of his hoodie.

'Don't you?' Ben asked.

Vedat didn't answer and instead turned to walk away from the bickering siblings. 'I'm going to get down there, before I change my mind again.'

Sadie walked away from her brother without uttering a word. She knew he was there, behind her, and she knew he couldn't possibly come along to the island with them. They couldn't risk having him there, though she was unsure why.

The island had sunk its teeth into her chest, the desire to return pulling on her muscles like fishing hooks. She considered protesting further, telling him to go home, but her body urged her to reach the island quicker. She turned back up the path to see Ben still following and sighed; she could worry about him once they were on the beach. She patted her hand across her backpack, feeling for the torches and her Walkman, though she knew she wouldn't need it. She could almost feel the creature's voice reverberate in the foam of the earpieces.

'What's the plan once we get there?' Vedat asked.

Sadie didn't know the answer to that; in truth, she was still unsure why they were going in the first place. Trying to explain that her motivations for returning to the island were wholly rooted in a feeling wasn't particularly simple. She was being drawn to an energy, a magnetism that she couldn't even begin to explain. 'I don't know, but I think we'll know once we get there.'

Callie brushed her hand over the branch that remained taped to her forearm, the smooth texture of the wooden object burning her skin and prickling her hairs with energy.

THE OARS SLICED through the still water with ease. Sadie had no idea what her plan was, how she would confront the creature she knew existed between the trees and shrubs. The air was still, the sea was calm, the group breathed in unison, holding in their words and concerns for now. Sadie's palms curled around the oars, the sticks of wood acting as an extension of her limbs, moving at her will and dragging the small boat closer to the island. Callie mirrored her movements, neither of them uttering a word. Every now and then one of them tried to catch the other's eye, but they didn't utter a word.

After a brief argument, Sadie had managed to persuade Ben to remain on the beach. Deep down she could sense his fear of the island and she played on it, convincing him that it'd be best if he waited on the shingle for them to return. He relented surprisingly quickly and sat with a heavy thud amongst the shells and stones with his knees bent, chin resting atop his legs.

'Sadie?' It was Vedat who shattered the silence.

'What are we looking for?'

'I don't know.' Sadie turned back to face Callie and continued rowing in silence.

Deep purple clouds rolled in off the island, unfurling across the darkening evening sky, casting a momentous shadow over the mainland. 'Something's coming and we need to stop it.'

None of them answered her; all of them swallowed their fears.

The boat slid up onto the shore, the nose of the canoe burying itself in the soft muddy sand. Sadie was the first out, jamming the tip of her ore into the ground and flinging her backpack over her shoulder. She clicked on the large torch and held it down to her right hand side. Her palms were cool with sweat. A nervous energy jittered through her limbs as she slung the rope around the nearest tree to secure the canoe.

'We'll go this way,' she declared, shining the torch through the thick layer of trees that ran around the ground, concentrating more and more towards the centre of the island. 'Before you ask, I don't know what exactly we're looking for, and I'm hoping beyond all hope that once we find whatever it is, we'll know what to do about it.'

'Solid plan,' Callie jibed.

The torch flickered amongst the trees, casting long shadows over the grassy ground. Tree roots and vines coiled across the forest floor, threatening to wrap around the group's trainers and pull them down into the mud. Their tenuous footsteps led them towards the centre of the small island and, within twenty minutes or so, they'd reached a wooded area they recognised.

'It was somewhere around here we found the heart thing.' Vedat was shining his own torch around the base of a large, old tree, searching for a hint of what they found on their last excursion to the island. He knelt closer to the ground, his nose inches away from a cluster of knotted plants.

'The *what* thing?' Ben asked, marching up behind him. 'What did you find?'

'Jesus! Ben, where did you come from?' Vedat turned to find Ben emerging from the undergrowth, his face red and clammy with sweat. 'You shouldn't be here,' Vedat hissed, urging Sadie to come over and talk some sense into her younger sibling.

'Ben?' She marched over, her eyes wide. 'What the fuck? You said you'd stay on the beach? What are you doing here?' Her face was bright with panic. 'You can't be here, go back. Please,' she begged, her eyes glistening with the threat of tears.

'Oh come on,' he teased, wiping the sweat from his forehead. 'I was hardly going to stay over there. I took another boat and followed you over. Amazing how little you looked back once you'd landed on the shoreline. Anyway, I'm here now. What are we doing? And more to the point, what thing is Vedat talking about?'

'Ben, you really can't be here' Sadie hissed, glancing over her shoulder at Vedat who shrank to the back of the group again. 'We think we found a,' she stumbled over her words, 'a dead animal or something. It freaked us out. Please, go home.'

'Right.' The disbelief resonated in Ben's voice. 'I'm not going home until you do. And that's the end of it, you can't make me leave.'

The group fell into silence again, only the sounds of their breathing puncturing the atmosphere. Sadie's limbs shook with a mixture of energy and nerves. She breathed a heavy sigh, and relented to the fact that Ben was not about to turn around and go home. 'If you're staying,' she said, 'don't leave our sight, understand?'

Ben nodded, a frown playing across his forehead. 'Don't worry,' he shrugged. 'Everything'll be fine.'

Sadie's feet pounded the ground, taking her towards what she knew she was searching for. The humid temperature of the forest seemed to drop the closer to the centre of the island they got, an almost icy chill settling around their ankles and biting into their exposed skin. Goose pimples prickled to the surface of Sadie's arms, contradicting the mid-summer sun that had been high in the sky just hours earlier.

'Can anyone else feel that?' Ben looked to the ground, convinced that the mud was becoming more waterlogged with every step the group took. 'The ground is getting wetter, but we're getting further away from the water,' he thought out loud, the soles of his shoes slipping around in the sodden earth. The ground squelched underfoot, the mud sucking and grasping at the bottoms of their shoes, trying to keep hold of their feet. The darkness bled from the sky, permeating the spaces between the trees and vines that strung themselves out across the forest.

Sadie swatted at a low hanging vine draped across a branch, holding it back for the rest of the group to pass under. 'We're getting closer, just a few minutes more.'

'How do you know?' Ben asked, ducking under another cluster of vines that hung down from the sky. 'What are we looking for?'

'I honestly don't know, I think you just need to trust me. And *please,* don't leave my sight.'

They walked for another ten minutes or so, the white lights of their torches sweeping across the floor and the ground sucking at the soles of their shoes. The further they walked, the quieter the island became. All sound was sucked from the upper layers of the island, absorbed by the squelching that was happening under their feet.

A deep grumbling emanated from the ground, shuddering up from the core of the earth. The trees shook, their leaves fluttering in the darkness, prickling with nervous energy.

'Oh shit,' Sadie hissed, grabbing onto the trunk of a tree as it quivered from the roots up. The ground jerked under their feet again, just for a second or two; long enough for the group to know it happened, but short enough for them to forget and immediately question their reality and the reliability of their memories.

'That did not feel like a good thing,' Ben stammered, holding himself upright with both hands resting against the bark of an oak tree. His breath had quickened with his fall and his words came out in short gasps. 'Sadie, whatever this is, you need to tell us now!'

'Shhh,' she hissed, edging her body behind an unusually

large trunk. She peered her head around the bark to summon the others and her body slipped behind, disappearing altogether.

'Sadie!' Ben called, following behind her and squeezing his own torso behind the bark.

'What?' Sadie's voice trailed off, whistling through the atmosphere as her friends and brother squeezed behind the tree to meet her. The forest melted away, revealing a small clearing about the size of two tennis courts side by side. The clearing was rimmed by a dense wall of trees and vines that matted together to block out any light that the moon attempted to give; the only light left in the harsh blackness was that from the torches that hung limply by Sadie and Vedat's sides.

The group stood a few feet apart from each other. The only sound that they could clearly hear was the in and out of each of their breaths, their lungs grasping anxiously at the air around them. Despite the muggy, humid temperature of the island and the beach back home, the temperature in the dingy, dark mossy bubble seemed to have dropped to that of a different climate, a different season entirely. Sadie eyed her brother and Callie as they rubbed their hands up and down their forearms, easing blood into their limbs in an attempt to warm themselves against the dropping temperature.

'What is this place?' Callie walked closer to Sadie, craning her neck up to the leafy ceiling of the space they found themselves in.

Sadie didn't answer; of course, she didn't know. She shook her head, her hands habitually travelling to her pockets, the torch limply hanging from the thin black cord by her side. The white light spilled from the lens, dripping in streaks onto the forest floor.

'Stop it,' Vedat hissed under his breath, looking over at Callie who was standing further away from him than he anticipated. She frowned at him, her mouth opening enough to convey her confusion.

'What are you on about?'

'Something touched me, you touched me! You swept your hand against my shoulder or something, I know it was you, Callie!'

'Vedat, quiet down,' Sadie urged, 'Callie didn't touch you, she's miles away from you. It's your imagination. And well, if it wasn't your imagination, do us all a favour and stop shouting to give away our exact location.'

Vedat hung his head in embarrassment, his chin lowering to his chest as Callie stood her ground, her arms crossed over her chest. Silence descended over the group again, its abruptness final and suffocating. The light dimmed even further as the last of the drips of moonlight failed to penetrate the thick foliage that coated the cell they'd found themselves trapped in. Sadie swallowed her bottom lip into her mouth, nervously chewing on the flesh and sucking on the skin. It was an old habit she'd developed as a small child; she'd chew on her lips, wrench them further into her mouth and make them sore. Sometimes they'd bleed but somehow it would make her feel better, like she'd regained control of the situation she was in. The pang of pain reminded her that she was present and not about to give in to the panic that threatened to consume her. The temperature dropped even further, the chill frigid in the air, drifting across the group's limbs.

'Should we head back?' Callie flung her arm up in Ben's direction, holding an outstretched digit in front of his lips. Her hand hovered inches away from his face, the white lights on the torches casting long shadows between her spindly fingers.

'Did anyone else hear that?' she questioned, ripping the torch from Sadie's hand and scouring the trees. Sadie winced as the torch was taken from her, but relented and allowed her friend to take possession of the light.

'I didn't hear anything,' Sadie answered, twisting around to get a better view of where Callie had thrown the light source. She reached her hand out into the dark, grabbing onto Ben's forearm.

'Shh,' Callie hissed again, 'stay still, don't say another word.'

Their limbs froze, the icy temperature continuing to drop and cementing their already cold feet into the forest floor. Was Callie right? Was there a noise that they had missed? Their nostrils flared, ears burning with the desire to hear further, to feel further, to know more than it was possible for them to know. Fingertips stretched into the air, desperate for a clue or a hint. What were they looking for? Why were they here? Hearts raced, thudding noisily against rib cages, sweat beaded on top lips despite the chill in the air. Their eyes roamed the darkness, straining against the lack of light, desperate to see something that would help.

And then it came.

Sadie was the first to see it. Two glowing orange spheres floating amongst the tree line behind the darkening outline of her brother. They rotated in the suffocating darkness, throwing a hot, burning light from their centre. The amber light buzzed a shimmering outline of his face, his neck, his torso, the light so bright that it cast shadows onto the once onyx floor of the forest. Ben didn't move, but it was clear by his face that he knew that there was something behind him, that something was not quite right in its existence.

The orange light swelled from the eyes, the halo forming around Ben's face and neck. The light grew in strength until the other three were shying away from it, Ben still rooted to the floor, unable to convince himself to move in any direction. Sadie inched away from her brother, fighting the conflicting urge to hold onto him for dear life and to run from whatever they were about to face. The brighter the light became, the more of the creature that became visible to the group, the more the creature allowed them to see. Its outline revealed itself to them as a hazy mirage of a person, unsure of itself but brimming with energy. Limbs hung heavily by its side, as if its hands were too much of a burden, pulling the closed fists towards the ground. The fiery light spread to touch its face, revealing what looked like the features of a young woman, dragged through age against her will. All noise from the forest melted away. The rustle of leaves, the breathing of the group of friends, the distant mewing of a forest critter or bird or insect, or the lapping of the gentle waves on the distant shore. All of it disappeared, swallowed by the presence of whatever it was that now stood at the head of the group.

The creature was coated in a watery substance, its body strong yet unconfident of the form it had taken. It occurred to Sadie that it was not comfortable, that it had not taken this shape in many years or that it was reluctant to relent this form to the group.

It stood, but still, it did not speak. Sadie opened her mouth, her tongue dry and sticking to the roof of her mouth.

'I - I....'

The group stared at her, confusion plastered across their faces.

'What?' Ben asked, a deep frown furrowed across his brow. He stood unnaturally still, his arms pulled straight by his side, palms flat against his legs, fingers rigid and pointing to the floor. He turned to face his sister, just his head moving on top of his neck.

'Ben?' Sadie whispered, leaning her body closer to her brother but not moving her feet. His eyes were his own, but something about his body and his movements weren't connecting.

A severity settled across his face as he picked up one foot and moved closer to his sister. A look flickered across Ben's eyes, a look of fury and of anger and of rage. A look that Sadie had never seen before and did not expect to see in the face of her brother.

She gripped her hands to her chest, her fingers knotting and twisting together. Words crawled up her throat as her stomach swelled with anxiety and panic. She could feel her glands puff and inflate and she drew in a rasping breath. *It's all in my head,* she thought. *This feeling in my throat, the swelling around my voice box. It isn't real, it's not really happening. I know it isn't.*

She turned towards the shadowed creature. 'What do you need?'

The head flicked towards Sadie, orange spheres burning. It registered her voice, but refused to answer.

'Sadie!' Ben yelled. His body remained rigid and stone-like as his head spun on his shoulders. The only part of him that was animated in any way were his facial features, and they moved as if controlled by strings behind his skin, jerking and pulling in conflicting expressions.

He'd shifted, his feet no longer planted and cemented to the forest floor. His legs were loosely bent at the knees but she could see clearly the power in them. The amber glow strengthened behind Ben, throwing the burning light over his broad shoulders. He was young, but even at this age he looked so much like their dad. She wondered what he might look like if he were given the chance to grow older. The flaming light crept onto his chest, consuming his upper body. No matter where he moved, it clung to him like a magnet, pulsating and glowing in the low light, a constant reminder that it would remain there forever.

'She needed to be appeased,' Sadie started, her voice cracking. She risked a glance up into the creature's eyes. 'She needed something from us.'

'No.'

And then silence. Stunned silence as the group came to the realisation that the growl did not come from Ben's lips as they had assumed.

'No.' The bellow came again. The creature brushed Ben aside, his once glowing body sinking back into the inky darkness and crumpling to the floor.

'Ben,' Sadie gasped, rushing forwards to get to his side. The creature leapt in front of Ben, guarding him from Sadie's reach. The group froze and stared.

The first time Sadie saw her brother hurt, he was only around six or seven. They were at the park with one of their cousins, or a friend, she couldn't really remember the exact details now. Ben and another boy were playing on a merry-go-round, one of those ancient rusting things that spun on its axis. It was a circular metal disk with bars running across the top, one where you hold onto the bars and spin, frantically running and pushing off with one foot and hopping up onto the disk. You held on as you spun and spun, around and around, hoping that you didn't fly off. Well, Ben didn't fall off at all. Thinking back to it, Sadie almost wished he had.

Ben held onto the peeling red painted handlebars, his right foot planted on the flat of the disk. His left foot pushed off against the tarmac. Him and his friend held onto the bar for dear life as they rotated, faster and faster. And then Ben's left foot folded in on itself. His ankle must have twinged or caught on the tarmac, planting his foot firmly underneath the spinning disk and jamming it between the tarmac and the metal. He howled in pain. And, of course, being the older sibling, the sibling that's meant to protect the younger, she ran to his side to check he was okay. He wasn't, but it wasn't all that bad. He'd broken his foot, but to a young boy with lots of friends, having a cast that they could all sign their names on made him a virtual hero.

This was different. This was a situation Sadie had no control over. There were no play-park rides here. There was no spinning, no laughing, no other family members and no cast to squiggle her name upon. More to the point, she knew Ben would follow them here. She had as good as brought him here. She made this happen.

Sadie craned her neck around the creature to see her brother, comforted slightly by the fact that he was now sitting up and seemed to be unhurt. Still, the confusion and concern were incredibly apparent on his pale face.

'I do not need appeasing,' the creature hissed. Its features seemed to soften somehow. The more it spoke, the more it appeared to humanise itself. Each word forming a recognisable feature, like a nose and then top lip, and then small yellowing teeth set amongst high, pink gums. 'That's not what this is, don't lie,' the creature said again, the hiss lifting from the timbre of its voice to be replaced by the sounds of a woman. A young woman, at that. The black shadowy form drifted to the floor, the harsh lines of the creature's shoulders softened and narrowed. The form changed to reveal a girl, barely old enough to be a woman, though the deep amber eyes remained, an unnatural glow against the pale, freckled skin that surrounded them.

Her frame was small but still held the enormity of the creature that stood in the same spot before it. Sadie leant curiously closer, desperate for an explanation and a guarantee of their safety.

Those amber eyes. They'd followed Sadie for days, a mirage in her dreams, in the shadows of the kitchen cupboards at night, between the trees in the garden. Under the shed. They remained as a whole, two glassy orbs swollen with flames that twisted and turned on itself. The features that adorned this unidentified woman's face were unquestionably young and yet Sadie knew that each one held years and years of history.

Vedat thudded to the floor, breaking Sadie's quiet concentration. She turned to see his legs give way, their support giving out amongst the unusual situation they had found themselves in - that Sadie had put them in. Callie rushed over to his side, her normal defensive demeanour melting into the ground up leaves and sludge underfoot. Callie kept her eyes on Vedat; she had this under control. Sadie knew they, at least, would be fine.

'Aren't you going to tell your friends what's going on?'

Sadie turned back to the sound of the creature's voice, oddly smooth and calming considering the body that housed it moments ago. She jumped back, her feet slipping in the mud. In the seconds that her attention was on Vedat and

Callie, the form had edged forward even closer to Ben. Its hands, pale and glistening with sweat, now rested on his shoulders, the skin under each nail a bright white with pressure.

'Ben?' Sadie choked. He showed no sign of physical discomfort; his face was statuesque, his cards as close to his chest as he could possibly hold them. But she could just about see it. She could see him shaking, the skin around his chin and chest quivering so slightly that no one would know, that didn't know Ben like the back of their hand.

'He's fine,' the thing responded, monotone, flat. 'But a deal's a deal.'

Ben turned to face his sister at that. A sharp, sudden turn, his eyebrows dipping at the centre.

'Ben, it's not --'

'Enough!' The creature's yell thundered around the small enclosure, the echo bouncing off the walls the trees made. The creature grew in size, holding onto its human features but stretching them up on grey and black stilts, reaching to the top of the closed-in space. Tendrils of smoke and black flames coiled off its limbs, swallowing any room to move and any room for the group to breathe. Vedat, Sadie and Callie inched away from the creature, its hold tightening around Ben.

'You came to my island,' it started, the volume of its voice lowering slightly. 'You came here and you trespassed. But I let you be. You stayed away from me, so I held my distance.' The human form slipped away inside the growing tendrils of smoke. 'I held my distance, that is, until you destroyed my property. Until you stole from me.'

'Stole from you?' Vedat croaked. He'd managed to drag himself to his feet, his torso leaning heavily against Callie.

The orbs spun to face him. 'You, the group of you, I don't care who specifically. But someone here stole from me that night. And by taking something of mine and dragging it over to the mainland, you gave me permission to join you. You *invited* me.'

Sadie flung her head round to see Callie holding onto her arm, the faint outline of the stick visible under her thin, long sleeved top. She shuffled her arms behind her as Ben struggled against the creature's words. His shoulders writhed amongst the growing shadow.

'We invited you?' Vedat wiped a weary hand across his cheek, smearing dirt from the forest floor across his olive skin. He pushed his glasses back up his nose, thinking about the weight of the creature's words. 'So we invited you to our home?'

'Yes.'

'And,' Vedat continued to think out loud. He brushed a hand over his forehead, glancing at Ben, and winced. 'And now what? The only way we can set things right is to give you something you want? To what? Appease you?'

The creature remained silent.

'To retract the invitation?' he shouted, desperation straining across his face. The creature didn't respond. 'Sadie?' He turned to face his friend. Sadie was leaning against a tree on the outer edge of the clearing, her body crumpled and curling inwards. Her legs strained underneath her, struggling to hold her up off the forest floor. 'Sadie?' Vedat urged, edging his way closer. 'Tell me this -thing - isn't telling the truth. Tell me what you've done.'

'I didn't do anything!' she screamed, pushing herself away from the tree trunk and lunging forwards towards her brother.

'Wait!' Callie yelled, making to follow her friend and reaching her outstretched arms towards her. Her sleeve lifted, revealing her pale skin underneath. And the branch. Sadie saw it as it fell from her sleeve, toppling to the floor. Her mouth hung open, Vedat mirroring her reactions.

'Callie?' Vedat uttered.

'I didn't bring it back, I didn't! It wasn't me!'

'I can't believe you're still lying,' he said, 'after all this. You'd let your friend take the blame for you?'

Callie's jaw clenched, her eyes clamping onto Sadie's.

'Let's not worry about that now,' Sadie said, shrugging Callie's glare from her shoulders and moving back towards Ben.

The creature's torso was still, but it was changing. Once pale, fleshy, human fingers stretched into smoky black talons, elongating down Ben's torso and wrapping themselves like ropes around his stomach. The face of the woman sank back into the effervescent blackness of the shadowy creature, the eyes swelling to fill most of the space where the face once was. The darkness of the thing was so final, so complete, that it swallowed any light that had managed to creep into the clearing. It was the darkest of blacks, the most final of shadows. Tendrils and tentacles coiled from the creature's body, snaking between the trees and coiling in and out of the group, teasing them, taunting them. Who would be next?

Ben's eyes strained to stay open.

'Why aren't you fighting?' Callie screeched into the forest. The orange eyes flicked to meet Callie's, the fire in them burning the brightest they'd seen it. The life from Ben's eyes dropped away, filling the fire in the amber spheres.

'He can't,' the creature growled, its voice so low that it shook the ground around their feet. 'He can't fight, and neither can you. If you come back, or if anyone else from the island dares come back here, I can't be held responsible for what will happen to your precious hometown.' The low rumble settled amongst the trees, settling the space back into the consuming silence.

Sadie stood, her mouth hanging open. She watched Ben's eyelids slip over his eyes millimetres at a time. They slipped, the thin folds of skin losing their strength and ability, the desire, to stay open. It wasn't so much pain as a drunk feeling, a slurring of movement, of words, of consciousness. The energy drained from him.

Ben chuckled under his breath, his head lolling into his chest and rocking from side to side.

'What happens to your body when you're swallowed whole by a creature that has no body itself?' he asked. His chin flopped back, his neck loose and head buoyant. And he stared at his sister.

Sadie launched her body at the shadowed creature, bracing for the impact of the huge mass that grew in front of her. But rather than feeling a wall, or limbs, or muscles, she felt nothing, and flew through the air, thudding to the ground on the other side.

'How?' She gasped for air, pushing herself up against the sodden floor. She craned her neck in an effort to see the precipice of the creature, but the shadow now reached to the canopy of the forest, perhaps even further.

'Sadie!' The yell came from Vedat, who was leaning against a tree on the other side of the shadow. He thrust his finger up into the air, pointing at Ben as he slipped into the centre of the shadow.

Her eyes widened, hot tears of shock tumbling down her face as she watched her brother slip away. By the time his body had been entirely swallowed, his eyes had closed and, in some sense, he looked at peace. She tried to take solace in the gentle expression that came to pass over his features, but of course she couldn't. Her brother had gone. And she had done nothing to protect him.

An icy cold feeling crept from Sadie's chest into her lungs, her stomach, her limbs. The muscle in the centre of her chest pounded irregularly, skipping beats and sending her into a frenzied panic. She couldn't breathe. Any second now, her heart was going to stop altogether. It would beat its final beat and then lay still, and take the breath right out of her lungs. And she'd deserve it. When that did happen, she would deserve every part of it. Every ounce of excruciating pain, every second of anguish; she would deserve it all.

Her eyes frantically shifted from side to side, searching for something that she wasn't entirely sure of. Was her throat swelling? She couldn't bring herself to lift her hands and see. To raise her fingers and find her neck swollen and bloated with some kind of adverse reaction to something. The skin on her tongue prickled as that blew up too, filling her mouth and pushing against her teeth. Her heart beat harder, faster, skipping beats and adding them back in wherever it fancied, a struggling drummer desperately trying to keep up with a band that raced ahead.

Her torso swayed on top of her legs. The lights around her eyes narrowed and she searched for a pulse within her body. If she stayed still enough and listened deep in the cavity of her chest, she could feel it. Trying.

'Sadie?' A male voice broke through her hypnosis. Was he talking to her? 'Sadie?' it came again. Ben? Was that Ben? The voice muffled its way to her eardrums. A heavy hand clasped her shoulder and spun her around on the heels of her feet. It surprised her to find that she was still standing, but even on tilting her head to meet the voice that spoke her name, she wasn't quite able to ascertain who it was. Her mind was foggy, her thoughts clouded.

'We've got to go,' the voice said. Vedat rested both hands on her shoulders, his fingers digging just a little too tightly into her arms.

Sadie glanced over her shoulder to find the creature, the woman, the *thing* that had her brother, had grown to fill most of the clearing and yet, any indication of its original form had completely dissolved into the space. Everywhere she looked there was shadow. A grainy, gritty darkness flooded between the trees, seeping between the faces of her friends, between the laces of her trainers, stretching tendrils of black every which way. The harder she stared, the more she tried to comprehend, the less she understood. But one thing was becoming incredibly clear; the shadowed creature was growing at an exponential rate and showed no sign of stopping.

The remaining light in the clearing had all but vanished into the creature's grasp. Callie, remembering the flashlight that hung limply by her side, fumbled with the power button, jabbing her cold finger into the soft plastic. The flat glass face of the torch illuminated the floor by her feet. She swung the cool beam around the space, nodding at Vedat to do the same.

'Can you see him?' Sadie said, swatching as Callie swung the torch around. Vedat shook his head. He lifted his own beam, the light shooting confidently from the end of his arm like a helicopter brushing a searchlight across a busy highway.

'It's moved,' he uttered under his breath, his head leaning

back to glare at the underside of the forest canopy. Callie and Sadie followed suit, all three friends standing inches from each other. Their shoulders touched as they closed in, huddled in an effort to feel some semblance of safety or comfort. Their necks craned up to stare again at the forest ceiling, all moving as one.

'It's still growing.' The words escaped from Callie's lips involuntarily, like a low hiss of air from a deflating party balloon. Sadie and Vedat nodded, Sadie's eyes following the right flank of the creature as it stretched out, pencil thin fingers coiling round the nearest tree trunk and heaving its lumbering body behind it. Body. If that's what you could even call it.

'It's swallowing the whole space,' she gasped, her voice getting louder as she realised that what she'd said was true. Her cheeks were wet with tears, salty droplets dripping from her lips onto her tongue.

'We need to go. Now.' Callie grabbed both of her friends by their free hands and began to sprint towards a small slither of light in the far side of the clearing.

'But Ben! Callie, I can't leave him!' Sadie tugged against her friend's grip, her voice frantic.

Callie winced, eyeing the creature. 'He's gone, Sadie,' she mouthed, her voice barely registering above a whisper. 'You saw that. Now we need to get out of here, before that creature swallows the entire island.'

Sadie shuddered, her cries silently jerking against her chest. The creature instantly registered their plan and sent a cluster of tendrils coursing down the tree trunks after them. It cascaded down the trunks, flooding the space from floor to ceiling in inky blackness. Their feet pounded the ground, picking up speed as they edged closer to their escape.

The gap was small, barely big enough for an adult to squeeze through. But it was doable. The three of them shed their backpacks, throwing them through the gap and onto the floor on the other side of the clearing's perimeter. Vedat squeezed through first, his slender shoulder slipping between the branches. He stumbled through, his feet tangling on some vines. He swept up the backpacks in his arms. Sadie pushed Callie through, watching as vines and twigs tangled with her hair, snagging and holding onto strands. Finally, Sadie twisted her body side-on to slip through the gap. She could feel the creature's presence on her back, hovering inches from the tip of her forehead, still trickling ever closer. But the speed and velocity it had had moments earlier seemed to have dissipated. It moved with a slow and purposeful drag, each muscle and joint stretching and cracking behind the shroud of shadow. She could hear it, though she wished she couldn't.

The three of them stood outside the opening, hands gripping their torches, backpacks forgotten on the floor by their feet. No one spoke, despite them all having the same questions growing in their chests. What now? What, after what they just saw, were they supposed to do now? And most importantly, what should they do about Ben?

'We can't leave him, we just can't.' Sadie had her fingers wrapped around the loop of her backpack, her knuckles white. She'd not turned away from the entrance to the clearing since they squeezed their way out of it. 'We need to go back in,' she cried.

Neither Callie nor Vedat could give her an answer any of them would be happy to hear.

'Of course we can't leave without him,' Vedat moved closer to Sadie and rested his hand on her shoulder.

'Right, okay then,' she stammered, 'so what do we do?'

Sadie leant her hands on the tree trunks that curved and twisted to reveal the small window back into the clearing - or where the clearing once stood. She placed her palms down gently, as if placing them too confidently would create noise and commotion enough to give the creature back its power and energy. The trees shook beneath her palm. Her head peered back into the space.

A wave of wind shot from the slither in the trees. The sheer power and speed of it knocked the breath straight from her lungs and wrapped its power around her shins, flinging her like a discarded item of clothing to the corner of her bedroom. She didn't really have time to react in any measured way and could only watch on as both Callie and Vedat were thrust into a tree beside her, their bags blown feet away from the group. Sadie pushed her hands into the ground and forced her shaky limbs to allow her to stand.

'Are you okay?' she shouted into the darkness, aware of her friends only because of the now flickering torch with a deep crack across the lens, letting out the meekest attempt at light. Callie cradled her arm across her chest but nodded, checking over Vedat who, given the speed at which they were thrown against the tree, seemed to have fared remarkably well. Sadie ran her hands over the back of her head, running her fingers deep into her hair. 'I think I'm alright,' she yelled, calming her breathing and trying with all her power not to lose control.

Vedat stumbled onto his feet, his hands hovering at the base of his neck and his knees bent slightly. He didn't look well. He swayed on his feet and made his way over to Sadie, ushering Callie along behind him.

'Can you hear something?' he mumbled, his hand still

hovering at the base of his neck, right at the bottom of his skull.

'No. Should I be able to?' Callie asked, moving off in front of her friend, her side brushing past him. Vedat stumbled as their clothes brushed past each other, falling onto all fours and resting back on his knees.

'Vedat!' Sadie rushed over to him, resting a hand on his back as he remained in a table top position, eyes staring at the ground.

'I just need a minute.' A mumble, from his body, but the voice barely recognisable. 'Can't you hear that?'

The other two shook their heads, eyes firmly glued to Vedat and full of concern.

'Are you sure?' he repeated, brushing a hand over his ear, trying to make his eardrums pop. 'It's like a —'

'Ow, shit!' Callie dropped to her knees, her hands clamped over her ears. Sadie followed, leaning heavily against the nearest tree.

'It's like that!' Vedat yelled over the piercing scream that came rattling from the clearing.

Sadie blinked, scrunching her eyes up and trying desperately to clear her ears. The scream wasn't just any scream; it was visceral, inhumanly high-pitched and somehow kept going without the need to stop and take a breath. The discordant shriek split through Sadie's ears and immobilised the whole group.

The longer the shriek went on for, the more the shadow regained strength. The blackness that made up the shadow thickened and glistened in the non-existent moonlight. It began to swell again, swallowing plants and shrubs around it, the darkness pushing against the remaining trees in the clearing that acted as its cage. The dark tendrils burst their

way through the gaps between the trees, absorbing everything in its path and continuing to bulge. It now stood at
roughly the size of a block of flats. Its entire shape trembled
and vibrated.

'It's coming straight for us,' Sadie yelled, turning on her
heels, grabbing Vedat and Callie by the scruff of the neck.
They ran towards the edge of the island. She risked a glance
over her shoulder. The mass of black tendrils swept up plants
and trees like a twister, throwing them around in the air
before they disappeared into the depths of the darkness. And
still, despite inhaling everything in its path and continuously
growing, it tumbled and cascaded towards them. The more it
swallowed, the more it accelerated.

'I can see the canoe!' Callie called, sprinting off in front of
the group. She heaved an oar from the sandy shore and
hopped straight into the small boat, her hands itching at her
knees as she urged her friends to run faster than they were
able.

The last time they'd run like this was far different to the
evening they were experiencing now: the school summer
sports day. The day that Callie thrived, Vedat hid and Sadie
participated as quietly as she possibly could. But in the relay
race, they decided to run as friends, and it always ended in
Callie forcing the baton from Sadie and sprinting as if her life
depended on it towards the finish line. Only it felt far more
serious this time round.

After what felt like a torturous few seconds, Sadie arrived
at the side of the boat, adrenaline preventing her from stopping and thinking about what had happened. Vedat wasn't
far behind, holding his chest, his ribcage heaving in the darkness as he struggled to draw in as much air as possible.

'Hey, breathe,' Sadie whispered to him, planting her hand

firmly on top of his before whipping it away and urging him into the canoe. The three of them sat in the small boat, Sadie and Callie both gripping their oars and ready to paddle for their lives, but Sadie couldn't move.

'We can't leave him here?' Her voice cracked under the realisation that that was exactly what they would end up doing.

'Sadie, we'll come back for him. When it's daylight. But we can't go back onto the island now, it's way too dangerous.'

Sadie went to contest Callie's statement, but swallowed her words. Her head dropped. Vedat remained silent between his friends' exchange, gripping the sides of the boat until his knuckles went white.

'My brother, Callie. You're asking me to knowingly abandon my younger brother?' Her voice squeaked and cracked, trailing off into the night air.

Callie straightened her back, her lips forming a tight line across her face. 'Yes, I'm sorry, but I guess I am. You heard what that thing said back there. We can't risk it Sadie.'

'We can't!' she yelled, but despite her desperation, her body remained stationary in the boat, still gripping onto the oar and staring at the edge of the island, terrified that the creature would emerge.

Since bursting through the line of trees onto the shore, the creature had retreated somewhat back to the centre of the island. Its tendrils could still be seen coiling and curling between the trees, dark writhing tentacles warning the group to keep their distance. But since reaching the boat, it seemed to give up pursuing them and hung back.

Sadie threw her hands up to her face, sobs jerking from her mouth in loud gasps. Callie and Vedat rested their hands on her knees, both unable to find any words that could comfort her.

'Sadie, the creature isn't going to hold off forever. We need to go,' Callie urged, her voice barely above a whisper.

Sadie looked up at her friends, the desire to fight dimming behind her glistening eyes. 'What do we do? What do we say?' she gasped. Her body shook as the weight of their situation settled across her chest. Cries burst from her throat, dry sobs as her eyes ran out of tears.

Vedat pulled his lips into a thin straight line. 'We don't say anything,' he said.

Callie and Sadie looked over at him in surprise.

'We can't say anything,' he replied, staring at the tops of his legs. 'You heard what the creature said back there? We can't go back, no one can, or else that'll mark the end of our hometown.'

Callie swallowed, her head making one short nod in agreement. 'He's right,' she said, turning to Sadie. 'Listen to me.' She squeezed her friends' fingers in hers, holding tight onto her hands. 'We need to go home, and we need to act like none of this happened. We need to wash up, go to bed and act like we were never here.'

Sadie's face was wet with tears. She blinked hard, swallowed and took a deep breath in, listening to her friend.

'People will notice he's missing, and people will look for him. But we can't say a word, understood? And I think it's best that we don't speak about it either. We've got to keep this quiet, do you understand?'

Vedat leant forwards. 'Callie, you can't be serious? We need to go to the Police, surely?'

'No,' Sadie interjected, her body sagging with exhaustion. Her eyes darted back to the writhing ropes of the creature's limbs. They were darkening, strengthening as they rested. A thick, deep black tentacle slithered from the centre of the forest, wrapping itself like the chain of an anchor around a cluster of trees nearest them. It clenched, solidified, and tore the trees up with an effortless sweep. The trees hung, suspended, their roots dangling like lace before the creature tossed them into the water.

Sadie jerked her head back to her friends. 'Callie's right. We can't say anything, not unless we want absolute hell to pay for it. We need to keep quiet, all of us.' She swallowed, rubbing a hand over her wet cheeks. 'And we need to go. Now.'

A cold chill settled over the boat. Vedat's motivation to run back to the island straight to Sadie's parents dissipated from his shoulders, lifting off into the cooling night air. There was no way any of them could risk opening their mouths, not now.

They rowed back to the mainland in silence, three of the closest friends, their bonds splitting and fracturing with each pull of the oars. Sadie's eyes glistened with tears. A frostiness settled across her shoulders and into her chest, an icy frost growing under her skin.

She'd had to do what she'd done, she had been left with no choice.

21

Summer 1995

The walk to the forest edge was more sombre than the group's half-sprint to the library. The weight of the suggestion held more than the old court, the three of them far more convinced that they would find what they were searching for amongst the thick blanket of trees and twisted roots. The second Ben mentioned the dense woods, the truth of the suggestion firmly planted itself on their shoulders, weighing down on their chests.

Callie held back with Vedat, walking a good few metres behind the others. Her hands were buried deep into her pockets, her shoulders curved around her spine causing her frame to shrink to a much smaller stature than normal. Vedat walked alongside her, his eyes often glancing up to meet hers. The fear did not hide itself well on either of their faces. It shuddered through every bone in their bodies.

Sadie walked at the head of the group, Ben and Lorraine a few steps behind and Vedat and Callie bringing up the rear. Sadie could hear the two chattering behind her, a nervous excitement clear in their voices. But she definitely did not feel anything like excitement. A cool sense of dread and anxiety had settled, a thin layer of frost across her chest - tightening whenever she tried to take a deep breath. She knew where they were going, and she knew what they would find, just like she knew the first time.

Sadie had spent the last five years living a life that was only half hers. She'd never properly grieved for her brother; she'd never allowed herself to. When they came back to Rose Bay that night, the group split off silently, agreeing to never speak of what happened to another soul. She'd swallowed the truth whole, her confidence and trust in herself as a person replaced by her constant sense of fear and panic. Her once calm nature had been replaced by a distant look, a set of empty irises and the obsessive need to check that her heart was beating.

All these years later and she was no closer to understanding how the creature on the island convinced her to do what she did, how it controlled her every move and her mood and her reactions to her closest friends. She was no closer to learning anything about it, largely because she'd vowed to push any memory of it as far back in her consciousness as her mind would allow.

Gloyer's farm was just up ahead, the old gates leading around the side of the farmhouse into the forest. Sadie and Ben had been up there a few times as children; the owners of the farm never seemed to mind them running around in the small alleyway that lined their house.

Sadie approached the perimeter and flicked open the

metal clasp on the gate. The wooden frame swung freely towards the trees, its hinges no longer as strong as they once were. One by one they walked into the tree line, slipping from view, their bodies sinking into the thick wall of forest.

'What now?' The question came from Callie. Sadie barely recognised her voice. The strength in it had seeped away, soaked into the forest floor. 'What do we do now?' she repeated, louder this time.

'We go to her,' Ben replied, striding off to stand next to his sister. 'We know where she is.'

Sadie's head jerked up to look at her brother, her eyes questioning his last statement.

'You know where she is too, right?'

Did she? She didn't know what she felt, she didn't know why she had so freely walked in front of the group, and she didn't feel like she knew where to look for this creature. The creature that was responsible for her brother's disappearance, for her family's pain, for her deteriorating mental state. The creature was responsible. It was the creature's fault.

'I...' she mumbled, glancing to and from Vedat and Callie. And as she said it, as that single syllable left her barely parted lips, she knew. She did know. She knew exactly where the creature was. The knowledge sat deep in her stomach like the needle of a compass, unwavering. Like the creature had reached into her throat and dropped a homing pin amongst her organs to make sure she could always find her way back. Her mouth dropped as she made eye contact with Ben again. He held her gaze but she couldn't read the expression on his face.

'Sadie?' Callie stepped cautiously towards her. 'What's going on?'

'I don't know,' she answered honestly, but she could feel

the eyes of everyone else on her. She knew that they were unlikely to believe her. 'We need to go this way.' She marched off, far more confidently than she felt, in an eastern direction. The rest of the group fell behind her and Ben remained at her side. Every now and then she could feel his eyes on her. Her heart thudded frantically.

'It's not far,' Ben declared around ten minutes into the journey. The forest was dense and sizeable, but the trees reached out in a large square rather than a sprawl of plants. They were reaching the centre of the copse.

'Is it just me,' Lorraine said, 'or is it getting cooler?'

'It's just where we're nearing the centre I think,' Vedat answered. 'We've been walking for a while. We're totally surrounded by trees, so it makes sense for it to be a bit colder I guess.'

Lorraine nodded, unconvinced. Sadie knew that that wasn't the case.

Back on the island, all those years ago, the temperature had dropped the closer they got to the centre. And when they reached that strange clearing, that cage of twisted branches and barks, it was dramatically colder than it was on the outskirts and the shore where they'd left the canoe. The temperature was a sign, a sign that they were close. That the creature was close.

'And what do we plan to do when we actually find what we're looking for? Do we actually have a plan, or are we just hoping that winging it will get us through this?' Her tone was laced with sarcasm, but Sadie knew deep down that she was saying what everyone else was thinking, what they didn't have the confidence to air to the group.

'I've done enough research to know who this woman, or this creature, whatever, is. Or was, I should say. I know what she was before this happened to her. I think I can get through to her.' Lorraine picked at a loose colourful thread at the edge of her cardigan sleeve. 'She took my daughter from me. I want to know why, and I want my daughter back.' Her hands travelled up to a tiny, golden half locket that hung around her neck. She rubbed the yellow pendant as she walked.

Sadie felt a pang of guilt deep down in the pit of her abdomen. Even if they could actually talk to the creature, would it relent its hold on Christine? Would it be able to?

Sadie's trainer went down with a squelch, the ground underfoot softening. She turned her head towards Vedat and Callie. They'd noticed that too. She turned to Ben. His face held no emotion, no clue of knowing what was going on. Still, after all this time, Sadie didn't know how much Ben remembered.

'I was wondering when you'd arrive.' The voice snaked between the remaining trees, curling atop the branches and vines. It was otherworldly. Ethereal. As if it hadn't been projected by a set of lungs more than it emanated from a person and lifted freely from their sternum. Sadie turned and motioned for the group to get together behind her. She crept forward, easing her way between two large oak trees in the centre of the forest. In a space eerily reminiscent of their visit to the island, the last remaining trees parted to form a circular clearing, a cave of branches and trunks and barks and leaves. It was quieter in the clearing, in the cove that the creature had formed itself.

Sadie felt Callie and Vedat edge up behind her. If they could gain just a few more metres of distance between their soft, fleshy frames and the creature's wrath, that had the potential to make a difference, right? She turned to face them, eager to present her strength and certainty. Her face gave her away, the creases at the corners of her eyes laced with fear and a deep-rooted sense of regret.

Ben placed a hand on top of her arm. She flinched at the suddenness of his touch, but knew what needed to be done the second the electricity flew from his palm onto her skin. She'd abandoned him for the last time.

Sadie moved away from the group, her front leg taking a long, lunging step out into the clearing.

'We're here,' she said. 'We need to talk.'

No answer came. The leaves rustled, their corners lifting and fluttering in the breeze.

'We already know you're here,' Sadie continued, taking another step forward. 'You've made your presence known already. There's no point denying it.'

A figure drifted from the far side of the trees, shrouded in a sooty black shadow. Its form was intriguing; the edges of her clothes and limbs and hair shivered. Sadie tried her best not to stare open-mouthed, but her eyes travelled of their own accord over the fraying mirage of a body, of the shimmering outline that bled into the trees. The creature appeared as a woman, oddly grey, as if the colours in her body, her clothes, her hair, were not saturated enough, as if the deep hues that should have pigmented her skin and the fabric of her dress had run out of energy and faded into sepia.

Sadie stood her ground and forced herself to hold her chest high, despite her legs trembling. Beads of sweat clambered to the surface of her forehead, her top lip, her armpits. Ben was a few feet away from her, his face oddly calm. The rest of the group were behind her still, not having moved since arriving at the clearing.

A shuffling noise broke Sadie's concentration. She turned to find Lorraine edging up towards her, her hands buried deep in the ends of her stretched cardigan. She'd hidden her fingers like an embarrassed teenager, but even so, Sadie empathised with the action, as if she were hardwired to react in that way.

Lorraine stood shoulder to shoulder with Sadie. Her bright, eccentric personality trickled into the forest floor as she faced the amber eyes belonging to the creature that had taken her daughter.

'It's been such a long time,' Lorraine said. 'You looked quite different back then. What happened?'

The creature's eyes rested on Lorraine. It remained silent.

'She'd be nearly twenty-one years old now, you know? My baby would be a full-grown adult.' Lorraine swallowed a sob, stretching the sleeve of her cardigan over her hand.

The creature edged closer, her ragged clothing traipsing on the forest floor, leaves and twigs clinging to the fraying fabric like velcro. The hessian-sack dress was torn at the edges, hundreds of tiny threads suspended around the edge of the garment that sat somewhere between a tunic and a long, shapeless dress or burlap sack. Her feet were completely bare, the toes encrusted with old, congealed blood and dirt. Paper-white ankles peered out from under the dress, grazed and brushed in a souring green and yellow smattering of bruises. Her hands looked much the same, as if her nails had gathered dirt under them from digging or scraping, clawing at inches of mud and soil. Every inch of her looked like it ached and, despite their eyes travelling over her entire body, neither Sadie nor Lorraine were able to put their fingers on her age, or, at least, the age she was presenting as.

Her beaten feet and thin, wavering body crept closer until she stood around six feet away. 'Christine?' Her voice rattled from her chest. 'Christine was yours?' Her head tilted to the side.

Sadie glanced over to Lorraine. Tears gathered in her eyes, spilling over her cheeks in silent streams. 'Yes,' she nodded, sniffing. Sadie wondered if she'd registered the use of the past tense in the creature's statement.

'Pleasant girl,' the creature answered, her amber eyes locking onto Lorraine's.

Lorraine only managed another nod, tears and snot flowing freely over her face. Sadie reached out for her fingers and held onto her hand, gripping it tight.

'You need to leave,' Sadie managed, her voice cracking. She hadn't planned to say exactly that, but now she'd let the words out of her mouth, she realised how true she felt they were. Sadie couldn't allow the creature to remain on the mainland, causing terror and destruction; she couldn't let it happen any longer.

'I can't see how you're going to make me do that.'

'By giving you what I should have five years ago.'

The woman tilted her head to the side, her eyes squinting inquisitively. 'Do you really want to do that?'

'Would it make you go away? And stay away?' Sadie's stomach squirmed. She held her hands out in front of her chest, picking and pulling at the skin around her fingernails.

'Sadie, no —'

'—I need to do this, Lorraine,' Sadie said, placing her hand on her new-found friend's shoulder and gently pushing her away.

'You don't,' Lorraine urged. She laid her own hand on top of Sadie's, her skin soft and comforting. 'Trust me, you don't.' Her eyes were wide and pleading. 'I know how to fix this.' She lifted her eyebrows, wrinkles settling between her glassy green eyes. She made an almost imperceptible nod and turned back to face the creature.

'We know who you are,' she whispered, pulling her hands down towards her sides and clenching them into tight fists. She marched closer to the creature, rage and desperation bubbling under the surface, tugging at her face in equal measure.

'And?' The voice echoed and reverberated from the trees.

'Your name is Ada.' Lorraine's voice cracked as she tried to steady her nerves.

The creature flinched, dark, snake-like tendrils coiling around its ankles like overstretched elastic. The shimmer in the amber of its eyes lifted and twinged, flickering to rest on Lorraine's face.

Lorraine rummaged in her cardigan pocket, the old wool stretching and warping under the force of her quivering hand. She extracted a small, torn piece of paper and, unfolding it, began to shout the lines that she had written as loud as she could.

'Your name is Ada,' she repeated, watching as the creature jerked and twitched at the recognition of a name she barely remembered. 'You had a younger sister, and her name was Nora.' The creature flinched again, the smoke billowing and darkening with each line that carried from Lorraine's mouth.

'You were exiled from this town for something you didn't do.' And that was it; that was the line that sent the creature over the edge. The trees around the edge of the clearing shook, leaves rustling and crackling in the gale.

'No one has spoken to me about this in many years. No one knows I exist. And those few that suspect I do, have never found those records,' its cracking voice bellowed. 'How did you learn of those things?'

Lorraine braced herself against the wind that billowed from the smoky outline of the creature. She held her shoulders strong, her body anchored to the ground, and shouted. 'A little digging around in the local history files, speaking to the right people,' she answered, pushing down the pride she felt for being the one to uncover the truth.

'You can't possibly know everything,' the creature, Ada, said, her voice trembling.

'We know you were blamed for your younger sister's death. We also know you didn't do anything to harm her.'

The amber orbs glistened as Ada narrowed her eyes, a pointed tongue flicking between her teeth. 'You think you know everything?'

'Yes,' Lorraine replied. 'I believe we do.'

'So you know that my sister, Nora, died at the foot of a tree somewhere in this forest? You know that she tripped and hit her head and, by the time I found her, she'd bled all over the roots and into the dirt between the plants and trailing vines? Her blood is as much a part of this forest as the tree you're standing under.'

Lorraine nodded again. 'Yes,' she said. 'I believe we do. I believe none of that was your fault, but you had to take the blame anyway.' Lorraine threw Sadie an encouraging smile.

'You think I didn't know where she'd hide in this forest? We played here almost every day. No matter the season, or the weather. I had to amuse my many siblings in some way, and playing here was about the only way I could keep them happy. You really think I didn't know where she'd be hiding before she tripped? Before she fell?'

'So you did know where she was then?' Lorraine said, inching closer. Sadie lunged forward, her hand reaching out to stop Lorraine seconds too late.

'Of course I did!' The roar shook through Ada's body as it twisted into a smoky cyclone of tendrils. Her eyes remained static amongst her moving body, her voice rumbling from deep within the pit of her chest.

Lorraine fell back against the nearby tree, exhaustion crashing into her chest. Sadie leant forward. Her limbs still shook, but she summoned enough confidence to fool herself. 'So how did this happen? Why did she die, Ada?' Sadie asked, glancing back at Lorraine.

'Because I let her.' The voice shook once more, trailing from a thunderous roar to a whimper. The smouldering tendrils of the creature retreated, the darkness billowing around Ada's body shrinking back to reveal the young woman in the soiled burlap sack cowering at the centre of it. 'I let her die.'

'But why, Ada? What happened?'

Ada collapsed onto her muddied knees, her frail frame dropping out from amongst the smoke. Her body was tiny, bones pushing against thin, greying skin that hung limply from her angular frame. 'I'd had enough. Of babysitting, of being the adult of the house, of shouldering the responsibility for my family. I couldn't cope with it. I just wanted to be a child.'

Lorraine pushed herself up from the base of the tree and walked over to Ada. She knelt by her side, ignoring the looks of concern coming from Callie, Vedat and Ben who were still cowering at the side of the clearing. She placed a wary hand on Ada's sharp shoulders, registering just how young she must have been when this all took place.

Ada looked up to Lorraine, moisture trickling from her nose. 'I'd met someone. We wanted to run away, get married,' she said, her dry, scabbed lips pulling into a smile. 'We'd arranged to meet on this particular day, I can't remember exactly now. It's not important. But Mother insisted I look after the children, so I couldn't go and see them. But I wanted to, more than anything I had ever wanted before. So I left the children playing on their own, not for long. And I went and found them. It was wonderful, they were wonderful. I was the happiest I had ever been.

I left the children for a while longer than I thought I had. By the time I came back, I found Nora crumpled underneath a tree, her head cracked along the side like an eggshell. Blood spilled onto the forest floor. So much blood. More blood than I'd ever seen before. Her tiny chest was still inflating, just a little bit. But I knew I couldn't help her - what could I have done? Nothing I could have done would have stopped her from dying. So I left her. I ran back to the house, pretended she'd run off when we were playing. And my father found her hours later, dead and frozen cold at the bottom of the tree. He saw right through me.'

'It was an accident, Ada,' Lorraine whispered.

The shell of the young woman peered up, the amber flames swirling in her eyes. They were less bright, the harsh orange glow petering out.

'You didn't do anything wrong. But you were alive in a time that could never understand that.'

Ada nodded, her eyes full of sorrow. The anger and rage and fire was burning out of Ada. Lorraine kept her hand on her shoulder, willing her to speak further.

'I was exiled to the island. I didn't survive very long, but I don't recall dying. All I remember is feeling so terribly lonely. All I wanted was someone to share the day with, a sister or a brother, someone that could be like my sibling. Someone I could take care of, properly this time. I thought that, maybe one day, they would risk trying to come to the island to find me, but they never did. I'm sorry I took your girl.' Ada glanced up at Sadie. 'And I'm sorry I took your brother.'

'I forgive you.'

'What?' Ada and Sadie's voices echoed together, the shock clear on both their faces.

'Why would you say that?' Sadie uttered, her mouth agape.

'You can't forgive me,' Ada agreed, shaking her head. 'I did something unspeakable. I have done many unspeakable things.'

'And I forgive you. Because forgiving you helps me heal. You need to forgive, Ada. You need to let go of this place.'

Ada plucked Lorraine's hand from her shoulder. 'You're right,' she whispered, standing slowly and brushing her hands down the front of her tunic. She shuffled a few steps away from Lorraine and Sadie and closed her eyes. All the hate, all the rage, all the fury and the darkness that coated Ada's soul lifted from her chest. She took one last, long, breath. Her head tilted up to the sky. The smoke and shadows returned, curling and coiling one final time, surrounding the tiny, frail body that now lay on the floor.

Ben edged forward, Callie and Vedat close behind him. 'Is that it?'

'That felt too easy.' Vedat shuddered.

'Hmm,' Sadie hummed in agreement, shuffling closer to the crumpled heap of clothing. Her eyes darted around the space where Ada once stood, searching for some confirmation that they were now safe. But she couldn't find anything that made her feel secure.

The air amongst the trees tensed, the trunks and barks clenching in suspense. Sadie checked over her shoulder and eased towards the bundle of burlap sack and pale limbs that remained motionless on the ground.

'Sadie...?' Ben breathed the question, his hushed tone settling amongst the still, stagnant air.

Sadie held her palm up to her brother and her friends, her feet continuing to carry her closer to the bundle of fabric.

'Ada?' Her voice carried the short distance to the body, but there was no response. She moved closer, a gentle breeze picking up around her feet, rustling the leaves that had gathered on the forest floor. Her heart thudded frantically in her chest, missing a beat and racing to catch up with the adrenaline that fizzed under her skin.

The breeze picked up to a strong gust, leaves and forest debris whipping up in tiny whorls, scratching Sadie's bare ankles. Ada's body juddered. Her back arched off the ground, thrusting her torso towards the sky. Familiar sooty tendrils burst free from her mouth, snaking coils of smoke writhing free and twisting in a knotted, expanding mass over her body.

'Get back!' Sadie yelled, her hands out straight in front of her, as if her wavering arms would go any way towards protecting her.

'Sadie!' Ben lunged forward, his hands gripping her shoulder. The tendrils paused, the slithering limbs frozen midair. The pointed tips quivered, waiting.

Sadie pried his desperate fingers from her arm, forcing him behind her as the thick, smouldering tendrils charged closer. 'Ben, it wants you, can't you see that?!' she yelled as the ropes of ash curled around her body to get closer to her brother. She shoved him, planting her feet squarely in front of him to form a barrier between her brother and the creature.

'Ada, you just need to forgive yourself!' Lorraine screamed from behind a cluster of small shrubs.

'That won't help now,' Sadie replied, her face trained on the mass of black snakes that continued to pulsate in front of her. 'It's too late for that.' The shadowy creature began to expand, the smoke of its limbs clambering up nearby trees and absorbing them whole. The darkness at its core grew, unfolding and stretching to fill the blue sky that once peered through the tops of the forest. The white cirrus clouds that dotted the sky moments earlier thickened, a deep grey bleeding into the wisps and rumbling with a guttural rage.

Lorraine fell silent, her mouth agape. A tendril tore away from the writhing pack, its pointed tip shooting down and slamming Ben into the floor as another ripped a tree from the ground, throwing it metres away from the group. Sadie rushed to Ben's side, curling her back over his body like a shield. For all she knew, it was only him and her in the forest now. Lorraine, Callie and Vedat dissolved into the tree line, their faces full of horror but of no help to Sadie. She squeezed her eyes, clearing them of the gathering tears.

'I won't let this happen again, Ben. I won't,' she gasped, her body arched over his torso.

'It's okay,' he replied, largely unscathed by the fall. He pushed himself up on his elbows and turned his face back towards the still-growing mass of tentacles. 'I'm okay,' he repeated, a tremble fluttering at the edge of his voice.

Sadie turned her back on her brother. She looped a hand through his, squeezing his fingers between her own. She knew what she had to do, but there was something she needed to learn first. Her chin lifted high towards the opening in the treetops, hoping that her voice would carry to whatever remained at the centre of the writhing mass.

'Why did you let Ben go?' she shouted.

The creature shifted. The tentacles pulled taut as the individual limbs twisted and distorted.

'I know you can hear me!'

The amber eyes pierced through the growing darkness, settling decidedly on Sadie.

'I was wondering when you'd ask that,' a deep, ethereal voice rumbled through the trees. 'It was never my intention to take Ben. It was you I wanted. But then you virtually delivered him to me - that was an offer I couldn't pass up on. You made it all so easy.'

Sadie swallowed, her heart smacking irregularly behind her ribs.

'But then you ran, and you left him behind. Your poor, defenceless, baby brother.'

Sadie looked over to Ben, her head shaking. 'No, Ben...', she whispered, but it was too late. The pieces had slotted together in his memory.

'You fled from the island,' the voice continued. 'Leaving me with Ben. Which worked for a while. He was a wonderful companion. But then, you'd basically given him to me. Didn't I have a duty to teach you a lesson? You should always protect your family, especially your siblings. I, of all people, should know that.' The voice echoed, any hint of sadness or remorse or humanity dissipating amongst the leaves.

Sadie shook her head, flinging her mind side to side and shaking out any memory she had of that night. As if the motion would relieve her of her mistakes. 'No, Ben, that's not how it happened. Please,' she begged, her face saturated with tears.

He blinked, the puzzle pieces of his fractured memory tumbling into place. 'You left me?'

'I couldn't save you, I couldn't. Of course I wanted to, I never meant to abandon you.'

'It wasn't just me you abandoned though, Sadie,' he said, the words travelling on his raspy breath. 'You abandoned Mum and Dad, too. When I was taken, you left them. And you left Vedat and Callie. And you left me. You left all of us behind.'

Sadie leant down towards her brother, her glistening cheeks sinking into her hollow face. The black tentacles whipped around amongst the trees, cracking and sparking between the leaves. 'You're right,' she mouthed, the tiniest hint of a whisper drifting from her lips. 'I have lived with that mistake. I will always carry that mistake with me. I'm so sorry.' Her wet lips drifted across his forehead, a fleeting kiss glancing over his skin.

'Sadie?'

She pushed herself up off the floor away from her brother and pivoted on her heels as another tree tumbled from the sky. She sprinted. One leap, two, three, four leaps and she was tearing towards the creature. The shouts and cries of her friends, of her brother, echoed in the back of her mind. Her limbs sprang her forward, adrenaline coursing through her veins.

It was time she paid for her mistake. It was time she protected her family, how she ought to have done years ago.

EPILOGUE

Her knees were wet from weeks of rain that fell like a cleansing blanket over Rose Bay. Rain, tears? She could hardly tell the difference any more. At least today was looking to be dry.

She couldn't see a great deal from where she knelt, but she knew risking a trip closer to the edge of the island would result in punishment. She couldn't afford any more of that, wasn't sure she could take it.

A small group of people had gathered at the edge of the shoreline. Each held onto a white paper lantern, a tiny flame flickering in the metal contraption at its centre. They began to let go of the lanterns, the wind plucking them from their wary hands and lifting them effortlessly into the grey sky. Their faces weren't clear from where she cowered, but she was sure they would be crying.

She'd lost track of how long she'd been between the trees. Long enough to be presumed dead, she assumed. Long enough to be watching her own memorial, long enough to witness her own family mourn her. At least they had Ben back. Her grazed, bloodied hands fell from their place on the bark. She closed her strained, exhausted eyes, willing the darkness to swallow her and drag her into unconsciousness. She could hope.

BEN STOOD BETWEEN HIS PARENTS, his hands empty having released the paper lantern into the air. His eyes roamed the edge of the island, rimmed red from the relentless tears. He fumbled in his pocket, slipping a small bottle with a curled up message within it into his palm. He turned it over, hoping above all else that it would reach its destination.

The small group of family and friends that he was with turned to make their way back up the hill. He could tell his parents were itching to be as far away from the beach as possible. The shingle and the sea and the clear, salty air held nothing but bad memories for them. No images of melting ice cream in the summer, no memories of donkey rides across the shoreline, their backs sagging under the weight of children that could just have easily walked. No fragments of laughter or smiles or family days out. Nothing but darkness.

Ben launched the bottle into the water, the glass object spinning and tumbling beneath the choppy sea. He took a deep breath, his nostrils flaring and eyes barely holding back the tears. He was exhausted and damaged, lonelier than he'd ever felt in his lifetime. But he could still hope.

ACKNOWLEDGMENTS

Gosh, where to start! *One Road In* is the most fun, complex, stress-inducing novel I have ever written, and I truly mean it when I say a heartfelt thank you to everyone involved in making this project a reality.

Thank you first and foremost to my brother, Karl, who spent days editing and critiquing this monster and helping me refine the mess of ideas that lives in my head. Thank you to Allie Ralph at Apartment 9 Media for somehow perfectly creating the vision I had in my head for the cover and artwork. Thank you, of course, to Dan for being my soundboard and listening to me ramble on about the most out there idea I've had (so far!) and Maria for being the best hype-person there is!

Thank you to my beta readers, Bethany, Victoria and Kent, for giving me much needed, invaluable feedback. And thank you to Richard for all your advice in the run up to the release.

I've said this before, and I'll say it again. If only one

person finds joy in what I've written, then I'll consider this book, well and truly, a success.

ABOUT THE AUTHOR

Hannah R Palmer is a thriller and horror author from a seaside town on the south coast of England. When she's not working her day job, she can be found writing in any of the local cafes or scribbling ideas down for the many novels that live in her head.

Her debut thriller novel, Number 47, can be found on Amazon. For a free preview, head to Hannah's website.

To keep up to date with new projects and what Hannah's up to, feel free to subscribe to her newsletter: https://www. hannahrpalmerauthor.com/subscribe

ALSO BY HANNAH R PALMER

Number 47

A Season of Darkness: From the Forest & Return to Sender

Printed in Great Britain
by Amazon

79504676R00181